ACTUALIZED

Book 3 of the Configured Trilogy

JENETTA PENNER

ACTUALIZED

Book 3 of the Configured Trilogy

By Jenetta Penner

ACTUALIZED

ISBN-13: 978-1717482990
ISBN-10: 1717482996

Printed in the U.S.A. First printing 2018

1044763

To the dreamers. Never let go.

CHAPTER ONE

I'm not who I thought I was. I never have been and never will be.

My mind tries to wrap around the fact that Cynthia Fisher—the ousted Director of Elore who served on the same council as Manning—is somehow my grandmother. Ben's grandmother. Bess' mother.

Bess. My heart breaks every time I think about her letter I lost. Somehow, she knew the truth and tried to tell me, but I wrote her off as delusional. Crazy. I'm wracked with guilt over the contempt I once felt for the woman who gave me life. Just as my heart was always searching for my place in the world, hers was too. *Is too*, I remind myself. I have to believe she's still out there, still safe, or I'll be the one who actually winds up crazy.

I stare up at the fabric of my tent. It's been four days since Aron, Ben, and I narrowly escaped President Waters, and I've barely slept or left my bed, save for checking on Ben. But, every time I visit the med tent, he's still the same—unconscious and out of my mind's reach. Which is way beyond frustrating. Cynthia says he's rebooting and they're doing everything they can. I know she's right, but she refuses to even let me try to help. "Just in case," she keeps saying. Just in case what? I don't even want to know.

Meyer's last words to Aron at the pod have repeated in my mind at least a thousand times a day.

"I know she doesn't need it, but take care of her," he had said to Aron, and then he left to board the Philly ship. That stupid Philly ship.

Why would he do that? Sacrificing everything for Aron, Ben, and me? He doesn't even like Aron, but Meyer didn't hesitate. I throw my head into my hands. A wave of longing for him ripples through my body as the memory of his scent, his touch, envelops me. Meyer can't be dead. He can't. I won't let him be dead.

My brain continues to swirl with endless questions, data, and doubt. All I know for sure is that I'm lonely.

Alone.

I reach for the necklace Ben gave me. It's somehow still around my neck after everything that has happened and all I have left from my former life. I pinch the gold heart charm between my thumb and index finger, rubbing the smooth surface. Love and loss is what it means to me now. Loss is painful, I've always known that. But so is love.

The charm slips from my fingers as I release a frustrated sigh. No one will tell me anything. Yesterday, I ran into Cynthia while she was speaking to a group of important-looking people and their conversation immediately switched to hushed warnings and whispers.

I push up from my cot and scan the inside of my tent. But staring at the speckled canvas walls won't do me any good. It won't find Meyer and it won't heal Ben. And it sure won't do anything about Elore or New Philly. I reach toward the chair next to my bed and grab the camo jacket folded across the back. I don't even remember placing it there. Nevertheless, I quickly push my arms through the sleeves and zip up the front.

Outside my tent, I raise a hand to my eyes, squinting from the morning sun. A crisp wind beats against my face and body, making my throat constrict. But the jacket does a satisfactory job of staying the chill overall.

The Affinity camp is nestled inside a valley surrounded by tall, looming snow-capped mountains. I have no idea if we are closer to Elore or New Philadelphia since I haven't bothered to ask. And with my EP on the fritz and no way to fix the implant out here, I'm not receiving extra information about anything. But, to be honest, I don't really care.

Two Affinity members in tan uniforms approach. One of them, a brown-skinned girl, flicks a look at me and then returns her attention to her companion. Does she know who I am, what I can do? That I'm Fisher's grandchild? I stare at the girl as she passes. Reading people's intentions is no simpler here than it was back in Elore.

There, I had to assume everyone was against me. But, here? We're all on the same team. At least, that's my hope. Without being able to see inside people's brains, I never really can tell. Too bad they're not more similar to computers—ones and zeros. Then life would be easy.

I lower my head and let the Affinity members pass without me uttering a word. I should force myself to be friendlier, but old habits die hard.

I compress all my troubles and relegate them to the back of my brain. If I let them out for too long, they'll consume me. I'll end up a basket case and never leave my tent. One thing at a time.

Sanda.

She's the one who needs support most right now. When grief finally hit her, she emotionally drew inward and pushed others out. Her entire family might be dead—most of them are— so I can hardly blame her. This is why I haven't confided in her yet that my grandmother is alive and right here in the camp. But maybe I don't have to. Maybe it doesn't matter.

With the pair of Affinity members out of sight, I cross my arms over my chest and trudge to the spot where I've seen Sanda sitting alone the few times I've ventured out. Tawny scrub-grass crunches beneath my boots and a cold breeze ruffles my hair. I pass a series of tents, some that are set up as housing and others as workstations for the rebellion.

Just beyond the last tent, a cluster of evergreens shades a large boulder where Sanda sits. Knees near her chest, she draws her finger in the dirt and through fallen foliage. I'm still not entirely used to her long hair being reduced to a short pixie cut. I miss the mop of loose, gold-tipped, dark curls she had before as it reminded me of everything Elore was against—individuality. Choice. Now Sanda looks as if she lives in Elore. But, that was the whole plan.

Hair doesn't matter, though. The person does. And Sanda

matters to me. She's like a sister. I once thought of Kyra like a sister. Now I have no idea if that sentiment was reciprocated. My stomach drops at the memory of Kyra's betrayal, but part of me still longs to help her. She's being used, and she can't even see it. But then, why would she? Living in Elore is all about taking your experiences and feelings and locking them up tight.

"Hey," I say, when I'm standing over Sanda.

She continues drawing in the dirt. Her black shirt and jacket hang loosely over her petite frame. A tiny hole in her khaki pants reveals a bit of her dark skin.

I lower myself to the ground and lean my back against the rock next to her. "I thought I'd find you out here."

"Well, you did," she mumbles.

Nervousness tingles in my chest. Maybe Sanda's angry with me. She probably blames me for the death of her entire family. My breath hitches at the thought. It's true, though; Jayson and Gabrielle might still be alive, if it were not for my mistakes.

"Don't be mad at me," I whisper.

Sanda lifts her head and narrows her brows in confusion. "Mad at you?"

"You're mad at me for everything that happened." Hot tears burn the corners of my eyes.

"Avlyn, I'm not mad at you. I thought you needed time to yourself to think, same as me." Her gaze darts away from mine. "I've always felt like I was doing the right thing by joining Affinity and following my dad's example, his passion. Even after he died, I wanted to follow in his footsteps and continue the work he started. But because of everything—I'm lost..."

I lean into her with my shoulder, desperate for human connection, as if somehow it will magically make the pain go away. It doesn't. Instead, the ache continues hovering somewhere between my heart and my head. A part of me still values what I used to have: self-sufficiency, emotional control. But trying to put my emotions back in the box is impossible. Not as if I really want to, now or ever. I'm pretty sure Sanda doesn't want to throw away everything she thought was important, either.

Sanda presses her shoulder into me.

"I miss my mom. I didn't even get to say goodbye," she says. "I mean dad had just died, Thornton was so out of the way, and she was outside town anyway. There was no chance she was going to die too, right?" Tears stream down Sanda's face.

Everything in me wants to fix it for her, bring her mother back. If Gabrielle wouldn't have come to Thornton in her pod, Ben, Aron, and I would have never made it out.

"Were they able to get her body?" It's a terrible question. But, when Mother died, they had to leave her body in Elore. If Affinity had retrieved her remains, I feel like I might have made peace with her death. Instead, it still haunts me. In a twisted, last-minute form of redemption, she pushed me away from the falling debris. Darline took death for me.

Sanda nods. "I've been told that scouts recovered her body two days ago. Fisher had her cremated immediately. But I'm not sure if I'll get the ashes. It's not exactly high on Affinity's priority list."

"At least it's something."

Sanda wipes her eyes. "How's Ben?"

"Cynthia says he's getting stronger. But I'm pretty sure they're keeping him sedated by MedTech, and I don't like it."

"If it helps him heal then you should be glad for it."

I sigh, thinking back to Lena's advice that the MedTech was, in her words, *bad news*. "I know Affinity is different but, in Elore, there were simply too many easy ways for them to control us. The meds, VacTech—Ruiz never trusted the food printers. Meyer told me so."

My heart winces at my casual mention of Meyer's name, and I wish I could take it back. Sanda flicks a look at me but doesn't say a word. Instead, she links her arm with mine and pulls me in tighter.

"You just want him to be okay," she says.

"I can't lose him." At this point, I'm unable to separate whether we're speaking about Ben or Meyer, and everything comes tumbling out. "Why did Meyer go? Why did he board that ship?"

Sanda slowly closes her eyes for a moment. "Because that's who my brother is. He's the most loyal person I've ever met. He doesn't let people in easily but, when he does, he's all in. Aron told me what Meyer said before my brother boarded the ship." She pauses, probably to choose her words. "I think it was Meyer's way of letting go of anything he held against Aron."

"What do you mean?"

She shrugs. "Meyer and I had talked before you left the bunker to warn Thornton. I told him to stop being stupid, that all this jealousy stuff made him look like a jerk. If he really loved you, he'd just focus on what he does best—caring. Aron's a great guy.

He knows his stuff. And if Meyer weren't trying to be all sulky, he'd probably like him too."

Embarrassment crashes into me as I remember my and Aron's kiss. Sanda doesn't know about that. Maybe Meyer had a reason to be jealous since my behavior was thoughtless. But the ache of missing him is so great, like an empty pit, not at all what I feel for Aron. And it hits me. Love can be different. I like Aron. He's nice to look at, he understands my background, and I get him. But my feelings for Meyer are infinitely deeper. Ever since I've gotten to know him, I've never had to justify wanting to be with Meyer like I did with Aron.

The twist of confusing emotions wrenches me, and a floodgate of tears lets loose.

"Oh Avlyn, I'm so sorry," Sanda says between her own tears. "I shouldn't have pushed you. I'm only trying to process the whole awful thing myself."

"I know," I choke out, trying to get a hold of my emotions. I draw in a full breath to settle again, and it somehow works. A measure of peace falls over my body. Not a lot, but enough. I quickly formulate a topic in my head to change the subject but, in my anxious state, the wrong words spill out. "Cynthia is my grandmother."

My stomach drops. I slap my hand to my mouth, but it's too late. The secret escaped.

Sanda eases back, her eyes wide. "What?"

I stay silent for what seems like forever, but there's no use trying to pretend. "She's my and Ben's grandmother."

"How do you know?" she whispers. "She told you?"

"No, not yet. But she is. I know it. Cynthia is Bess' mother. Bess tried to tell me in a letter how the identity of her bio parents would put me in danger. I didn't believe her, but this is what she meant.

Sanda raises a hand to her mouth. "Bess is the baby Cynthia was pregnant with when she escaped Elore? Wow. I would never have thought." Her sad demeanor shifts to intrigue as she tries to work through this new mystery. "Who's your grandfather?"

"My grandfather?" I consider the question. "I don't know. I guess whoever Cynthia was paired with before she disappeared."

"Well, it sounds like you need to talk to her and find out all the details."

I lean away from the stone behind us. "Yeah. I think it's time."

CHAPTER TWO

A soft rumbling rolls out of the clear sky. From the east, a medium-sized hover pod shoots across the air toward the camp's far side. The sun glints across the metallic hull, making me squint.

"Wonder who that is?" I ask, holding a hand to my eyes.

Sanda shrugs. "Could be supplies. They come in occasionally."

"Maybe," I mumble, still watching the sky even though the pod has already vanished. I stand and dust off crushed pine needles from my tan cargo pants. "I think it might have landed near the medical facility." It's a good excuse to check on Ben again and gives me extra time before I attempt to talk with Cynthia. "You want to come?"

Sanda stays seated and gazes up at me. "No, I think I'll stay out here a bit longer. Come tell me if it's anything interesting, though, or if there's news about Ben."

I give her a soft smile. "Sure thing."

I leave Sanda and work my way back toward camp. Part of me hopes to run into Cynthia and get everything over with, and another part wants more time. Why would Cynthia send her baby back into Elore when she had her safely outside the city? It makes no sense. She knew very well Elore wasn't safe.

The camp now bustles with men and women, both outside the tents and in. But there's no sign of Cynthia. Aron either. But I haven't spoken to him much over the last few days. He always seems to be busy working on his drones when I ask anyone about him.

As I approach the camp's west side, near the medical tent, I take in a long draw of air. Ben is probably not any better. I need to be prepared. Manning's virus really did a number on his nanotech, maybe even his brain. Closing my eyes and concentrating, I reach out to him again with my thoughts.

But, it's a black nothing. Defeat settles over me. What if I can't speak to Ben in my mind again? It's not like we've been successful at it for a long time, but the experience allowed me to grow closer to him. As if somehow this connection made up for all those years we were separated. And mind communication is unique to us. Dread simmers in my chest and I cross my arms, wishing I could disappear. A feeling that's not foreign to me.

The camo-patterned medical tent comes into view, and I slow my pace. *Ben will be okay,* I remind myself. *You are not going to lose him too. He just needs time.*

To the tent's left and a few-hundred feet away, waits the hoverpod I saw a few minutes ago. I check for any activity— maybe someone unloading supplies, something to help Ben, or some food—but there's no one. The vehicle simply sits parked and abandoned. It's probably nothing to concern myself about.

The tent's front flap is pulled closed. I release a trembling breath and grab the fabric, pull it open, and then step inside. Six cots occupy the space and Ben lays in the one farthest on the right. He's still asleep, with a medic sitting in the chair next to his bed, her back away from me. Her long dark hair falls down her back, loose, instead of pulled up like most of the medics I've seen. Strange, she's also holding his arm. Panic rises in my chest. Is something wrong?

I march toward the medic, grabbing her shoulder when I reach her side. "What's going—?"

The woman turns to me, and I snap my hand back. A jolt of memories flashes across my brain like lightning.

Bess.

A weary smile crosses her lips, and the area under her eyes is colored a pale purple, as if she hasn't slept in days.

"Avlyn," she says in a near whisper as she stands, but she doesn't make a move toward me.

My mind rounds with questions. Should I hug her? Should I ask her about my grandmother? Where she has been? "Why... why are you here?" is what tumbles out, instead.

The smile disappears from her lips, and she glances back at Ben. "So many reasons."

Tucked under Ben's arm is the small stuffed rabbit I found in Bess' apartment on my Configuration day. I always figured it must've been Ben's from when he was little. Otherwise, the stuffed rabbit probably wouldn't have been in the hidden wall space inside his old room.

I don't make any move toward her. Much of me wants to get to know my bio mother better, but all the years of pent-up bitterness and prejudice won't quite let me. Not yet. "I... I found your letter."

Her eyes widen as she returns her attention to me. "You did?" She looks down. "I had no idea if you would, but I couldn't leave without telling someone. I'm so sorry for everything that happ—"

"Cynthia is your mother," I blurt out.

Bess flicks her gaze my way and clenches her jaw. "She is."

I drag a second chair from a nearby cot to Ben's side and lower myself into the seat, back straight, eyes level. Nodding to the chair Bess vacated when I had arrived, I say, "Sit." I know my words are rude, but I'm too upset for pleasantries.

Reluctantly, she takes the suggestion.

"How did you know about Cynthia?" I say, and nervousness roils around in my stomach when she hesitates to reply.

"It's a long story," she eventually says.

I look at Ben again, still completely out. "There's time and I have a right to know."

"Yes, you do." Bess nods and inhales deeply. "Growing up, my parents were different. I was aware I wasn't their bio child, and that was fine—normal."

As she speaks, I study her face—the freckles sprayed across her nose match Ben's and mine, same with how her dark hair falls across her forehead.

"But a few times we had... guests. Which was odd," Bess

continues. "The meetings were always in secret and late at night. I should have been in bed, so I held my ear to the door to listen."

I lean closer to her, my eyes wide with attention.

"The topics ranged from genetics to whispers of black market MedTech. I generally couldn't make out much, but what I did hear stuck with me. Of course, when I was seventeen I moved out and Devan and I made our pairing contract." She pauses for a few seconds and looks away, softly adding, "Life was pretty normal and, by that time, I'd all but forgotten the meetings."

I remain quiet as new questions spark to life and join the others already swirling around in my head. For a moment, I think the conversation is finished. But, with a heavy sigh, Bess continues.

"Then, one day towards the end of my pregnancy with you and Ben, my mother I was raised by showed up unannounced. I hadn't seen her in a couple of years, since a few months after my Configuration. Immediately, she analyzed my body with a hand-held scanner. Satisfied with the results, she had pulled a small metal lock box from her bag."

My bio mother looks at her hands as her fingers knot and unknot. "She told me not to be afraid but not to ask questions, either. That my life and the lives of you two depended on it. But I *was* afraid, and all the memories of my parents' secret meetings came flooding back. I didn't have much time to think on the memories, though. From the box, my mother removed a thin, silver device the length of her forefinger and pressed it to my neck. I flinched when something sharp shot into me." Bess touches her neck, her brows pushed together. "I demanded explanations, but all she did was hush me in reply. I wanted to know more but I let my mother do what she wanted. She hugged me right after the injection and then she left with the device. And, after you and Ben were born, things got crazy and I kind of forgot about the whole thing for a while. Then, Direction wanted you to take part in those experiments—"

Why?!" I snap, cutting her off, my pulse pounding. Pent up emotions boil to the surface. "Why did you allow them to manipulate us? We didn't have a choice!"

Shame blankets Bess' face. "We didn't know better and hoped you and Ben could have a better life. But, really, we did as we were told."

I release a long sigh, remembering the night in Bess' apartment when I found data outlining our part in the experiments. I went from an Intelligence Potential of One to a Two in a short amount of time. But, Ben was experimented on for *nearly four years*. Tightness squeezes at my chest. A flash of Ben and I as infants receiving a dose of painful MedTech lights up my thoughts. "The test subjects don't last long," the tech had said. But, somehow, Ben and I survived.

"Those experiments did more than upgrade my intelligence potential, Bess."

"I know. Cynthia and I have been in touch. What you and Ben are doing is amazing." Her eyes beam with pride. "But I don't understand it at all. The ability must've been a side effect of the experiments."

"I think the last VacTech activated it for me. Ben's started after all the extra experimentation he went through."

Bess shifts her attention to her still sleeping son and gently strokes his hand.

"Devan is gone. Dead." I say.

"I was afraid of that." Her voice shakes.

"Maybe Ben can tell you more later." I dip my head and force her to look at me. "But give him time. It's still a pretty sensitive subject."

She nods.

Sunlight streams into the tent from the doorway. "I knew I'd find you in here," a raspy female voice says, and I turn toward the sound. Cynthia stands in the doorway with a tentative smile. Dressed in a pair of slim-fitting black pants and a camo jacket left open, revealing a loose, blue button-up shirt, she appears casual despite her rigid posture.

"Avlyn knows," Bess says to Cynthia.

"I thought she might. She's a highly intelligent girl," Cynthia replies.

Bess walks to meet her and the two embrace. My hands curl into fists as I stare at the scene. How could she hug her bio mom like that? Cynthia had left Bess in Elore and for what? She could've kept her. It would have been safer outside of Direction's influence. And Bess simply accepts this?

I study Ben, whose brow is furrowed, even in sleep. As if he somehow senses our awkward reunion too. Maybe he does—through me. Though, I'm still not sensing any emotions or thoughts from him.

"I need answers," I demand, now standing but not ready to approach them.

Cynthia and Bess step back from one another.

"You deserve them," Cynthia says, hanging her head.

The heat of anger tingles in my chest. "Then why haven't you given them to me yet? What are you hiding?" The questions come out more forcefully than I expect. But I mean each word, so I don't regret voicing them.

Cynthia moves toward me, leaving Bess' side, and I step back a few inches. She stops.

"Avlyn, it was my fault," Bess pleads.

My gaze switches from Cynthia to her. "Your fault?"

Cynthia turns to Bess and holds up her hand. "No, it was—"

"It was *my* fault," Bess stresses. "I asked her not to share anything with you until I arrived."

"Avlyn." Cynthia returns her attention to me. "Your offense is understandable, and I'm sorry. Since Thornton, I've been attempting to balance my new position as the leader of Affinity while also being reunited with my family. I should have, but I never believed that Ruiz would be killed. I didn't even know if I'd ever see Bess again, let alone Ben and you. It's a lot to process, I know."

"Why would you dump Bess into Elore?" I spit, ignoring her excuses. "You of all knew it wasn't a safe place."

Cynthia cocks her head, arching an eyebrow. "You of all know it's not a safe place *anywhere*."

Her words punch me in the gut. She's right. This world is very unsafe.

"But you could have done something to protect her. Not left it up to people you didn't know," I say.

Bess still stands farther back near the tent opening. She takes a deep breath but says nothing. Isn't she angry? Doesn't she want answers?

"And why do you assume I didn't know the people I entrusted her to? Assume I didn't play out every option in my mind?"

"How could you know them?" I demand. "You were Level Three, a Director. Bess' parents were Level One. You'd have no interaction with them."

"Ruiz and I were Directors of Social Rights. We had more interaction among all citizens than other Directors. Level Ones were not looked down upon as much then as well." Cynthia loosely crosses her arms over her body. "Remember, this was over thirty years ago, things were different. Manning is the one who has changed Direction for the worse."

I look away and close my eyes for a second.

"It was dangerous for Bess to be seen with me in the Outerbounds. I couldn't keep her."

"That makes no sense," I argue, unable to accept her vague answer. "Others can be seen with their babies in the Outerbounds, why not you?"

She looks to Bess, and Bess shakes her head slightly.

"Because, I could not," Cynthia says, finality in her voice. "My goal was to keep my child alive, and placing her back in the city with a family I knew who would care well for her was all I could hope for at that time. I know it doesn't make sense to you, but my options were extremely limited."

I pump my fists and stare at Bess, but she refuses to look my way. What are they not telling me?

To my side, Ben moans, and I fling myself toward him. But, as soon as I do, he relaxes again.

"Well, at least tell me where you've been all these years," I start up again. "It wasn't Philly."

"How about you let me come out of the doorway?" Cynthia asks kindly. "We're all on the same team, Avlyn. I have no wish for anger to exist between us."

"I've been able to move on," Bess says. "You need to as well."

"How am I supposed to move on from anything? Look at how many people are now dead. Gabrielle, Ruiz... the whole town of Thornton." My voice trails off as I plunk into my seat. "Meyer." I plunge my face into my palms. "Everything's a mess, and you refuse to make sense."

Cynthia lowers herself into the chair Bess had used a few minutes ago. "You're right. Absolutely nothing makes sense." She places her palm onto my shoulder and I allow it. "We can't change the past. We can only move forward and hope to make a better life in this world."

"I'm okay with what happened, Avlyn," Bess says. "The reality is, Cynthia and I were not an intelligence potential match anyway. If she had stayed in Elore, she wouldn't have raised me."

"But she didn't stay in Elore," I mumble, my mind moving back to the words Sanda asked earlier. "Did your pairing know?"

"No," Cynthia says flatly, patting my shoulder before removing her hand. "After I left Elore, I had no further contact with my pairing."

"Do you think he cared?" I ask.

Sadness sweeps over Cynthia's slightly wrinkled face. "I don't know."

Bess walks around to the other side of Ben and runs her hand over his dark hair.

"For the last ten years," Cynthia begins, changing the subject, "I've been living in a small, transitional outpost operated by a group who isn't directly affiliated with Affinity but who have similar goals. We would get news of what was happening in Elore or Philly and work as a think tank on solutions. Most of the people there were outcasts or didn't want to be found. It was peaceful, and I was still able to be a part of the rebellion. It was better than being on the run, which was how I spent my time before then. Ruiz knew about Bess and kept my secret. She and I have been in contact all these years." Cynthia gives Bess a soft smile and looks back to me, holding my stare. But I won't soften. After a couple of quiet beats, she says, "I have additional news for you too."

"What?" I ask.

"Your father, Michael. He's alive and safe."

CHAPTER THREE

"He survived?" My heart beats wildly in my chest at this news. My father and I were not close in Elore but, back in New Philly, I felt like he was trying to make a connection with me in his own way. Then, when the attack happened, I abandoned him during the escape. He must hate me. Even so, I'm flooded with relief that he's safe.

"Apparently this Dr. Sloan of yours did you another favor. He must've liked you. I've heard he's not an easy person to get to know," Cynthia says.

Memories of him flicker in my mind. He was an odd, reclusive person for a citizen of New Philadelphia. But he took part in saving me in Thornton and now this. Dr. Sloan keeps on surprising me. "Yes, he's interesting."

Cynthia nods. "When everything exploded with President Waters, Sloan arranged for your father to get out of New Philadelphia. It was a close one too. Waters' guards were on the way to arrest Michael."

I pinch the bridge of my nose. I was afraid Waters would go after Michael. But, the weight of not knowing my father's fate leaves me.

"Would you like to speak to your father?"

Instantly, the calm evaporates. What if he's angry and doesn't want to talk to me? Our relationship was already hanging by a thread, and I still think he blames me for Mother's death.

"He's here?" My voice comes out in a squeak.

"No, we couldn't bring him to the camp." Cynthia shakes her head. "But, I can arrange a secure comm."

Her words help my tightened shoulders relax. "Um... yes. Maybe in a while, if that's alright?"

She arches a brow and stays silent for a few seconds. "Okay, that's fine. But let me know when you're ready."

"Yeah, I will." I just don't know if I can deal with him right now. Since Michael is safe, I need to focus on sorting out my own problems. I glance at Ben again and attempt to connect.

Are you there?

Black nothingness blankets my mind. I exhale a steady stream of air from my nose and look up at Bess who's now standing beside me. She places her hand on my shoulder.

"I'm just glad to be back with the two of you."

"I'm glad too." And I realize I mean it.

She gives me a soft smile. "Ben will recover. I know it."

Everyone but me seems confident everything is going to turn out well. I wish I could join them. I bring my hand up to my shoulder and lightly touch hers. Then I pull my hand back to my lap.

Cynthia clears her throat. "I wanted to wait until Ben had healed more to discuss Affinity's plan for the war between Elore and New Philadelphia, but I think we need to move that up. Keeping you out of the loop was foolish. I see that now. Some part of me wanted to be your grandmother, I believe I wanted to protect you. You are as much a part of this as any of us, maybe more so. Later today, I'm holding a council meeting. You should join us."

I'm somewhat torn, and cringe with being part of the solution. But the war is much greater than my life and happiness. Too many lives are at stake.

Still, I stand to leave the medical tent, and say, "Come get me when you're ready. Right now, I need to speak with Aron."

Bess makes a motion as if she wants to hug me. I reach out and catch her upper arm, stopping her from doing so, but squeezing her instead. The thin smile stretching over her lips tells me she's disappointed, but the squeeze is the best I can offer right now. I'm not sure I'm ready to make room for meaningful attachments with others. Loss is too painful.

I release Bess' arm and nod to Cynthia before I step toward the tent's opening. Then, I push the flap aside and leave my biological family.

A breath loosens from my tightened chest as I rub a hand over the back of my sweaty neck. I lower the zipper on my jacket to let in the brisk air and release pockets of nervousness. How do I balance all these emotions? The reality is that I have no clue. The weight of it drags me down again.

I step from the tent and amble in the direction of where I

know Aron's lodging to be. The situation with him isn't any less complicated than the one now behind me. But at least Aron and I share a common background. As a Level Two, he knows what I'm going through.

In no hurry to get there, I take the long way around the campsite's perimeter, hoping to spot birds flying across the sky. Only a few wispy clouds that look like someone smeared something white across a blue background greet me, however. Slight warmth from the sun radiates onto my face and chest, and I pull the zipper to my jacket all the way down. Lost in my thoughts, I nearly miss the row Aron's tent is on. But a shout in the distance snaps me out of my head, and I make a right. His shelter is five tents in on the left.

Dread consumes me over the thought of addressing our kiss, or even discussing the night he flew us to safety in Gabrielle's pod. I have no recollection after I passed out. But I push all my anxiety aside and keep walking. His tent's flap is pulled to the side and fastened open. Inside, he sits on a chair with a tablet in hand and large computer screen in front of him. Over his shoulder floats, what appears to be, his favorite micro drone. It zips side to side as Aron works feverishly on the tablet. If I didn't know better, I'd think that little thing was alive, like a curious friend or something. I've always thought computers are easier to understand than people; I'm sure Aron does too.

The whole scene makes me smile and I forget my problems for a minute. I really do like Aron and have no wish to lose him over something stupid like a kiss we had shared in a stressful moment. I walk to the entrance and clear my throat. Aron peers up from the tablet. The golden micro drone zips over to me, encircling my body, letting out a few excited beeps, then flies back to Aron as if to tell him I'm here.

Aron's lips quirk into a smile, forming the dimple on his cheek I like so much. "Avlyn," he says warmly, placing his tablet on the table in front of him. "You're up."

I release a small sigh. "I'm up."

The smile falls off Aron's lips, and he looks away. "You know he was fearless."

Heaviness pushes on my chest because I know exactly who he's talking about.

"I don't know if I could have done what he did," Aron adds. "But he didn't think twice."

"And I stupidly tried to stop him."

Aron shrugs. "That night was insane. I know I wasn't thinking clearly, either. I was so nervous I think I almost crashed three times." He chuckles.

"We need to talk," I say.

He nods. "Yes, we do."

I scan the room for a second chair, but there isn't one. Aron's cot sits directly behind him, so I walk over and lower myself onto the edge of it. I sit for a second not saying anything and then open my mouth to speak. "I—"

"I should have never kissed you." Aron's words spill out before I get the chance to say nearly the same thing.

I stare at him, attempting to process what this means. A tiny part of me is sad to hear him say it. Aron was my pairing. I chose him, and no one forced me. Not even Affinity. But my feelings for him are so different than I have for Meyer.

"Um," he says, now fidgeting in his seat and looking away. "That doesn't hurt you, does it? Because you need to know I like you, Avlyn. Those feelings were always true, and they still are. But I think you were right back at Gabrielle's bunker. You are familiar and safe for me and so being with you is comfortable."

"Yes," I say. The whole thing is true. And he's a safe place for me too.

"But I've thought about this a lot for the past few days. Sanda and I spoke about it as well. And I can't get over what Meyer did for you... for me. He doesn't even like—"

"Like you?" I chuckle.

"Yeah." A sad smile crosses his lips. "I don't believe he's gone." Aron locks eyes with me. "If someone who's willing to sacrifice himself for others wants to be with you and you want to be with him, I have no right to interfere."

Aron's words shock me. He's so much more in tune with his emotions than I would have ever expected him to be by this time. He truly is becoming the person I thought he could be back in Elore, and I'm so glad he's not there anymore. If nothing else good comes from this mess, at least his freedom is something.

"You're a good friend, Aron."

He smiles again. "I hope so, because I want to remain friends."

"Me too."

"But, one thing. When Meyer comes back—"

"When?"

"Yes, when."

"There's been no word from him. And, even if he's still out there, how's he going to find us?" I ask.

Aron pauses for a second. "He took my drones. I built beacons into them to find each other."

My stomach clenches as I watch Aron's little drone buzz around the room. "Have you picked up on the ones he took?"

"No, but Meyer could've disengaged the trackers on his end for whatever reason. He knows how to do it. That's one of the things I showed him that night at the bunker before we got in the fight." Aron blushes and looks away.

That night? Oh, he means the night he kissed me.

He turns back and looks me straight in the eye. "Meyer's coming back, and when he gets here, you have to tell him."

My chest clenches. "About the kiss? Why? He'll probably hit you."

Aron nods his head. "Maybe. But to be honest, I don't believe so. I think he's mostly talk when it comes to that. Promise me."

"Promise I'll tell him?"

"Yes," Aron says. "Honesty is the right choice."

"I promise." But I mostly do it because I want to change the subject. "Now, what is it you're doing?" I stand and walk to the table where he works.

Aron's face lights up at the question. "Oh... a new upgraded drone project."

"Now, *that* is your first love, isn't it?"

Aron looks up at me and flashes a smile. "Yeah... it kind of is."

He chuckles as the little drone of his sweeps closer into him.

"I was able to meet with a handful of Affinity's engineers who Cynthia has on the council out here. They had a few upgrading ideas to test on the project I worked on in the bunker. Though, they were pretty impressed with the work I've already done."

I lean over and study the screen. The data includes specs, diagrams, failure and success projections, as well as other vaguely familiar information from my experience with computer hardware. But the information is still out of my realm of expertise since my talents lie with software. Aron is far more knowledgeable in hardware. It's no wonder SynCorp in Elore already had him working on special projects just a few weeks after his placement.

"I don't know exactly how they plan to use the drones yet," he says, "but I'm confident they'll play a big part in taking down both Elore and New Philly. All the information is here for the engineers to build the tech."

"You're okay with that?" He never had a choice in leaving Elore or not. The decision was forced on him by Affinity because of me. And I guess he had the option to leave New Philly, but it was under pretty stressful circumstances too. In the end, I forced him to do that as well.

"Am I okay using my skills to make the world better?" he asks, tapping at his tablet and watching as the data shifts on the screen. "Of course, I am."

"But Elore was your home."

He stops what he's doing and looks to me. "Yeah, it was. But

I never felt at home there. I was always trying to be someone I wasn't. I think that's why it was a relief to find you and ask you for a pairing. I knew I wouldn't have to spend the rest of my life being completely fake." Aron spins on his chair and looks out toward the opening of his tent. "But in the Outerbounds, it's nothing like that. The whole world is waiting. There are so many people who like me—for me."

His words hit me, and I couldn't agree more. "With all the awful things that have happened, I think that's one of the aspects I've enjoyed the most in the Outerbounds too."

"And the food bars, right?" The dimple appears.

I press my lips together. He knows I hate them. "Um, no." The rations I've had out here over the last few days have not been any better either, and my stomach rumbles for a printed meal or one of Sanda's home-cooked dinners. "When this is all over, I'm going to ask Sanda to teach me how to cook. If I never had a food bar again, I'd be happy."

Aron chuckles. "They're not too bad. But yeah, I sure could go for another sandwich like the one I had at the cafe with you, in Elore. That was a good lunch."

"The food was good. Our first meeting wasn't."

"We won't talk about that. How were we supposed to become friends without a little conflict to start us off?"

"I guess it made me memorable."

"Yes, it certainly did." Aron nods. "So what kind of duty has Cynthia assigned you to?"

"I'm not sure yet." I decide not to tell him that Cynthia is my grandmother. He'll have too many questions that I won't know how to answer. Instead, I change the topic again. "But she did tell me they were able to transfer my father out of New Philly before President Waters got to him."

"That's great news. Are the two of you on speaking terms?"

Aron knows my past, because he had a similar relationship with his parents. "Michael and I actually had a good connection before I left him in Philly." I turn from Aron and cross my arms over my chest.

"You're still feeling guilty about leaving him, aren't you?"

"How else should I feel? I ripped him out of Elore and then left him to die at the hands of Waters."

Aron places his tablet on the table again. "Hey, I know we were brought up to try to be perfect. But, it's okay that we're not. Who knows? Your father might be angry, but he might not be, either."

"Cynthia said she'd arrange a comm for me to contact him."

"And?" he asks, tipping his head.

"And I told her I'd do it later."

"Why would you do that? We've lost enough. If you say you had a connection with him, then you need to get that back. Don't let a good thing slip between your fingers. It's not worth losing him over your pride or uncertainty."

Tears burn at the corners of my eyes and one tear slips out. I quickly wipe it off my face, a little embarrassed to cry in front of Aron.

"You need to go back and find her. Tell Cynthia you want to set up the comm right now."

I smile and wipe more moisture from my eyes. "It's a good

idea. You have good ideas."

Aron's lips quirk into a silly grin. "Yeah, I do. Now get out of here. I have work to finish."

"Fine, fine, I'll go."

His little golden drone does an excited spin around my shoulders and Aron tips his head up toward me. "See you at dinner?"

"Sounds like a plan." It'll just be rations tonight, but I haven't eaten outside of my tent for days. Plus, it'll be good to experience moral support for a change. Maybe even the company will make the meal taste better. I doubt it, but I can hope.

CHAPTER FOUR

Outside the shelter, my heart lifts a minuscule amount at the thought of talking to Michael. Aron's right. Throwing away the connection I made with him back in New Philadelphia simply because of my shame is a stupid thing to do. I need to hang onto what is important to me.

Looking around at the rows of tents, I'm a little unsure of the fastest route to Cynthia's location. My chosen seclusion these past few days—no Flexx, and with my EP still broken—has left me uncertain of the camp's layout more than I'd like. But I can wing it.

Trying to find my bearings, I wonder if Cynthia is still in the medical tent or at a different location, tactical planning? A few people mill around a series of larger tents where I assume most of the work around camp happens. She's probably there.

As I walk straight for the group of tents, a single brown bird flies overhead. Maybe it's a good sign. I pick up the pace and enter the first shelter I come to. A low buzz of voices fills the room. Half-a-dozen people glance my way, but most stay deep in conversation or with eyes trained on the devices they work on. Cynthia sits in the corner at a small table across from a man who appears to be around my father's age. My shoulders droop and I blink back my disappointment. I start to turn around, not wanting to interrupt her conversation just to arrange a comm. But, before I can escape, Cynthia glances up and locks eyes with me, then waves me over.

I give her a reluctant smile and obey, angling around tables and people to get there.

"Avlyn, meet Commander Torres." She gestures to the man sitting beside her. "It's a bit soon for the meeting we discussed earlier. But this is as good a time as any to go through a few details."

Torres stands and extends his hand to me. "It's good to meet you, Avlyn. Fisher has told me so much about you." His grip is firm, and he gives me a few shakes before removing his hand from mine.

I'm her granddaughter?

"Really? What has she shared?" I ask, trying to be friendly but also attempting to get more information about their meeting.

"That you have an amazing talent," Cynthia says. "And your—what are those abilities called again? Oh... *immersive* abilities have the potential to be extremely useful to us—"

"We simply haven't figured out the best way to use 'immersion' without putting you at risk," Torres finishes.

"What are you saying?" I ask, nerves swirling in my stomach.

He tips his head slightly. "Your ability is valuable. So,

keeping you off the front lines is our highest priority," he says, gesturing for me to sit in the empty seat next to him.

I should be braver, but relief tingles in my chest. Maybe I *can* hang back and do some good. Being far away from the war sounds wonderful to me right now. I'm not sure I could handle witnessing more death. Maybe all of us—Sanda, Aron, and Ben—can stay behind where it's safer. I flit my attention to Cynthia and then lower into the chair. Does my relation to her play any part of this decision, or is my safety merely because of my ability's value? Right now, I'm not sure I care if immersion keeps Ben, my friends, and I safe. But Cynthia is looking at her handheld, unaware of the questions in my head.

"Your brother is awake," she says.

I lurch forward, eyes wide. "What? When? Is he okay? I just left him not too long ago."

"Well, apparently he's alert. But I don't have all the details."

My gaze wavers between Cynthia and Commander Torres.

"You should go," Cynthia says. "We can pick this up later."

I pop up from my seat, heart pounding against my ribcage. "Thank you."

I dash from the tent. Outside, I glance right to left, but my mind is too wound up to figure out what direction to head.

"Which way to the Med tent?" I ask a young guy walking past. He points to the left, and I don't even bother sticking around to see if he had anything to say.

I follow the row of tents until something looks familiar. My shelter. I race past it toward Ben, relieved when a few of the tents look familiar. I know where I am now.

Nearing his tent, I slow my pace and focus my mind. *I'm on my way, Ben.*

This time a warm glow of orange fills my mind. It's something.

I rush inside and find a medic alongside Bess. Ben is sitting up on his cot. There's even a smile on his face. He turns his head in my direction, and the grin widens. He tries to swing his legs to the floor, but the medic holds out her hand, stopping him. Ben scowls but doesn't try it again. But it doesn't matter because I'm already beside him. I sink to the edge of his bed and throw my arms around his shoulders.

"You're back," I say, my voice thick with relief.

"I think I am," he sighs. "And Mom is here." Ben looks up at Bess, his eyes full of wonder and questions.

Bess smiles at Ben, but the medic redirects her to the tablet she's holding and points to the screen. Bess purses her lips as the woman directs her to the exit.

"Ben, Avlyn?" she says. "I'll be right back."

Concerned, I push up off the cot.

Bess shakes her head. "Don't worry. Everything is fine. We'll all go over it later. Stay with Ben."

I lower myself back down beside my brother. I hate being in the dark at this moment, but it also means I can talk to Ben in private.

As soon as Bess and the medic leave, I turn to my twin. "I couldn't reach you this whole time."

Ben shakes his head. "I know. I tried too. But nothing." He holds out his hand and examines his arm. "Though, I feel myself growing stronger right now. And I sensed you trying to contact me before you came in. It was kind of like a far-off voice. I think it was the sleep MedTech blocking me from responding, but it's wearing off. I guess I received the final dose last night, according to the medic."

I click my tongue and shake my head. "I told them not to give you any."

"Something did happen while I was out, though."

"What?"

Ben pauses to think. "I don't know. It's hard to remember now. But it was like I was connected to someone."

My heart skips at his words. Before she died, Ruiz mentioned Waters' experiments to recreate our ability. "Another person?"

Was someone else able to connect to Ben when I couldn't? A shiver caresses my spine. What if Waters in New Philly is controlling our thoughts or influencing us somehow? The idea fills me with dread. Ben has been in a weakened state. What if they do something to harm him?

I study Ben, and his eyes are full of concern. "It's not like they were trying to control me or anything," he says as if he read my mind. Maybe he did. "It was like I was watching something from the outside. I just don't know *what* yet. To be honest, I'm not one hundred percent sure it was even real."

"But it could have been real. Waters was working on a project to mimic *us*. He could have figured out that you are my twin."

Ben opens his mouth to speak and quickly snaps it shut. I

glance over my shoulder, surprised to see Bess and the medic return so soon.

"We've been able to slowly restart Ben's nano tech and purge his system of any lingering negative effects from the virus Director Manning uploaded into his system," The medic says while looking at her tablet. "I don't want to get anyone's hopes up. But his recovery is progressing at a rapid pace." She holds the tablet in front of Ben and scans his head, then nods. "Yes, he's already seen a 10% general improvement since regaining consciousness. I believe the temporary stasis coupled with the upgraded nanotech data Avlyn was able to provide from the DPF soldier was effective. The regeneration is amazing."

"And his aneurysm?" I ask.

Bess' mouth falls open. I guess a medic or Cynthia hadn't shared with her yet.

"We've been monitoring his anterior communicating artery closely, and the aneurysm is nearly isolated. Once the internal tech stabilizes the area, the nanos will begin the removal process. It's still early to tell, but I expect a full recovery, or close to it, by tomorrow morning."

Ben smiles widely and looks toward me. Warmth fills my mind again, and relief floods my body.

I'm not sure if I could ever forgive myself if I had lost him. Cynthia wouldn't allow me to help, but I would have forever wondered if I could have done something.

An alarm outside pierces my ears, and I jump. The look of happiness disappears from the medic's face.

"What's that?" Bess asks, covering her ears with her palms.

The medic swipes at her tablet and taps something in. "We all need to go to the mess tent."

"Why? Me too?" Ben asks.

"I don't know yet." She stares at Ben and rubs her forehead. "But yes, you. Normally I'd say no, but I think you are strong enough." Her gaze slides over to me. "Help him, please."

To the cot's side is a pair of Ben's shoes. He swings his legs over the bed's side and puts them on. I stand and grab for Ben's arm and pull him up. He rises easily.

"Follow me," the medic orders as she hands Ben a jacket.

Without hesitation we obey. But, to be honest, if we're under attack, I'm not sure the mess tent is going to provide us any more protection than we have here.

"Fisher will brief those who are not automatically dispatched," the medic shouts over the blaring alarm.

Bess keeps pace with the medic and Ben, and I follow behind. At least five others pass us, moving in the same direction. At the mess tent, around fifty people have already arrived. Some of them pace and others wait patiently for Cynthia's presence. But no sign of Sanda or Aron.

The medic waves the three of us to a table and then walks over to another person donning a medical emblem on his shirt. Ben sits, and Bess and I fall into the chairs next to him. His breathing is more labored than usual, but I try not to let it bother me. He's healing.

Cynthia walks into the room and I pop out of my seat ready to voice my questions, as do five other individuals. However, others beat me to it and begin demanding information. I don't want to bombard her with similar requests, so I plop back into my seat. A few more stragglers fall in behind Cynthia as she moves away from the tent's entrance.

A hush falls over the group as Cynthia raises her hands. "We just received word that an unidentified ship was spotted in the vicinity."

More questions ring out from the group in a jumbled mess of shouts. Cynthia raises her hand once again to quiet them. "Scouts were dispatched. But you need to prepare yourselves for the possibility of evacuation. It's only one ship but, if it's a spy craft, there are sure to be more en route."

Nervousness twists in my belly. Despite Cynthia wanting to keep me away from the direct war zone, it may be coming to us.

Sanda appears at the tent opening and races to Cynthia's side. She leans in and whispers something into her ear. Cynthia nods, and then Sanda rounds and disappears outside again.

"Our new drone tech has located the ship and our ground team is closing in," Fisher says.

It must be Aron's drones. That's why he's not here.

"Since we don't know anything else," Cynthia says. "Please return to your tents and start preparations for Evacuation Procedure Three. If that changes, you'll hear three short beeps on the emergency alert, and then it will stop. Then, wait in your shelter until further notice."

The group erupts into a roaring sea of questions again. But, Cynthia quiets them. "Evacuation Procedure Three," she says again, and then turns and walks from the tent.

Ben looks to me, his eyes wide.

"Maybe you should have stayed asleep," I joke, trying to lift my own anxiety.

"No doubt. You think I should head back to the med tent?"

I squeeze his hand and look around for the medic. But she's not here anymore. "You and Bess should come with me." I lean past Ben to see a pale-faced Bess who remains silent. "Bess? We're going back to my tent."

She breaks her trance with a hard blink. "Um, yes."

The three of us rise and weave around a few clusters of people. Where would they evacuate us to? And would it even do us any good? If Waters or Manning knows we're here, there's little chance of us getting out.

Someone grips my arm from behind. I turn, expecting Bess, but instead I'm met with a stern Commander Torres.

"Ms. Lark," he states in a deep voice. "I need you and Mr. Porter to follow me."

"We're heading back to our tent to prepare for the evacuation," I say, pulling from his grip.

Torres clutches my arm again. "Fisher's orders."

I look toward Bess.

"She'll need to stay here," Torres says.

I have no idea if Bess will be okay by herself.

"It's fine," she says. "I made it out here alone in a pod. I think I can figure things out."

I yank my arm from Torres' grip, "Lead the way."

Before Ben follows, he wraps his arms around Bess. "I don't want to leave you here. I just met you again."

Bess folds him into an embrace and then lets go. "We'll see

each other again. Be safe."

Ben answers with a sad smile. I'm filled by a sudden urge to hug her goodbye as Ben had, but I don't. I don't know why, but I don't.

"Goodbye, Bess," is all I say.

She raises her hand chest high and waves once. "Goodbye, Avlyn."

With that, we leave her in the walkway and follow Torres.

"Where are we going?" I demand.

"All I can share is that I'm escorting you to a pod with orders to head south," he says.

Ben and I look at each other. If nothing else, at least we're together. He tips his head.

"Why *is* Mom here?" he asks me. "It seems odd Cynthia would bring her here just to see us."

That's right. Ben doesn't know that Cynthia is our grandmother yet.

Before I get the chance to answer, Torres hurries us out of the tent city. Up ahead I spot, what must be, three hoverpods under tarps. Torres races forward and throws the fabric off the first craft, revealing a similar small, four-seater pod similar to the one we came here in.

The commander activates the back door and it slides up. "Get in!" he yells over the camp's blaring alarm.

Without question we obey. Ben climbs into the back seat first. I lift my foot to slide in next when the blaring suddenly stops. Torres holds a hand to his ear and shakes his head. He must be receiving instructions in his comm.

Three long beeps of the alarm sound and then silence. The metallic roar of a large hovership fills the sky. A New Philadelphian ship, similar to the ones that attacked us at Thornton, zooms by overhead. It's here. The sight shoots panic into my stomach and I almost double over, the pain like a stabbing knife. I swing my attention to Torres and catch his gaze.

"It's fine!" he yells over the noise. "Fisher has it under control."

Three of Aron's drones, from seemingly nowhere, zip past us toward the center of the camp right as Torres finishes speaking. The ship slows and hovers about two-hundred feet ahead of where we sit, and I stare, my breath coming quick.

"What's going on?" Ben asks, studying the panic on my face.

I ease from the door, and he emerges to watch what's happening too. Did Affinity capture a ship? Because that could be really helpful.

The New Philadelphian ship kisses the ground. My hair blows from my face and I squint against the hovering gusts. The engine rumbles to a stop, bringing a moment of silence before the hatch lowers with a whine. Three armed Affinity members march out—bulky, serious men, just like Commander Torres.

And then another male steps out. This one, however, slumps and drags his feet.

My heart nearly leaps out of my chest.

Meyer.

CHAPTER FIVE

My knees buckle at the sight of him. I catch myself on the pod's top, tears stinging at the corners of my eyes. Meyer's alive. *He's alive.*

"Is that Meyer? How'd he even find us?" Ben asks from beside me, but somehow it sounds as if he's a million miles away.

On shaking legs, I take a step forward. Torres throws a hand in front of me.

"You can't go yet," he says. "It's too dangerous."

I draw in a deep breath as Cynthia and ten guards hustle toward the ship and Meyer. "Why?"

"You need to stay with me," he says.

Eight of the guards dash for the ship, surrounding it, and two board. When Cynthia reaches Meyer, he holds his hand out to her and says something I can't hear. Cynthia seems to reply, and Meyer grows agitated and stumbles back. My breath hitches and I clap a hand over my mouth. Cynthia reaches out to stay him but struggles to hold up his weight. The shorter of the two guards clamps onto Meyer's upper arm, preventing his fall.

Exiting the hatch, two tiny golden drones zip toward Meyer and buzz about, disturbed it seems. They must be two of the four he took when he had left. The guard helping Meyer stand waves the bots to the camp. I'd swear the drones hesitate but then they zip off toward the tents.

"I need to accompany both you and Porter back to your quarters," Torres says.

I don't want to go back to my tent. I want to be with Meyer. "When will I be able to see him?"

"I'm not sure, Miss," he says. "He'll need to be debriefed first."

How long is that going to take? Is he okay? But I don't ask him any of my questions because I'm pretty sure he won't answer them.

Torres waves us away from the pod, and I turn to watch Meyer being escorted to the camp's north side. He doesn't even see me.

Ben comes up beside me with a thin smile. "I can't believe he found us."

"Aron's drones have a beacon in them," I mumble.

My heart pounds, wanting to escape and find Meyer. Adrenaline races through my veins. And, as if my feet have a mind of their own, they start off in Meyer's direction. There's no way I'm waiting to see him.

"Meyer!" I yell at the top of my lungs.

He twists toward me. The exhaustion appears to lift from his body as he pushes from his escort and makes a beeline for me.

In the middle of the open field our bodies collide. Meyer wraps his arms around me so tightly that I can barely breathe. But I don't care. His strong arms pick me up off my feet and swings me around until, at the end of the twist, our bodies collapse into a heap onto the ground with a thud.

I meet him on my knees and loosen a fluttering sigh of relief that originates from somewhere deep within my soul. This doesn't fix all the terrible events over the last month, but it's a start. Immediately, my lips are on his face, kissing his tear-soaked cheeks, his chin, his lips. Meyer's mouth crushes onto mine and his arms coil around my back, pulling me closer, as if he's trying to meld us together.

This is home. Meyer is my home.

"You're alive," I gasp in-between kisses, not bothering with how many people are watching us, including my brother and grandmother.

He eases back, placing his hands on the sides of my face. "*You're* alive. Fisher wouldn't tell me if you were here." Meyer slides his fingers down my arms, still clutching me as if I might disappear. He sits back, some of the exhaustion I saw a few minutes ago returning to his demeanor.

"Meyer, Avlyn," Cynthia's stern voice calls.

I tear my gaze from Meyer and snap my attention onto her.

"We need to debrief him followed by a medical examination before he's cleared," she says, holding her hand in the air to signal to the guards to hold their posts.

Feeling momentarily bold, I look up at her. "I'll walk him there myself if you give us a few minutes. Leave a guard if you want."

She crosses her arms over her chest and scowls. "We are in the middle of a war, Avlyn. We don't have time for this."

Frustration burns inside of me. "Then make time for it," I snap. "If it weren't for Meyer, Ben and I would be dead. And we are your best chance at ending this war." I stare at her for a beat. "Now please, give me a minute with him."

She drops her arms to her sides and turns, shouting to the guards. "Head back." She gestures them to the camp then twists back to us. "I'll give you ten minutes."

"Thank you," I say. But she doesn't respond as she walks away.

I look back to Meyer. Despite the weariness on his face, his dark eyes sparkle in the sun, and a full grin pulls across his lips.

"You in charge now, or something?" He chuckles. "Because I like a girl who's in charge."

Heat rakes up my neck and under the back of my hair. "I'm not in charge," I mutter under my breath.

Remembering Ben, I turn to where the pods are parked, but he and Torres are gone. I'm sure he didn't want to see Meyer and me kissing. And, as I think about it, more heat spreads to my chest. I kissed Meyer. *Seriously* kissed Meyer in front of everyone.

Meyer struggles to rise but, once he stands, he reaches out to me. I take his hand, and he pulls me up. Not releasing my grasp right away, he gently tugs me close to his warm chest, and I run my hands across his shoulder blades.

"I had to get back to you," he whispers, leaning his face into my hair. "You were all I could think about."

My chest buzzes at his words. "Don't leave me again, okay?"
Meyer's hand finds mine. "I won't if I can help it."

I stare at the camp and know we need to get back. Meyer's
pants have an old blood stain on the thigh, and it reminds me he
should be checked for injuries. I gesture with my head toward the
tents.

"Can you talk about what happened?" I ask, pulling him
slowly along.

Meyer shrugs. "Aron's drones and I took over the ship. One
of the soldiers got a shot off before I blasted him. Real bullets."

I glance down at his pant leg, torn and stained with blood.
My breath hitches.

"The other soldiers were dead," he continues. "But the pilot
and one other person were on board. The drones took them out
before I even got to the front."

"Other person? Like a copilot?"

A tiny crease forms between Meyer's brows. "No, I don't
think so. She wasn't exactly conscious."

I stop walking. "What are you talking about?"

"A girl. She was somehow immersed. But, I'm not sure
exactly what she was doing."

Panic twinges in my gut. Waters is farther along than we
thought. "Do you still have the body? I could examine the tech in
her."

Meyer looks away. "No. As soon as I destroyed the Philly
ships that were following your pod, I disarmed the ship's tracker,
landed, and dumped the bodies. I had no way to tell if they had
tracking devices in them."

I stare down at my feet, disappointed.

"But, while I was laying low, I had the chance to check out the tech on the ship. You're going to want to take a look. I couldn't make out most of it, but it sure seems like bad news for Elore. And us."

He's right. It's the strategy Ben and I attempted to use to infiltrate the Elorian mainframe and grid structure. But, if Waters has immersion tech, who knows how many people are now hacking into the mainframe and waging a real-world war. He could decimate Elore.

"Cynthia needs this information." I begin to walk again, pulling him beside me. Meyer doesn't move, and his muscular frame prevents me from forcing him. "Let's go."

"We still have a few minutes before she gets upset." Gently, he tugs me back to him and closes his eyes. "I love you, Avlyn Lark."

My stomach flutters with joy. "I lo—" But he doesn't give me a chance to say it before his tender lips are touching mine. He holds the kiss for what seems like a lifetime, and, yet, not long enough still. Slowly, he moves his lips up to my forehead.

"Okay, *now* it's time to go."

❈❈❈

Inside the meeting tent, Cynthia paces. Upon seeing Meyer, she directs him to take a seat at a table where three other people wait.

"You can go, Avlyn," she says, and then paces back the other direction.

"No way." I cross my arms over my chest. "I need to hear what Meyer has to say."

She twists toward me. "We'll fill you in later."

I plant my feet. "Cynthia, I'm involved with all of this whether you like it or not. My abilities helped set this entire war into motion. I'm sure it would have escalated eventually, but Waters is trying to develop immersion capabilities of his own, and, once Manning finds out, he'll want them. You're not going to be able to end this war without my involvement."

Cynthia narrows her eyes and stares at me for what seems like minutes rather than seconds. But I don't let the discomfort get to me and stand my ground. She pinches her lips together and gestures for me to follow. As she turns, I let out a tight breath.

Meyer leans in, grinning at me. "I really do like a girl who's in charge."

I elbow him, and he feigns pain in his side.

At the table, Meyer's smile returns to a serious expression. We take seats across from each other. Cynthia leans away from the back of her chair with her hands folded and resting on the tabletop.

"These are my advisors." She gestures to the others at the table.

The first woman is near Cynthia's age, but with darker skin. She clears her throat. "I'm Susan Redmond. I've been with Affinity for many years and served as an advisor to Adriana Ruiz." Sadness darkens her eyes, but her expression remains stoic. "Thomas Hayes and Joanne Perry served with Ruiz as well."

At the mention of their names, they each dip their head in

acknowledgment.

"Fisher has shared information concerning your abilities, Ms. Lark," Thomas says. "They are quite remarkable. And we understand your twin, Mr. Porter, has similar capabilities."

I nod.

"This is why you're going to want to hear what I have to report," Meyer interjects. "The Philly ship has a form of immersion tech on it. Back in New Philadelphia, Avlyn believes she stumbled onto information of how Waters is using her test results to develop immersive abilities on select citizens. He called it Project Ascendancy. And it seems he might be farther along than we originally thought."

"If Waters infiltrates Elore's mainframe, he could remove any defenses. Take out the grid," I say.

"Which is good for us," Joanne adds.

Cynthia shakes her head. "Yes, if only it were Affinity marching in to take over Direction. But Waters is dangerous. More dangerous than we were previously aware. What he did at Thornton was an atrocity."

"This is why you should have more than foot soldiers," I say. "Ben and I will destroy this immersion tech. But we'll need to discover where he's housing the immersive test subjects first."

"Do we have leads on plausible locations?" Thomas asks.

"Not yet, but we'll be working through every possible option," Cynthia says. "If we don't need to go in directly, we won't."

Meyer slumps down in his seat an inch or two. He's trying to hold it together, but any adrenaline that had kept him alert is now wearing off.

Joanne gives Cynthia a quizzical look and opens her mouth to speak.

"Ma'am," Meyer interrupts. He reaches into his pocket and produces a small data drive. "I have all the information you'll need on here, from what happened outside of Thornton all the way up until I landed. I'm sure the explanations are a lot more coherent than I'm going to be right now. I haven't slept in days."

Cynthia takes the drive. "Go to the medical tent for evaluation... and then rest." Cynthia sets her attention to me. "Will you escort him?"

Part of me knows she's using this as an excuse for me to leave, but I stand anyway. "Let's go, Meyer."

He stands. "If you think of any questions, you know where to find me."

"Thank you, Mr. Quinn," Cynthia says.

I take Meyer's hand and interlace my fingers with his. Outside, Meyer and I amble through the maze of tents; the med facility isn't far, no need to hurry.

I lean my head onto his shoulder. "Cynthia is my grandmother."

Meyer turns his head to me. "Is that why she shot down your idea?"

"I think so."

He chuckles. "Well, I want you safe too. But I know we're never going to be safe if Waters' immersives are strong enough to destroy Elore from the inside. And, there's no way he's stopped searching for you, anyway."

"Maybe." The med tent is ahead of us. "For now, let's take care of you."

Before we arrive, one of Aron's drones flies in next to us, settling over Meyer's shoulder. It whines happily, and Meyer softly laughs.

"Did you make a friend on that ship?" I ask.

Meyer nods. "I think the two of us bonded."

We enter the tent, the drone following behind, and the same medic from earlier sits at a table while working on a handheld, now folded out into a tablet.

"I brought you a new patient," I say, trying to sound cheerful.

"Fisher messaged you were coming," she says, rising and pointing Meyer to the first cot.

Meyer has a seat and lets out a sigh. The micro drone hovers near him.

"I'm going to take some scans, but my preliminary diagnosis is that you are dehydrated and need sleep, Mr. Quinn."

I place my hand on Meyer's shoulder. "May I stay?"

She runs her fingers through her hair and then twists to retrieve her tablet. "No, I think if you stay, he'll not get the rest he needs. Why don't you come back in the morning?"

"But—" I protest.

"Go make yourself useful somewhere else," she says.

I scowl at her and then bend down, planting my lips square onto Meyer's. When I release him from the kiss, he gives me a goofy grin.

The medic scoffs. "See? No rest."

CHAPTER SIX

"Hey," a far-off voice echoes as something touches my shoulder.

My lids blink open to Ben's smiling face. He's standing over me, wearing a dark puffy jacket and a stretchy hat pulled over his hair. I curl the blanket up to my chin to ward off the crisp morning air in my tent. It's not working. Sleeping outside would be far more comfortable in the summer.

"What time is it?"

"Earlier than we should be up, but I want to go look at the ship. Cynthia cleared it, and Aron and Sanda are already out there."

I pop up from the cot and peer out the open tent flap. A pink hue paints nearby tents. The sun is just now rising. "Why didn't you get me up earlier, then?"

Ben shrugs. "I don't know. You looked so peaceful... and warm."

I am peaceful. Having Meyer back renews my spirit, and I

slept better last night than I have in days. Sure, he's in the Med tent for the night, but apparently, his nanos continuing to heal the injury on his leg just fine. "Is Meyer at the ship?"

"No. Sanda said they have him under observation until after breakfast." Ben reaches into his pocket and pulls out a food bar. "Speaking of breakfast..."

My stomach nearly turns over at the sight of it, but I snatch the food bar from him. "What flavor?"

"Apple."

"Haven't had this flavor yet." I glance at the bar again and grimace. "You sure you're healthy enough to check out the ship?"

"Yeah, I'm fine. The Medic cleared me. Ninety nine percent back to normal."

I look at the bar and back at him. "Give me a few minutes to get dressed?"

Ben nods, pulling the flap shut as he leaves.

I down the bar in as few bites as I can manage. It's no better than the cherry, or any other flavor for that matter. But it does the job. I toss on a pair of gray pants and a black sweater, lace up my boots, topping it all off with a thick camo jacket. Then, I make quick work of my hair.

Outside, Ben hands me a stunner. His is holstered to his side, but I tuck mine into my pocket since I don't have anywhere else to store it. The air outside the tent is even colder than inside and the packed-down grass glistens from a sheer film of frost.

"Did you get a handheld issued to you yet?" I ask.

Ben shakes his head.

"Me either. I think Cynthia is trying to keep me out of the

loop a bit."

"Why?"

I stop walking and round to Ben. "You asked me yesterday why Bess is here. Has she told you anything yet?"

Ben shakes his head.

Here goes. "Cynthia is Bess' mother."

Ben's eyes grow wide. "Her mother? How?"

"I don't know the full story yet, but, yes, she is. Cynthia is our grandmother."

Ben narrows his eyes in thought. "Well, that explains why she's holding back on you. So, who else knows?"

"I'm not entirely sure yet. Bess... and I told Sanda and Meyer." I grab my twin's arm and pull him along. "You'll have to talk to Bess about it later."

"I'll be doing that."

Cynthia had the ship relocated last night to a more secluded spot a little farther out from the camp. Ben and I jog the rest of the way, and I will admit the exercise feels good to me. The last few days of lying around hasn't helped my mood. After a few minutes, the ship comes into view. Now, it's covered by an elastic tarp—I suppose to camouflage it from the air—staked to the ground and stretching out over the hull's top.

Aron appears at the hatch. Seeing him reminds me of a conversation I promised to have with Meyer, one I dread. Aron steps out from the ship's gangway and descends to the ground, a drone hovering above his shoulder. Sanda rounds from the ship's back and presents the tablet in her hand to Aron. A second drone follows behind her and flies around her head. She points to the screen, and then looks up in our direction. Her face lights up. She waves and leans into Aron, who is focused on the tablet. So much so, he raises his hand and waves without looking.

"What did you two find?" Ben says when we reach them.

"Like Meyer reported, this ship has some pretty amazing tech on board," Aron says, finally looking up from his tablet. "It surprised me since Elore is so advanced. I didn't expect any of New Philadelphia's tech to be more so. I do think his new immersive system is still in beta, though. But Waters is onto something."

"Which is bad," I say, looking to Ben.

"Which is very bad," Aron echoes. "But, if we can figure out what he's doing, we'll be ahead of the game, especially if he's not aware we have his ship yet."

"We should take this data back to Cynthia," Sanda says to Aron. "Go over what we found."

Aron looks at her. "I probably should show Avlyn and Ben inside first."

"Oh, they're smart." Sanda glances at me and smiles. "They can figure it out themselves. Now come on." She grabs Aron's arm, nearly knocking the tablet from his hands. "Sorry."

He smiles, making the dimple on his cheek appear, and returns his attention to Ben and I. "It's also been combed over by Cynthia and the other techies last night." He swipes on his tablet. "One of my drones will stay here with you."

The drone that was beside Sanda buzzes excitedly to the left of Ben.

Sanda leans in and hugs me. "See you soon," she whispers in

my ear as I return the squeeze. This kind of human contact is becoming more and more comfortable for me every day. I'm not sure how I lived without it the first seventeen years of my life.

She releases me and taps Aron on the shoulder. "Race you," she calls, already sprinting forward, not waiting for Aron to make it a fair race. Aron barely misses a beat and chases after her. But Sanda is faster.

Ben bumps me on the elbow. "Let's check it out." He walks up the gangway and I follow, Aron's drone gliding in behind us.

The ship's interior is mostly a long open corridor. Benches line the sides with straps for the soldiers to affix themselves to the seats while in flight. When the soldiers attacked us on the ground, there were maybe twenty. It's all a blur now. But, looking around, there are thirty seats. Makes me grateful the ship wasn't loaded to capacity during the attack. Who knows if we would have made it out with ten more, even with the help of Aron's drones. I wipe my now sweaty palms on my pants.

"You okay?" Ben asks.

I look at him. "Yes, why?"

"I think our ability is returning. I was getting a pretty strong wave of emotion from you."

Just bad memories, I say to him in my mind to test his theory.

Ben's lips bend into a thin smile. Part of me is glad I was barely conscious for much of that night.

The sensation of yellow sunshine strangely mixed with waves of blue fills me. *I guess the ability is back. Good thing, I missed it.*

Me too. We should get busy.

I study the area around the cockpit and notice a seat near the front that is constructed differently from the rest. *That's what we're looking for*, I think, and gesture with my head toward it.

The chair has armrests with metal cuffs at the ends. Not very inviting.

"You want to try it out?" Ben asks, but nervousness glints in his hazel eyes.

The drone emits a high-pitched whirring and floats over the seat.

Not really, I think to him. But, I shoo away the golden orb and take a seat in the chair anyway. This is what I'm here for. I brace for anything. But nothing happens.

Maybe put your hands in the cuffs, Ben thinks to me.

I hesitate, then lay my wrists into the open cuffs. Without warning, the cuffs snap shut, and a metal restraint emerges from the chair's back, affixing my torso in place. Panic waves through my body for a split second until my vision goes white and bursts into a sea of code for a schematic of the ship's interior. My body relaxes.

I have complete control of the ship.

"Welcome, beta immersive," a soothing, robotic female voice says in my mind. "How may I assist you?"

"What is my purpose?" I ask.

"To assist in piloting the ship," she replies in her flat tone.

There has to be more to this position. No way is Waters wasting immersive abilities on piloting. I take a long shot.

"What is the primary function of..." I pause to recall the name of Waters' immersion project. "Project Ascendancy?"

"This is classified information. Warning: if you continue to inquire about Project Ascendancy, you will be deactivated."

I groan. Apparently, the project name is the same, but Waters has built in more safeguards than in past systems I've explored. I'm going to need to hack into the tech. But, since I'm not sure what I'm looking for, it could take a little time.

"Okay, fine. Your system needs repairs," I say. "Grant access to the data stores from the last four days."

"Working," the unseen voice says and, in a beat, a wall of code flies in front of me. I reach to touch it, and it vanishes.

"Warning: I have detected an incoming hovercraft ten miles from our current location."

Chapter Seven

"What's going on?" Ben says as his form materializes in my mind.

"The ship's computer system has detected a hovercraft in the area," I say to him. To the system, I order, "Identify ship."

"Scanning," the voice says and pauses for a few seconds. "Elorian vessel. Unknown model. The ship landed three-point-five miles southeast from your current location."

Ben's stares at me, eyes wide. "Elore? We need to alert the camp. It's likely a spy."

"Download coordinates and any data concerning this Elorian vessel," I order the computer. A slight electrical jolt runs through my body as the information downloads to my nanos.

"Got it. Let's go," I say.

We release from the hovercraft's system, and my vision returns to the real immersion tech chair within the ship. In my mind, I command the system to release the cuffs off my wrists and the restraint on my chest. When it does, I pop from the seat. The micro drone zips right to left, agitated. I wave to it and hold out my hand. The bot floats to me and lands on my palm.

"Give me a second," I say to Ben.

"Don't take too long. We need to go."

I close my eyes and immerse with the little drone. In my mind, I push all the location data into the bot. I flick open my lids. "Find the Elorian ship and report back to me."

The orb beeps what I guess is a yes and then zips down the ship's interior and out of the open hatch. Ben grabs my upper arm and we race from the vessel, the metal flooring pounding under our feet.

Outside, the sun hangs low in the morning sky, melting the blanket of frost on the ground. The air is still. No alarm blares in the distance to indicate the camp's knowledge of the nearby Elorian ship. I pull my jacket in tight as I follow Ben toward the encampment.

Once there, we weave our way through the tent rows to the central meeting place where people are already bustling with activity.

Aron, Sanda, and Cynthia sit around a table, deep in conversation with Commander Torres, who's wearing a tan uniform today. Ben and I hustle to them.

Ben stares at Cynthia anxiously, not saying anything. The wave of nervous energy he emits overtakes me. But this isn't the time for familial introductions.

"A ship has been detected," I inform them, out of breath.

Cynthia flicks her attention to me. "What? There's nothing on our scanners this morning." She rises and heads for a woman with short blonde hair who is working on a tablet. "Have you picked anything up out of the ordinary?"

"No, ma'am." The woman's fingers dance over the screen. "Nothing since the ship yesterday."

"Stand by. We may be headed into alert mode again," Cynthia says.

The woman nods.

Cynthia turns back to me. "Are you positive?"

"Ben and I were out at the Philly ship. We were testing the immersion capabilities and I tapped into the ship's computer. I was barely in when the system informed me of an Elorian ship barely ten miles out. While I had the computer scanning for data, the ship had landed only a few miles from here."

"Where? Why didn't we pick it up?" Cynthia asks. Sanda and Aron come up behind her.

"I don't know. Maybe Elore has a new cloaking ability you are not aware of, but New Philly is." I twist to the woman holding the tablet. "May I borrow that?" I say, pointing to the device.

The woman defers to Cynthia, but my grandmother nods approval. I take the tablet from the woman and push the upload stored in my nanos to the tablet.

"It's all there." I hand the device back to her. "Plus, I sent the drone Aron left with us after the Elorian ship."

"You did?" Aron produces his handheld and folds the screen out wider. He swipes his finger across the surface, considers the information, and then holds it up for us to see. "I'm locked on." He turns the screen back to himself and studies the data. "The drone located the ship. It's a medium hover, built to carry three passengers, including the pilot. The model has a limited amount of walking room and storage. Here, you can see."

He waves us back to the table and places his tablet in the center. Above it, a small hologram appears of the oblong ship. Disembarking are three soldiers who are wearing the same drab DPF uniform as the soldier who crashed outside Gabrielle's bunker. Feelings of guilt for letting the man die swirl in my core. But, there was nothing I could have done, so I push the feeling away.

The hologram shows the soldiers setting up camp. At least, I guess that is what they're doing. The ship is parked beneath tree cover, and two of soldiers busy with removing supplies from the vessel. I don't see the third anymore.

"Looks like a scouting mission," Cynthia says. "If we're lucky, they may not even know we're here yet. Well, not our exact location. Go ahead and call the drone to return, Aron."

"It could take them out right now. The drone could stun them," Aron says.

Cynthia raises her hand slightly. "No, not yet. I need time to figure out the best course of action." She looks to Ben and me. "Thank you for your quick thinking. I'm sending out soldiers to take it from here."

I open my mouth to reply but Cynthia shifts away.

"The camp is on Silent Alert Level Two," Cynthia announces, raising her voice to those inside the tent. "No one is to leave unless I order them to do so." She returns to the woman with the tablet. "Please inform the rest of the camp over handheld devices. There are not enough of the DPF to warrant evacuating.

And I want to see what the Elorian soldiers are up to first."

"Orders?" A tall Affinity soldier approaches Cynthia.

"Douglas, arrange a team of ten to surround the intruder ship. Have them meet here in twenty minutes," Cynthia says.

"Yes ma'am," Douglas says, and promptly exits the tent.

I step up behind her with Ben still at my side. "Ben and I should be able to help." I look to him, and he nods. "You know I came across that DPF outside Thornton in the crashed ship. I've been able to study the data I downloaded before he died. I think I might even be able to shut off these soldier's programming with that information."

Cynthia scowls at me. "This is risky, Avlyn. I have the information you obtained from the incident. And you were not able to download his data without killing the soldier."

"I know, but..." I say.

"We are going to send in the micro drones and a team," Cynthia insists. "They should be able to handle it without endangering you."

"Right," I argue. "But the DPF soldiers have a self-destruct feature built into their nanos. If you can't disable it, they will die. Ben and I are the only people who might be able to flip their programming quickly. This is our one chance at the information in their tech."

I look away, remembering Jensen, the DPF soldier and how he allowed himself to self-destruct so I could try to save Ben. These Level One citizens don't deserve being experimented on or made into living weapons and need our rescue just as much as anyone else.

"We can get better insight to what Manning is planning to do and how he's using the Level Ones for the DPF," I press, "and if plans changed since the attack on Thornton."

Cynthia grasps mine and Ben's shoulders and leans into us. "I won't value their lives over yours," she whispers. "Beyond any personal feelings, your abilities are too great to throw away on three soldiers. Please return to your tent and await my orders."

"But—" Ben begins, frustration filling his face.

"No," Cynthia says firmly. "Return to your tent." She looks back at the table and catches Aron's attention. "I need you to program a few drones."

Aron nods and taps on his tablet.

This is getting nowhere. "Fine. We'll wait for you," I say, grabbing Ben's arms and pulling him toward the exit without even saying goodbye to Sanda or Aron.

One of the microdrones heads straight for us and buzzes to my side. It must be the one I sent to the Elorian ship. I wave for it to follow and it trails behind us as we walk in the direction of my tent. I hold out my hand and the drone lands on my palm. I join its tech and order the bot to stay with us even if Aron calls it back.

"Take us to the Elorian ship." I release the bot again, sending the drone ahead since it knows the way.

So, we're not headed to your tent? Ben says in my mind.

I don't think Cynthia understands what could happen to the soldiers. And how we can be of help in this situation.

Ben keeps pace. Then why didn't you try harder to explain it to her? She's letting her emotions get in the way of herself.

Because she's not going to listen and we'll run out of time. I break into a sprint and Ben tails right behind. Hurry. If we don't get out of here now, the guards will stop us.

Are you sure this is the right thing? Cynthia's plan might work.

Probably not, but I feel like I owe it to the soldier who let me download his information for you.

For me?

Yeah, his nano upgrade helped save you.

At the encampment's edge, guards have yet to arrive. The bot hovers alongside me, waiting for us to move again. We must get to the ship before the Affinity guards do. If we can't, I have a feeling this will not end well. Possibly for either side.

"We don't have long," Ben says. "But, if we're quick, we should be there by the time Affinity leaves."

"Then we need to get going." I race in front of him, following the drone.

Keeping silent, Ben and I try to stick close to the trees so we are more difficult to spot. Eventually, the microdrone leads us to the ship and two of the soldiers have set up camp outside of it. The other must be in the pod. We duck farther into the tree cover. I pull out my stunner and check the settings. It's set to stun. I don't want to accidentally kill any of them if I don't need to.

"We need to achieve physical contact with at least one of the soldiers for our plan to work. Once we flip him, hopefully he can help us complete the rest," I say. "Back at our camp, a few days ago, I went over the data from the DPF we had brought to Gabrielle's bunker. Manning is using a form of tech called a

Neuro-link to connect them. But Jensen, the crashed DPF, was able to disconnect and control his nanos for a short period of time by focusing on his emotions. There wasn't time then for me to figure out how to completely disarm the system. But, if we work as a team, we can overload the flipped soldier's system and then release him. I can disable his nanotech if you can distract him with emotions, like love. It's the emotion that allowed Jensen to regain control of himself."

"How am I supposed to know what one of these guys loves?"

I fall into a squat not knowing the answer to his question. Jensen broke the connection himself and I knew part of his story when I saw the picture drawn by his child. But, I don't know anything about these people.

"Maybe fear will work then, or loss. The Level Ones have been in fear since Manning initiated the draft. But I'm sure it was long before that. They were always the last to receive the VacTech and never gained the same privileges as the rest of us."

Ben drops next to me and looks away. "I remember. I was one of them."

"Do you think you can convey to him what you... *we* went through? You could show him the experiments. Show him your fear."

Ben's face turns white.

"We are going to need to talk about it eventually," I say.

Ben nods, but his dark emotion clouds over me. "I can do it," he says in a low tone. "The more people who know what happened to us, how they used us, the better."

I touch the tips of my fingers to Ben's shoulders.

Now to get one of those soldiers away from the rest. Maybe a diversion?

But it's not even necessary because, the second I form the thought, a soldier with blond hair steps from the pod. For whatever reason, he walks towards the wooded area on our left.

Ben looks at me, raising his eyebrow. *Maybe he needs to use the... facilities.* He grips his weapon at his side.

Well, I'm not asking questions. I turn over my stunner and recheck the settings. Low stun. We only want him out briefly, just enough time for us to immerse and flip him back to normal.

We set off as quietly as we can, keeping the soldier within our sights. I signal for our drone to keep an eye out, and it buzzes away toward the ship.

The guard walks behind several trees and I crouch, training the stunner on him. Hopefully, we are far enough away from the ship to conceal the blast from the others. I check my aim, since I only have one shot, and depress the trigger. The brief pulse vibrates my hands, and the shot hits the guard in the back. He falls to the ground with a soft thump.

"Let's go," I whisper, but Ben is already on the move.

We reach the guard, flip him over and kneel, placing our hands on his chest. The world fades to white, and his internal nanotech surrounds me. Ben appears to my left, muttering words I can't make out for some strange reason. He throws his head back, eyes closed, and raises his hands as if in a trance.

"Take me to his nanos!" I scream in my mind. Furious emotion from Ben floods our surroundings and the space dots with glowing red. The color brightens and glows, spreading and taking over, cracking and spidering through the whiteness.

My head spins with the sensation, and I push off Ben's emotional state and focus again.

The nanos appear, floating around us, fading in and out as if in a dream.

"Wha–what are you... doing?" a new groggy voice echoes in the space.

"I'm trying to help you. *We* are trying to help you. You need to let us." I grapple for the nearest nano bot and pull up its code. The tracker appears, as well as the self-destruct sequence—a kill switch in the programming—and I quickly disarm them both.

"Who *are* you?" The voice demands, sounding stronger than before. I think what Ben is doing is working.

"I know Direction hurt you," Ben's voice instantly becomes clear in my mind. "They hurt us too..."

"I have a family... my pairing... they took her," the voice says, panicking.

In an instant, the nanos vanish and the white left in the space turns blood red. Heat overtakes my body. I scream at Ben, "We need to get out of here!"

Ben's eyelids snap open and he races for me. I suck in a breath, and my eyes open to the real world where my twin and I kneel before the soldier.

The man gasps and his eyes fly open. He shoots up straight to sit. Without thinking, I throw myself on top of him, knocking him back to the ground with a thud, and shove my stunner in his face.

"Don't even think about calling out," I growl. "If you do, you are dead."

Ben stands and trains his weapon on the soldier. Terror fills the man's face, and he shakes his head. Very unlike when his actions were being more controlled.

I'm ninety-nine percent sure we did it, I think to Ben.

Ben lowers his gun, and I do the same.

"Please don't kill me," the confused soldier pleads, pulling his hands up near his head.

My shoulders relax just as the crunch of a footstep sounds behind me. I twist toward it and throw my stunner out. One of the other DPF soldiers stands before us, our little micro drone clutched in his palm. Without warning, a blast from his weapon comes our way. On instinct, I depress my trigger, hitting him flat in the chest. He crumples to the forest floor and drops the golden bot, which now appears to be unworking.

Next to me, Ben's body hits the ground.

CHAPTER EIGHT

I need to flip the new soldier before his tracker kicks in or he dies, but, instead, I drop to my knees and throw my hand to Ben's chest, feeling for his heartbeat. I sigh with relief. A healthy pulse drums against my hand. He's alive. Only stunned.

Relieved, I swing my attention around and find the already-flipped soldier sitting up with a dazed look on his face. He won't be any help for a while, if ever. If I can't purge the DPF upgrade on the stunned soldier quickly, he'll die. I glance back to Ben, but he's still unconscious. I've no idea if I can complete both sequences in time without him. But I'll have to try.

I scramble to the passed out soldier and place my palms onto his chest. The forest around me vanishes. I connect to his nanotech and visualize the code for the kill switch. The symbols appear, and I work to disable the code, rearranging and removing the patterns.

As I work, I also call up my memories from Elore to show this soldier. Flashes of the experiments Ben and I were subjected to blink in and out of focus. An infant's screams echo around me. The voice of the medic who said, "None of them last long," murmurs in the background. I grit my teeth.

I arrange the last bit of code just as I did on the other soldier. Hopefully, it works. The other one didn't die, so that's a good sign. I wave the code away and let the memories and emotions come to the forefront of my mind. I remind the soldier of the chaos in Level One on the day of the draft. Families were ripped apart, and I'm sure his was one of them. Anger wells inside me. The haunting image of Naomi Jensen being stunned for trying to protect her child while her pairing was led away flashes in my mind.

"Get out of my head!" an unseen voice shouts.

"You have to remember. Don't let Direction take everything from you."

"They've already done that," the voice seethes.

My heart leaps. He's hearing the truth. But then my being fills with heat and resistance as the DPF programming fights for control.

"Did you know that Virus three-zero-zero-five-B was not an accident?" I yell. "Direction intentionally set that virus loose and Level Ones died because of it. Manning is doing the same thing now by controlling you for the DPF. It's a means of population control."

"No, that's not true. The Direction Initiative was formed to protect the citizens of Elore from viruses in the Outerbounds," the voice booms.

"What dangers have you seen? You're in the Outerbounds,

and it's healthy. Direction has decided to kill Level Ones with the virus to frighten Elorians away from the Outerbounds and keep citizens under control."

His fear and anger surround me. But, there's another emotion too. Hope. Just a fraction. This man knows that what I've shared is all true. He probably always has. But the program has a firm hold onto him.

"Direction is always lying to us. They have from the very beginning," I yell. "They took away your life with lies and expected for you to die for them!"

The voice screams back, piercing my ears.

"You can fight it. I've disabled the kill switch Direction installed. You have nothing to lose."

The temperature rises higher, and my entire body feels on fire, inside and out.

"You must listen to me!" I scream, my head spinning.

Everything blacks out.

My eyes shoot open. A gasp of air inflates my lungs and the overwhelming scent of damp earth fills my nose.

"It didn't work. It didn't work," I want to shout, but it comes out in mumbles.

"Is she dead?" a shaky voice I don't recognize says from my left.

I twist my head toward the sound, and the soldier Ben and I flipped stands at my side.

"Ben? Where's Ben? Did you hurt him?" I mumble as I attempt to sit up.

The world carrousels and I fall backward. A hand grasps my

arm, and another supports my back, pulling me up to a sitting position.

"Are you okay?" Ben whispers.

I look at him and blink several times, confused. I have no idea if I'm okay. "I... I need to go back in. I didn't finish. He'll die."

Movement comes in front of us and I flinch. The soldier whose nanos I just immersed with rises. He tips his head and narrows his eyes at me in thought, as if he's trying to recall lost information.

"What's going on, Barrett?" he says to his comrade, then pauses. Studying me, he says, "You're the traitor we're searching for." He glances back to Barrett and then eyes his weapon on the ground in confusion.

"Maybe it did work," Ben whispers in my ear.

Barrett steps between the solider and us. "I think we can trust them."

"She's... she's a traitor," the soldier growls. He scrunches up his face, perplexed. "Isn't she?" Then the soldier's expression shifts again. "Of course we can't trust her."

My head is still spinning, and my thoughts barely come together. "We're trying... to hel–help you."

I look for my stunner but it's too far, and I'm pretty sure if I tried to get up I'd fall over anyway.

"Carver," Barrett whispers, holding his hands out to calm the other soldier. "She could have killed us, and she didn't. They released us from whatever Direction did to us."

"Direction lied to us?" Carver mumbles as if he's trying to

work out the truth. His shoulders relax, and his gaze bounces back and forth between Ben and me. "You released us from the DPF programming? How?"

My mind clears. "We did. Manning is lying to you. Do you remember anything else I showed you?"

"I do," Barrett answers instead.

"We don't really have time for this," Ben insists, pulling me to my feet. "We need your help disarming the other soldier. There are people from our group on the way to intercept you. And, if Avlyn and I are unable to flip the other guy back to normal before they get here, we can't guarantee the tracker Manning installed won't kick in if they shoot him."

"What do we need to do?" Carver asks. "I don't want anyone to die."

Nausea whirls in my stomach from the last immersion, but I push it down. "I need you to pick up your weapon and capture us."

"What?" Ben asks.

Barrett takes in a deep breath, and his eyes fill with fear. "I'm not a very good soldier in real life. I just want to get back to my family."

"Well," Ben says. "If that's what you want, you'll need to pretend you know what you're doing."

I grab my stunner and the broken drone off the ground. After, I tuck the weapon into the back of my pants and pocket the bot. Ben conceals his stunner, as well.

I look to Carver. "Do you know anything about the other guy? Who he was in Level One?"

Carver wipes his hands on his pants. "Not much. A bunch of us were detained together before we were upgraded, if that's what you want to call it. We talked before the medics took us in for the procedure. Thompson is his name. He's young, just arranged his pairing."

"Do you know if he had any emotional investment with her?" I ask. It's a long shot, but Level Ones are often more emotional than Twos or Threes and might choose a pairing based on attraction or even love.

"I... I'm not sure. I had just met him," Carver mumbles.

"There was something," Barrett says. "He mentioned her name several times. Diana, I think."

I look at Ben. "It's something extra to go on. I think the programming had a stronger hold on Carver. Knowing some of Thompson's past might be helpful to trigger his memories."

"So, what's the plan?" Carver asks.

"The two of us will put our hands behind our heads," I say. "And you'll escort us to the ship. When Thompson is in view and close enough, maybe fifteen feet, you need to stun him. Ben and I will take it from there, hopefully before Affinity arrives."

At this point, I don't know how far I'll get without vomiting, but it's our only chance.

"Affinity?" Barrett asks, his eyes wide.

"Yes," I say. "You both are working for them now. Let's go."

I put my hands onto the back of my head and Ben does the same. Barrett steps behind me and shoves his stunner into my back. My heart leaps into my throat. Other than the fact that we hadn't killed him, he has no reason to trust us. Even if they believe our story, they have years of Direction propaganda under their belts.

"Keep in mind," I say, "if Thompson suspects you are normal again, he'll probably shoot you, and not on stun. So, helping us is your best chance." I hope my angle will add enough gravity to the situation to keep them in check.

They both nod and, without speaking, we march past the thicket of trees and into the slight break where the pod landed. My pulse races as the stunner's barrel pushes between my shoulder blades. Sickness waves through me, but I continue placing one foot in front of the other. *Keep it together, Avlyn,* I mentally encourage myself.

"Thompson!" Carver calls from behind Ben. "We require your assistance."

I look to my twin, whose face is whiter than usual. He must be questioning their loyalty too.

When they start shooting, you need to get out of the way, I think to him.

Hopefully, it's Thompson they're shooting at and not us. Ben raises his eyebrow.

I train my eyes back onto the ship as Thompson emerges from the exit. He's about my age and not very tall, maybe my height, with short, dark brown hair. He immediately un-holsters his stunner and points it our way.

"What do you have?" he asks.

"Found these two patrolling in the woods." Carver then calls out, "One of them appears to be the traitor we're looking for. Avlyn Lark."

I grunt as he pokes me in the back with his stunner again.

"We need to secure them," Carver orders.

"And the male? Is he one of the missing?" Thompson asks.

Carver doesn't answer immediately. The pause causes my stomach to drop.

"An Affinity member I thought we should question."

Thomson narrows his eyes. "Orders are to kill—"

Barrett flings me aside and I topple to the ground and cover my head. Barrett and Carver throw out their weapons and shoot. Thompson crumples to the ground.

I turn to Barrett, and he nods for me to go. With that, I push up from the ground and meet Ben, who's already crawling for the soldier. I help him up and we race to slide to Thompson's side.

"His pairing's name is Diana," I remind Ben.

We place our hands onto Thompson's arms. As before, everything goes white and his nanos appear. Ben is at my side, frantically calling up his own memories and reminding Thompson he needs to get back to Elore to see Diana again.

A sharp pain shoots through my skull, and I gasp. I shake it off and throw my hands to the nearest nano, ordering its coding to appear. But it doesn't obey. I muster up my focus, but the stabbing pain in my head resurfaces. Flipping these soldiers must be overloading my nanos and my brain.

I grit against the pain and order the code to appear. Strings of information blink in and out and then materialize fully. My fingers fly toward the symbols and rearrange the patterns. But my eyesight blurs, so I squint to sharpen the targeted sequences. My hands shake, and the shivering advances up my arms and into my chest. The sensation continues through the rest of my body and light-headedness overwhelms me. I fight to stay conscious as the code fades in and out.

A jumbled voice that isn't Ben's resonates in the space. It must be Thompson's. But I can't make out if he's following Ben's lead or if he's resisting the flip.

I must finish. I stretch for the last bit of code, deactivating both the tracker and the kill switch, and then swipe it back into place. My hand withdraws, and my body goes limp and falls.

Crack!

I gasp as the sound thrusts me into reality. I snap back from Thompson's body just as one of Aron's drones zips around me, forcing me to collapse backward.

Did... did we do it? I think to Ben, but nothing comes back.

As if in slow motion, the scene warps and fades. Ben stands with his hands raised as a hazy group of Affinity soldiers surrounds us.

The sound of a stunner's pulse echoes in my ear, and both Carver and Barrett buckle to the ground beside me.

"Are we secure?" A male voice asks, who sounds a long way from where I lie.

"Why are *they* here? Get them to safety," another voice shouts, this one furious and almost certainly my grandmother's.

CHAPTER NINE

Beep... Beep... Beep...

I awaken to a splitting headache and someone squeezing my arm.

Beep... Beep... Beep...

"Can someone shut that sound off?" I mutter.

I turn my head and find Meyer sitting next to me, frowning. A medic runs a relentlessly beeping handheld scanner over me. She's also frowning.

"You're not invincible, young lady," she says. "Your body was trying to tell you to stop, and you didn't listen. What you did out there nearly shorted out your nanos. And since they seem to be so highly integrated with your brain, I'm afraid if you take on too much too fast, your actions might cause brain damage."

"She's not the best at listening." Meyer eyes me.

"How was I supposed to listen when someone's life was at stake?" I mumble.

The medic's lips form a thin line and then she picks up my

right hand, placing it on her device's screen. "I'm giving you something for the pain."

My heart races at the thought of MedTech. But the stabbing in my head is unbearable.

"My stomach—"

"Nausea?" she questions. "Yes, this will take care of nausea too."

The device vibrates but, other than that, I feel nothing in my palm. Though, before she finishes, the headache subsides, and the nausea dissipates. When it stops, she returns my hand to my side.

"Now get some rest." She walks over to a table, sits, and folds the scanner out into a tablet.

I look to Meyer. "Is Ben okay? What about the soldier. He's still alive, right?"

"They're all fine," he assures me. "Ben immersed with Thompson and made sure everything was correct. Cynthia has all the DPF detained. I'm not sure what she's going to do."

I push up from the cot. "I need to see them. Check the disabling for myself."

"You are not going anywhere until I finish your scans," the medic says without looking up.

I roll my eyes and plunk back down.

"Why did you risk your life to go out there, anyway?" Meyer asks, keeping his voice down.

My stomach tightens with guilt. "I felt like I owed Jensen. If I could've kept him from dying, I would have. Getting to these men before Affinity was the only way to save them. Plus, if they were stunned the kill switches could've brought more Direction soldiers before we were ready."

"Why didn't you tell Fisher?"

"I tried. But she refuses to let me finish my explanations. She's trying to protect Ben and me, and it's clouding her judgment."

Meyer nods his head. "Well, while you're waiting, why don't you get some sleep?"

"I don't want to sleep," I huff.

"I know." Meyer chuckles and leans closer to me, smiling widely. "But unless you want me to take this medic out," he whispers, "I'm not sure you're going anywhere."

"I heard that," the medic says flatly.

My lips quirk into a smile. "Fine. But just a short nap."

Meyer squeezes my hand and leans back in his chair. "I'll be here. She won't let me leave the med tent yet, either. More tests to run."

"I heard that too," the medic says. "You two are very impatient."

I inhale deeply and close my eyes, but there's no way I'm sleeping. Visions of Thompson's code scroll over my thoughts. I replay the sequences I changed and the ones I left. Everything seems right until I get to the last one. I focus on the pattern and what it should take to disarm the kill switch. An electric jolt fires in my chest and I shoot up to a sitting position.

"I can't stay here." I swing my legs to the floor and then bolt out of the med tent.

Both Meyer and the medic shout behind me, but I pay them no attention. I need to find Cynthia. Now. As fast as I can run, I head toward the meeting tent. In a fury, I burst through the door flap. All eyes land on me.

"Avlyn." Cynthia turns from Ben and the other people she is speaking with.

I race toward her and grab her shoulder. "I need to talk to you."

Ben steps to my side, eyes wide. *What's wrong?* he thinks to me.

"I did the coding incorrectly," I say to them both. "I need you to take me to the DPF soldiers."

"I double checked, it was fine," Ben says.

Cynthia gingerly removes my hand from her shoulder and massages her temples with her fingertips. "Avlyn, the soldiers are detained, but they're healthy. I do recognize after speaking to Ben that you were correct. We needed to disarm the programming, and you did that."

"But—" I say.

"No, you have been through a lot, and I need to ensure you are healthy as well. I'm glad to let you take a look at them, but not until you've been cleared by the medic."

Meyer appears beside me. Somehow, he escaped the medic too.

Anger burns in my core at Cynthia's words. I square myself, plant my feet, and lock onto her eyes. "Okay. I get what you're doing here. And you need to stop." I pause for a second and clear my throat. "Ben and I are Cynthia Fisher's grandchildren. Our biological mother is here at the camp too." I say to everyone in the tent.

A hush falls over the room.

Cynthia's eyes widen. "I... I—"

"They need to know," I interrupt her. "It's a secret you can't keep." I round back to the Affinity members in the tent. "I don't want this fact to stop anyone from using my abilities in any way they can. The outcome of this war is much more important than any one person, even me."

"She's right," Cynthia announces and gestures to Ben and me. "These two are my grandchildren. Avlyn is also right, this connection may have interfered with my decision making. I won't let it happen again."

Cynthia turns to me, a scowl on her face, and her cheeks become ruddy. "Can you come with me?"

I look to Ben. He gives me a nod of approval, and I follow my grandmother out of the tent. Murmurs come from the Affinity members as they turn back to each other or whatever they were doing before.

Once outside, Cynthia crosses her arms over her chest. "You didn't have to do that."

"Yes, I did, and you know it. But there's no time to talk about this right now. I need to see those soldiers."

"I think you're overreacting," she says. "You went through a major stressor overriding all the coding."

"Stop dismissing me every time I try to speak with you. We're wasting time."

Wrinkles form between Cynthia's eyebrows, but some of her frustration falls away. "Fine. Follow me. I'm not sure if I want to deal with the storm of questions anyway." She waves for me to follow her.

"It needed to be done," I say.

Cynthia doesn't answer and leads me to a tent flanked by two guards stationed out front. They each step aside, allowing us to pass. She pulls back the opening and enters first.

Inside, there are three more armed guards, one for each of the DPF soldiers. Thompson lays on a cot, still unconscious, with his hands and feet restrained. And Barrett and Carver are each seated on a chair with hands secured behind their back. A male medic, who clutches a scanner, stops inspecting Carver, and all eyes fall to us.

"Ms. Lark needs to review the work she did to disarm these men's DPF nano changes," Cynthia announces.

The medic steps aside.

"Please tell them to let us go," Barrett pleads to me. "We helped you. The programming is gone."

"It's probably nothing," I say, trying to convince myself.

The tension in the man's face is palpable. And I believe he thinks the program is deleted. But there are aspects of it he can't control. No matter what he wants, the program could force him to die or kill any one of us if still active.

"We are just taking precautions," I say to him. "We need to give Fisher any information that could be useful."

Barrett stares at me.

Carver nods his head. "We only want to go home."

I have no idea if he'll be able to go home and, even if he can, what Elore will become. Hopefully, it will be a better place, but there are no guarantees. "Everyone is working hard to make that possible," I reassure him and then complete my diagnostic on both Carver and Barrett. "They're both clean."

I break away from them and walk over to Thompson, squatting at his side. "Why is he still unconscious?" I ask the medic. "I thought Fisher said he was healthy? Did you give him something?"

"No," he answers. "He's been that way since we brought him in."

I don't know if it should, but something about him not waking up bothers me. The other two woke immediately after I disengaged the program.

"His vitals are normal?"

The medic nods.

I inhale and take his hand. I focus my mind on the programming, and I'm in. I search the patterns as fast as my brain will allow. The sequences scroll through my mind, and everything appears in order. No, something *is* off. I didn't imagine it. I reach and grab for the pattern, but several of the strings don't make sense. I reread the surrounding patterns to work out the meanings, but the code shifts again.

"It's as if the code is mutating to survive," I mutter. I must not have finished disarming the DPF program, and the code is trying to stay active.

The symbols continue to change and rearrange on their own. My hands fly forward as I try to decipher the new code and my body temperature rises.

"You... you have to go," a voice says weakly. Thompson.

"No, no... I can complete the flip."

"I know you want to. I can sense it in you," the voice says. "But I can feel it taking hold again, and this time it's stronger. Just let me die."

"I have to do this!" I yell, as a portion of the code becomes clear to me. "The tracker is attempting to reengage. If that happens, Direction will be alerted. They'll send out more teams to scout the area."

The rogue code shifts in color from white to pale orange. The color worms it's way over to the pattern. Spreading.

I reach for it and a shot of electricity jolts me back and off my feet.

"You need to go. Warn your people," the voice booms. "I'll hold it off as long as I can."

I struggle to my feet and reach for the now bright orange code. "I can do this!"

"No!" the voice screams, and Thompson's energy blows me back again.

Nausea twists in my stomach as tears roll down my face. My mind races with what to do, how to solve this problem. "I'm going to download the data. I need to understand what is going on. So, if it happens again, I can stop it."

I clear my mind and pull the information into my nanos. When it's complete, a flash of electricity releases me to the real world. My eyes fly open, and I snap my hand back from Thompson.

"Did it work?" Cynthia asks.

I twist out of my seat toward her. "We need to evacuate. Now."

"Is he okay?" Carver starts to stand, but one of the guards points his pistol at him and he plops back into his seat.

"Heart rate elevated," the medic says, standing over Thompson, scanner in hand.

"No, he's not okay. He's dying, and he'll end up killing us," I say. "The DPF code for the tracker and kill switch is mutating and gaining a hold again. I can't stop it, not without more time."

"How *much* more time?" Cynthia paces with a hand to her head.

"The code is moving too fast. Thompson's brain is his own again, but he's not able to stop the programming from killing him. He said he'd block it for as long as possible. But I don't think he can hold back for long."

"What about these two?" Cynthia rounds to Barrett and Carver. "Is the same thing going to happen to them? Are they time bombs?"

Horrified looks cross both soldier's faces.

"No, I completed their flips. The code didn't mutate before I disengaged it."

Thompson's body begins to shudder on his cot.

A medic races over and runs a scanner over his body. "I have an idea."

"We don't have much time," I say.

Cynthia stops pacing. She raises her arm and taps at the device on her wrist. "Emergency evacuation procedure. Immediately."

I glance back at Thompson and guilt sweeps over me. I've always had this notion that Level Ones were somehow less—it's shameful. But, the Level Ones I've recently known are the bravest most selfless people I've ever met.

"Orders concerning these two?" The guard nearest to Barrett asks.

Cynthia exhales but doesn't speak.

"You are not leaving them," I say before she has the chance to announce anything horrible. "And I need at least one of them to travel with me to Elore."

"Travel to Elore?" she says. "You're coming with the camp."

"No." I stand my ground. "I need to access the Neuro-link and flip all the DPF soldiers. Trying to do it from the outside is too risky."

"But look what happened to him." Cynthia gestures to Thompson. "You could make a huge mistake. It's not worth the risk of going in directly."

I shake my head and lead Cynthia outside the tent. "Waters will attempt to take out the mainframe and grid with his new immersives. The tech in the ship Meyer had brought in shared how the program is still in beta. But who knows how many test subjects Waters has. He doesn't care about their expendability. And, at any time, their abilities could take off like mine have. We must find a way to take over Elore and dismantle President Waters at the same time. It's our only chance at survival."

Cynthia's nostrils flare. "And I suppose you need to take Ben too."

I quirk my eyebrow at her. "I need Ben, Meyer, Aron, and Sanda." I tip my chin at Carver through the tent opening. "And him. You need to promise to take Barrett."

Cynthia shakes her head in frustration. "I promise."

"We'll also need the coordinates for the tunnel system leading into Elore." I think for a beat. "And we are taking the New Philly ship."

Chapter Ten

As if someone hit a switch, Affinity members are now bustling, pulling tents down and preparing the camp for evacuation. Flyaway strands of hair flutter across my face as several people rush past us.

"We don't know enough about the ship yet to know if it's safe for travel," Cynthia says, crossing her arms over her chest.

"Meyer was in it for days, he knows enough. And, it gives Ben and me the chance to learn more about the immersive tech Waters is developing. On the way, we can study his new tech and the DPF upgrade on Carver. The more information we have on those two things, the better off we'll be when we get into Elore."

Cynthia opens her mouth to speak.

"Look," I interrupt, "this isn't the way I wanted operations to turn out either. But, if going into Elore is the only way to stop this war, then we need to be flexible. Flipping the DPF to our side *is* the only way. Then, we need direct access to Elore's mainframe to fight Waters' immersives." I rest my fingertips on her shoulder. "I get wanting to run, to remain invisible. But, we can't this time. We'll have to get dirty."

Cynthia gently touches my hand, and the expression on her face softens. "You're right, and I've made choices I'm not proud of. I'm simply not sure you understand how dangerous it is for you and Ben to go back. And the dark information Elore holds? You may not want to know."

I doubt there's much that can surprise me after learning of all the experimentation Ben and I endured. But Elore is also a city of lies.

"If you are leaving, go soon." Cynthia sighs. "I need to make sure a few things are in order, but please see me before you leave."

I squeeze her shoulder affectionately as Meyer appears.

"We're headed to Elore," I say to him.

He furrows his brow. "Now? Why?"

"She'll give you all the details on the way," Cynthia says. "Please find Ben, Aron, and Sanda. They'll be accompanying you."

Meyer looks at me, and I nod.

"Okay," he says and sprints from us.

"I'll get Carver," I say to Cynthia.

"Now to figure out what to tell the rest of Affinity about this new plan." She raises the device on her wrist to her mouth and taps the face. "I'm on my way."

I race back inside the holding tent. Thompson is still unconscious on the cot. My heart seizes at the thought how he now might be dead.

"I gave him something to slow down his entire body

function," the medic says. "Essentially, he's in a coma. It should give us more time. And the kill switch hasn't activated. Fisher is transferring him to a small, remote location. I'll stay with him."

"Thank you," I say, and to Carver, whose restraints have been removed. "Are you willing to come to Elore? It's going to be dangerous."

Carver eyes Barrett. "If it'll help release the Level Ones from DPF's programming."

"I believe it will," I say to Carver, and turn to Barrett. "I'm sorry I couldn't save Thompson."

Barrett nods. "Thank you for trying."

I gesture to Carver and lead him outside. "I need to make a stop." There's something I need to deal with before I leave.

Wordlessly, he follows me as we zigzag through crowds busy with evacuation procedures. As we approach, I find Bess packing her tent.

"Please give me a second," I say to Carver. I saw enough in our immersion to know he's not going to bolt. He nods and stops walking as I continue my approach.

"I have no idea what I'm doing here," she says to me without looking up. Inside the bag is the small stuffed rabbit that had belonged to Ben as a child. I stare at it for a second.

"Bess? Ben and I are leaving."

I know," she says, rifling through the bag. "We're *all* leaving."

I touch her hand and she pauses. "Ben and I are not going with the camp."

She looks up at me, eyes wild. "Of course you're coming.

We're together now. All together."

"I know you want that, and part of me does too. But this is bigger than our family being together."

Bess pulls out the stuffed rabbit and thrusts it into my hands. "Take this."

I shake my head and push the worn toy toward her. "You need it. Maybe, when we get back, Ben or I can have it again." I'm sure getting back is a long shot, but I need hope. So does she.

"I have a task for you to do too. My *whole* family isn't together. Michael is still out there. Cynthia told me he was safe, but I didn't speak with him. It was stupid. I don't really know why I didn't. Actually, that's not true. I thought he might be mad at me for abandoning him." I look down at the ground, ashamed at myself. "But, when you get to safety, will you please try to contact him? Tell him I'm glad he's safe and... I miss him."

Bess slowly takes the stuffed animal from me. The tension on her face clears, as if giving her the instructions had freed her mind.

"Okay, I'll do my best," she whispers, her lips stretching into a thin smile.

"Thank you. Now you be safe too."

She closes her eyes and draws in a shaky breath. "Both of you come back to us."

"I'll do my best." I tip my head to Carver, indicating we should go.

The two of us jog to where the New Philly hover waits. From the distance, I can see the rest of the group has already arrived. Aron's drones buzz around the hull as Meyer, Ben, and Sanda load supplies into the cargo bay.

"When will everything be ready?" I say when we reach Meyer's side.

"Aron is inside, programming all the coordinates and running a double check on the ship's function," he says.

"What are you packing?" I ask.

Sanda stops what she's doing and looks at me. "Weapons to bring to Affinity in Elore, ration packs, and food bars. Fisher said that, as long as we have the room, we might as well bring additional supplies with us. If a full-fledged attack starts, it might be more difficult for provisions to get into the city. We need to be prepared."

"Delicious," I scoff. "At least in Elore maybe we can get some real food."

"Printed food," Meyer says.

"Yeah, the kind that tastes good," I say as my mouth waters at the thought of a blueberry muffin.

"Are you coming along?" Meyer says to Carver.

Carver stuffs his hands into his pockets. "Apparently so."

"Good," Sanda says. "Why don't you help us with this?"

Carver's shoulders relax right before he picks up a crate and begins to load it.

I mouth a "thank you" to Sanda, and she smiles.

"I'm going to check on Aron," I make my way to the ship's entrance and reach for the bot still in my pocket.

Inside, Aron sits in the pilot seat, running his hands over the navigation screen. One of his drones hovers alongside the console, making a soft, contented whirring sound.

"Hey," I say and plunk the broken drone onto the console beside him. "What are you doing?"

Aron pockets the bot. Then he spins toward me in his seat. "Running diagnostics. This is a fascinating ship. But, I wish I had more time to understand all the tech."

"So, it will get us there?"

"Oh, yes." Aron glances my way. "It has a cloaking or scrambling system built in. Meyer showed me."

"You're getting along with Meyer now?" I ask.

"He's not the same since he got back. Told you. More bark than bite." Aron returns his attention to the console. "The cloaking tech will come in handy, especially as we get closer to Elore."

"But it also means that New Philly's other ships have signal invisibility potential as well. And, if they launch an attack, they might be on top of Elore before we know it."

"Well," he says. "Then you and Ben should explore the code on the way. Maybe you can figure out how it works."

"Yes, we already planned to do this."

Aron turns back to the controls. "I have some ideas. I'm just not there yet."

"Are you nearly ready to leave?" Cynthia's voice comes over the ship's comm.

Aron glances at me and taps the console to speak. "I think so. Ship functions are a go and the supplies should be almost loaded."

"I'm on my way then," Cynthia says. "There's one thing I need to bring Avlyn."

"We'll wait for you," Aron answers and clicks off the comm.

He spins in his seat toward me. "You should head out to meet her. I don't want to waste time."

Outside, I wave for Ben to follow me as the others load the last of the supplies into the ship.

"What's up?" Ben asks when he reaches me.

"Cynthia needs us."

We walk toward the camp, and, within a few minutes, Cynthia's shape appears. As she comes closer, Ben leans into me. "Do we bring up the grandmother thing?"

I chuckle nervously. "No clue."

Cynthia holds a small box in her hands. "I have something you'll need in Elore." She opens the box, revealing a thin, silver device.

"What is it?" I ask.

Cynthia picks up the device and holds it out to me. I take it.

"It's a DNA masker," she says. "Everyone, except Meyer, will need to use it to falsify any scans. When you arrive in Elore, give your data to Melissa Rice. I've spoken to her, and she's your initial contact. She's aware you're on the way and will get you into the city. She'll also set up your new identities based on the changes made by the masker."

"What?" Ben asks, eyebrows pushed together. "No way that works."

Cynthia's lips form a tight line, her eyes narrowing. "The masker doesn't truly alter your DNA, but it provides an illusion of alteration. Bess had her DNA masked as a baby, and you two had it done in utero. As for Meyer, his DNA is still not on file with Direction."

"That's what Bess' mother did to her when she was pregnant," I say.

"Yes," she says quickly. "We used the maskers to hide the markers linked to sharing DNA with me. Bess was assigned a false background, and, because she was downgraded to Level One, no one questioned anything. It kept her and you two safe all these years."

"But we need to do it again?" Ben asks. "Is it safe?"

Cynthia sighs. "It should be, but I'm going to be honest. There's not a lot of public data. This is a black-market piece of equipment."

"Well, don't want the mission ruined at the start." I say. "But it's not like we have a choice,"

Cynthia offers Ben a sad smile. "I'm sorry I didn't personally tell you that I was your grandmother."

Ben thinks for a beat and then opens his arms to her. I marvel at my twin's ability to easily forgive and be affectionate. Maybe it's because he was raised in the Outerbounds, unlike me.

"Better late than never," Ben says, a genuine smile warming his expression.

Cynthia squeezes him and releases from the hug. "Yes, yes, it is." She reaches for my upper arm and clutches it. "Don't take any unnecessary risks. We'll be in contact with further instructions."

I softly smile as she releases my arm. "We'll do our best." I tap Ben on the shoulder and motion for him to follow me back to the ship.

"And don't go looking for things you don't want to know," Cynthia calls to us.

I stop and twist toward her. What does she mean? She delivered a similar warning before. The information on the experiments? But there's not time for me to ask, so I only wave and turn to catch up to Ben.

My brother and I race toward the ship and pound up the gangway. Sanda is already strapped in, Carver across from her. Aron is still in the pilot seat, and a few of his drones buzz around the cabin. And Meyer's doing something at the back of the ship; I can't tell what. The chair with the immersive capabilities is open next to the pilot seat.

"I'll take it this time," Ben says. "You can scan over Carver's nanotech."

"Okay," I say and plop down next to Carver.

"You ready?" I ask him.

"Not really," he sighs. "But I want to be helpful."

"Okay, we'll start in a few minutes once we're in the air." I give Sanda, who's sitting across the way, a weak smile that she returns.

"Everyone strapped in for lift off?" Meyer shouts from the back of the ship.

I grab my belt and affix it. "Ready."

I look around at everyone, their faces somber. Who knows if I'm ready. But, if I have to go on a mission, these are the people I want with me.

Carver is asleep, now in the seat across from me, exhausted after I had immersed with him. Unfortunately, it appears that the upgraded nanotech completely purges itself of all data on the

DPF programming once the host has been flipped.

It's as if Carver was never a DPF.

"Ten minutes to our destination. Return to your seats," Aron calls from the pilot's chair.

My heart thumps faster at his words. This is it, there's no turning back now. I peer out the front window at an uninteresting, brown autumn landscape.

"You sure this is it?" I say to Aron.

"Yeah, Ben went over all the coordinates and map data." Aron tips his head to Ben who is still co-piloting in the immersion chair. "Big surprise, the whole operation is underground. Our tunnel access is going to be from there."

Everything still okay? I think to Ben as I take the seat nearest him.

The entire system is full of new information. Too bad the trip wasn't longer. His voice comes to my mind.

But you got everything you needed? I ask. Should I try immersing with the system?

No, I downloaded everything about the new cloaking device to pass on to Affinity. But there wasn't really any information I could access on Project Ascendancy. It looks as if the technology on the ship is only a tool for immersives, not the project itself.

But there might be something you missed.

I got everything. Ben impresses a sensation of slight agitation mixed with sarcasm on me. *You know, you should trust me more.*

Fine. I grin. Aron says we're almost there.

Yes, I'm already in contact and sent the security codes. If you look out the ship's front, I think you can see the bunker's entrance.

I refocus on my surroundings and gaze out the window again. A hatch in the ground mechanically opens with our approach. Aron begins our descent toward it. It's as if we're flying directly into a giant mouth in the earth.

"Meyer, you need to sit down!" Aron yells, loud enough to rouse Carver with a jolt.

Meyer slides beside me and places his hand on the small of my back as we descend into the bunker. Once inside, people in orange uniforms direct the hover to a landing pad. The ship lands with a hiss just as Ben releases from immersion.

A woman's face appears on the screen in front of Aron. Her hair is sandy blonde and cut short. Her eyes crinkle as her lips twist up into a tentative smile.

"Greetings. I hope your trip was comfortable," she says.

"Yes, thank you," Aron replies. "It was uneventful."

She nods. "My name is Melissa Rice. I'll be debriefing you before escorting your group into Elore."

Memories of the last time I was in Elore flood me, making my legs shake. What made me think I was strong enough to do this?

CHAPTER ELEVEN

"What is this place?" I ask as we disembark into a cavernous hangar. Behind us, workers begin boarding our ship to unload supplies.

"Welcome to the Sub. It's an underground habitat built before the Collapse," Rice says. "But it was never used. Most everyone involved died from the virus before it could be finished. Then, it sat vacant for over one hundred years."

"And Affinity just came across it one day?" Sanda asks, her bag slung over her shoulder.

"Yes," Rice says. "The maps were located, quite by accident. Affinity decided to keep the information under lock and key until we really needed it. We've spent time over the past few years digging access into Elore from the underground tunnel system. So, when this war between Philly and Elore broke out, we decided it was time to finally move in."

"What is our plan of action and timeline?" Meyer asks, slipping into soldier mode.

Rice waves us forward out of the main hangar and into a series of reinforced tunnels, dimly lit by yellowish lighting over our heads. The circles it casts under each of our eyes only serves to make us look even more exhausted than we already are. She leads us into a room and gestures us to sit at a rectangular table. I walk straight to the closest chair and sink into the seat and keep my bag snug on my lap. Meyer sits next to me and scoots his chair in closer a few inches. I give him a quick smile and touch his upper arm, grateful he's here.

From the head of the table, Rice begins. "I'll admit, when Fisher briefed me, I was not pleased about your group coming. The whole plan sounded too far-fetched and as if she were grasping at the wind. But, now that I've gathered all the details, I believe you all may be our best chance. If we can turn the entire DPF army to side with Affinity, we might actually have a chance to overtake Elore."

"Ben and I will need direct access into the Neuro-link for the plan to work," I say.

"I realize that," Rice says. "And it's not going to be easy. And, even if we can get you access, that still leaves us with New Philadelphia and the problem with Waters' immersives. Until we know more, you will be staying at a central location in Level Two. This way, when we do send you on a mission, you can dispatch immediately. Otherwise, don't go above ground. There's no use in taking on additional risk and moving out of Phase One until it's time."

"So, in the meantime," Aron asks, his companion drone buzzing above him, "what are we doing?"

Rice eyes the bot. "Fisher sent me data on your drone production work."

"I'm still working on the programming to improve them," Aron says. "I've been training Sanda to help me."

Sanda shoots Aron a proud smile. It's nice to see her at least a little happier.

"Affinity doesn't have access to a hover fleet," Rice says. "But we do have raw resources to create a small army of drones, courtesy of our alliance with Dr. Sloan's insurgent group in Philly."

Carver sits across from me with a nervous look on his face and continually squirming in his seat.

"Meyer," Rice directs with a level stare, "Your orders, as usual, are to protect Avlyn and now Ben in any situation where that is deemed necessary. Ben and Avlyn, you should focus only on accessing the mainframe to gather information, but without making any changes. We must fully understand the consequences before we attempt anything. Is that clear?"

I'm pretty sure Cynthia filled Rice in about my stubborn nature and our group's tendency to go rogue. "What about Carver?" I ask.

"Mr. Carver will remain here."

Relief washes over Carver's face and he immediately stops fidgeting as much.

"What about handhelds?" Meyer asks. "We'll need them to stay in contact with each other and Affinity."

Rice reaches into a bag at her side and hands us each a new Flexx. "I was getting there." She peers at me. "Fisher shared how both you and Mr. Barton have CosmoNano tech embedded in your nanos?"

"Yes," I confirm. "Aron and I can change our hair and eye colors."

"Anything you can do to conceal yourself while in Elore should be done," she says. "Propaganda vids have broadcast your face multiple times over the last two weeks. Mostly in the new ones Ms. Kyra Lewis is heading up for The Alliance of New Adults."

The mention of Kyra's name sends a shiver down my spine. I hope when Affinity sets everything right, she's not one of the citizens who fights us on change. Maybe she'll join us if she can just see why we're trying to liberate the Level Ones and Elore.

I touch Aron on the shoulder, and his blond hair shifts to dark brown and his eyes change from blue to brown. I focus on my own hair and watch as the brunette wisps tickling the side of my face transform into a sandy blonde.

Rice nods her approval. "Fisher also informed me that you have a malfunctioned EP implant. I'll personally walk you to our medical facility where medics are ready to examine your defective tech. They also have standard EPs for the rest of you, except Mr. Carver, of course."

I reach into my bag and pull out the masking device. "And our DNA?"

My newly working EP lights the bottom of my vision, displaying limited information about our surroundings as well as the new identities we've been assigned. Everyone else in our group has also been given regular EPs for the mission.

My new name is Alana Miller. It's a simple name and I kind of like it. But, hopefully, I won't really need to use this alternate identity much.

"Is everything you need loaded?" Rice asks. "We're experiencing trouble with moving supplies inside the city from all the increased security. But, I believe we were able to provide each of you a few sets of clothing in the Elorian styles."

Sanda nods and slings a bag into our transport vehicle. "Yes, and we have enough rations and food bars to last the group a week. I'm leaving the rest for your bunker."

My stomach sours at Sanda's words.

"The facility where you'll be housed has a food printer too," Rice says. "It's easier to obtain ink, since it's local, over supplying outside food."

I know Affinity doesn't trust the food printers, and for a good reason since the programming and ink production is controlled by Direction. But, I ate it all my life. A big stack of printed pancakes sounds a million times better than a food bar— any day.

I consider Carver, who waits to the side of our group. "Thank you for coming with us."

"I wish I could do more," he says, then sighs. "Have you heard from Fisher yet? Do you know what happened to Thompson?"

I shake my head. "I know they were able to evacuate the camp, but that's it. Maybe Rice can keep you updated."

Carver hangs his head.

I gently touch his upper arm. "I spoke with Thompson when I was immersed. He was willing to do what it took to save others."

"Still, I feel guilty," Carver says. "I'm here and he could be dead now."

I lower my hand. "Well, if it helps, I'm sure Rice will have plenty of opportunities for you to fight. This is just beginning."

"I'll figure out someway of being useful while I'm here," Carver says, his eyebrows furrowed.

"Time to roll," Rice says, "Your contact is scheduled to meet you soon."

I force a smile. "Goodbye, Carver." Pivoting away from him, I jog toward the transport, and Meyer helps me climb into the back. I place my bag on the floor in front of me. Even though it's driverless, this tan vehicle looks ancient and nothing like the sleek new taxis in the city.

"The trip through the tunnel system takes around thirty minutes," Rice says. "When you arrive, unload and take the elevator up. The palm scanner is programmed to lead you to the correct floor where you'll meet up with your contact. The code is 'looks like it may snow' and their answer will be 'the trees are still green.'"

"Got it," Aron says.

"Good luck," Rice calls out as our transport rolls away.

As our transport travels the tunnel my mind wanders to Naomi Jensen, the woman who tried to protect her son from the DPF when she was chosen in the Level One draft. Manning used her as an experiment and converted her husband to a soldier. He died in Thornton helping Ben and me.

What happened to their son? I made Naomi's unconscious body a promise before she died—I would find her child. I don't even know if that's possible.

The transport stops at the beginning of an empty corridor, and each of our Flexxes buzz. Words glow in the bottom of my vision.

Arrived. Follow the corridor 50 ft to the elevator. Upon entering, scan your palm on the hand scanner.

"Everyone ready?" Ben asks, but the uncertainty on his face and the emotions radiating off him tells me he's not. I'm not, either.

We pile out of the vehicle, each grabbing our bags. And, when we've all exited with our supplies in-hand, the vehicle automatically reverses direction and drives away from view.

"Well, I'm hungry, so let's get going," I say and start off down the hallway. Soon enough, the elevator appears, and I push the call button. I'm the first to enter when the elevator beeps and opens. As instructed, I place my palm on the hand scanner inside. The others do the same, and the door shuts. The cab vibrates and moves up as we stare at the closed door.

"What was the code again?" Meyer says behind me.

"You don't remember the code?" Sanda scoffs. "What's wrong with you?"

Meyer's lips drift up into a soft smile. "I remember. Just trying to lighten the mood. You're all a little too serious."

Sanda punches Meyer in the arm. "This *is* serious."

He shakes his head as the smile falls from his lips. "I know."

The elevator jolts to a stop and then opens. A tall, thin, and short-haired girl stands at the opening. It's a face I never thought I'd actually be glad to see.

She stares at me, brows furrowed. "Nice hair."

"Corra?" I step out of the cab and touch my newly blonde locks.

"Looks like I'm stuck with you again." She rolls her eyes.

"Are you our contact?" Aron comes to my side and looks from me to Corra. "What about the code? Looks like it may—" he starts.

"Yes... 'looks like it may snow' and then I answer, 'the trees are still green,'" she says.

Aron looks to me, and I nod.

Corra places a hand on her hip and sighs. "They figured Avlyn would have a measure of trust with me. And, I was *lucky* enough to live in the building that houses the bunker Affinity wanted to use for your group."

Aron shrugs and gestures in front of Corra. "Okay, then lead the way."

She spins on her heels and leads us down the white hallway. "The facilities here are pretty new, so you should have everything you need." She points at a door on the right. "Sleeping quarters are in there."

She takes us to an open room containing several tables and chairs with computer screens on the right. On the other side is a seating area with two couches that face a large MV on the wall. "This will be your main workspace and just beyond here is the lab and the eating area. You'll be able to figure everything else out."

She twists back to us, her face tense. "Now, I'm heading back to my apartment. I'm exhausted after getting everything ready for your group."

"Thanks, Corra," I say, dropping my bag and supplies in a corner.

"All the latest intel is loaded into the system. It will give you a sense of what's going on outside." She tips her head toward a screen. "Circumstances are different than before you left." She turns and heads back toward the elevator. "I'll check on you first thing in the morning."

I look at Meyer and he shrugs. "We'll figure it out."

I know we will, but I follow Corra anyway, catching her right before she presses the elevator button. Somehow, seeing Corra comforts me. She's someone from my past. Albeit not my favorite person. "How are you?"

She swings her gaze toward me, scowling. "Do you really care?"

"I wouldn't have come and asked if I didn't."

Corra crosses her arms over her chest. "It's bad out there. The Guardian drones are everywhere. Curfew is earlier now. We're required to return to our apartments immediately after work. Direction is watching my every move at GenTech."

"Do they suspect you of anything?"

She shakes her head. "I keep my head down these days. Do as I'm told. They're simply watching *everyone* more closely."

I study the lines that form between her eyebrows. "We're here to try and do something about it. Big changes are coming."

"Big changes are already here," she mumbles, lowering her

head.

I reach out and grab her arm before she tries to hit the button again. "What's going on with Kyra?"

Her eyes go wide for a second and then relax. "She's Manning's new darling. A spokesperson for how a newly configured citizen should behave. Just activate the MV... she's on all the time. She even let Direction pair her without any input."

"Kyra is paired?"

"She signed the contract a few days ago. Some guy from GenTech. But I wasn't paying attention. As if it matters."

Corra hits the elevator button. I try to sort through the idea of Kyra being paired. It shouldn't be a shock to me. It's the way we're supposed to act as good citizens. But, if she had no choice in the pairing, then there's no way she's doing it for even the tiniest bit of love—only duty. And that makes winning her over to our side feel like an impossibility.

The elevator dings and opens, breaking my thoughts. "I'll see you in the morning," Corra says before the elevator door shuts.

I spin back toward the meeting room and, when I get there, Ben, Meyer, and Sanda are sprawled out on the couches. The room is sparse, with grayish-white walls and a concrete floor. Two of the micro drones Aron brought buzz around the room, checking things out.

"Shouldn't we get to work?" I ask.

Meyer smiles at me and pats at the empty seat next to him. "Probably, but we agreed on eating first."

I look around and see nothing to eat.

"Okay," Aron says from behind me. "I got us drinks. Food is

on the way." He places a tray carrying mugs onto the table next to the couch. The ceramic cups are filled with some sort of hot beverage, maybe tea. "Can you help me get the rest, Sanda?"

"Sure." She pushes forward on the couch and stands, following Aron from the room. They're spending a lot more time together lately.

"We're going to work tonight, right?" I decide not to dwell on Aron and Sanda and snuggle in next to Meyer.

"Avlyn," Ben says. "Everyone is tired from traveling all day. We're not much use if we're not at our best."

"It's not as if Direction or Waters is taking a break, Ben," I reply back quickly. "We don't have a lot of time here. Right, Meyer?"

Meyer sighs and crosses his arms over his chest. "A fresh start in the morning would be nice. I still haven't gotten much sleep lately."

I huff and shake my head, sliding a few inches from Meyer.

He tips his head toward me. "See? I don't think *you* are at your best either. We'll wake up early, but let's eat a little, get a few hours of sleep, and then jump right in."

"It's the reasonable thing to do," Ben says, taking a sip of his tea. "You know it is."

"Fine," I say, distracted as Sanda and Aron step back into the room, holding two more trays.

"Dinner," Sanda says with a smile on her face. "It's not my cooking of course, but it *is* better than food bars."

"Nothing is like your cooking," Aron says, and his dimple appears.

Sanda gives Aron a shy smile.

He grins back at her while holding the tray out to me. I look back and forth between the two of them and then down at the tray. On it are three plates of spaghetti and meatballs. Steam wafts from the plate, bringing the spicy aroma of tomatoes and oregano to my nose. The food looks delicious, but I'm not in the mood to eat anymore.

"No thanks," I wave my hand at him.

He gives me a quizzical look. "Are you sure?

"I'll have dinner in a while."

Aron shrugs and presents the tray to Meyer, who doesn't hesitate. "If you're not hungry, I'll take it," Meyer says while grinning.

I reach over and grab the plate and place it on the side table next to me. "I said, I'll have my meal later."

"Mmkay," Meyer says, his mouth already full of food.

I look around at the rest of the group, already enjoying their meals. I shake my head and stand. "I'm going to go check out the rest of the place," I say.

"You want company?" Ben says. His emotions of concern resonate through me.

"I just need a few minutes alone," I say. By the look on his face, he knows I'm lying.

You sure? Ben says in my head.

Enjoy your dinner. I'll be fine, I think.

I turn and walk from the room, but not before I grab my bag.

"No, she's fine. Let her be alone," Ben says to someone. But I don't look back to see who.

I pick up the pace and soon my boots are thumping across the hallway's concrete floor. Within a few steps, I spot the entrance to the sleeping quarters. I touch the panel to the side and the door slides back. A dim auto light flicks on overhead and I release a tight breath. Five bunk beds line up against the wall. I plop down on the closest bed's firm, lower mattress and throw my bag onto the floor. Hugging my knees, I feel for the necklace around my neck and find the smooth heart pendant. The room's silence is welcome as I rub the metal between my fingers and thumb.

Thoughts of Kyra, the job we are here to do, and, for some weird reason, the way Sanda smiles at Aron, tumbles through my mind. But, touching the heart charm soothes me. I take a long draw of air and push it out again. Maybe I could have some dinner now.

I begin to rise, but a sharp pain stabs at my head, and I fall back into my seated position. The room spins, and my stomach roils.

Avlyn! Ben's voice comes into my head. Some... something's wrong.

My heart nearly leaps out of my chest at his words. *What?*

Crash. The sound resonates from the other room.

CHAPTER TWELVE

Ben lays sprawled on the meeting room's concrete floor, his plate still intact near his unmoving left arm. Aron kneels beside him, one knee in a tangled puddle of noodles and sauce.

"What happened?" I scream. Flashbacks of how Direction's computer virus nearly killed Ben flicker in my mind. "Is something wrong with his brain again?"

"We... we don't know," Sanda says, her eyes widen with fear as she slides a shaking finger over her handheld. "He said he felt dizzy and tried to stand... I have a med scanner app on here."

I push her aside, "I'm faster."

"Avlyn," Meyer calls.

But I'm already on my knees, taking Ben's hand. I close my eyes as nausea swells in my gut.

"Ben," I call out. My voice echoes in the space.

He doesn't answer.

Breathing deeply in and out, I push the feeling of sickness down and call up his code. A nanobot appears in my mind and I place my hands on its shimmering body. Next, I bring up Ben's brain function, and, although I'm not an expert, cranial activity appears to be normal.

I search through string after string of code, but nothing unusual presents itself. I grit my teeth. This isn't working. The nausea I felt before continues to churn and grows, as if whatever is wrong with Ben is spreading to me. Or, maybe, he's projecting it onto me. So, I focus on the feeling. And, instead of pushing the sensations away, I try to embrace the varied emotions. I try to understand.

As I let go, the sickness changes and becomes a gray cloud surrounding me with emotions. I reach out to touch it. The cloud moves away from my hand. Is it actively avoiding me? I attempt again, slowly. This time, I rake my fingers through the strange fog. Cold and thin. I do it again, and the gray cloud's energy writhes and shifts, as if it's alive.

I squint at the cloud. Then I realize it's not a cloud at all. Just like everything else in the immersive world, it's code. Tiny pieces of code that hover like a swarm of gnats.

I plunge my hands into it again. *What are you?* Hot emotions move through my body and demand an answer from the code. My chest fills with cold, and I snap back. The chill instantly dissipates. I tip my head to the side and stare at the lines of code that twist and turn into the cloud's structure. This time, using less force, I move my hands forward and barely touch the surface.

I fight to stay calm and force myself to take steady breaths. Coolness and shades of gray consume my mind as I give in and allow the data to transfer to me. The feeling racks my body, but I take it in.

My eyes fly open. The cloud disappears and my entire body tingles. This isn't good. We should have listened to Ruiz when she had said not to eat the printed food.

Quickly, I call up Ben's nanos again and apply a temporary patch. I push into the bot, and the surface gives slightly under my fingers. The intruder code's energy dissipates. I concentrate harder to ensure it's gone, but a tiny amount still pulsates beneath the surface. The invader is bound to the cells, similar to a Trojan. But, instead of being tech based, it's organic.

Ben's emotional energy lightens and fills me with warmth. His mind is waking up.

I release from his nanos and into the real world. All eyes are on me, and Ben blinks as he moves into consciousness.

"Are you okay?" Aron asks Ben as he helps him sit. "You scared us."

Ben inhales deeply. "I'm not sure. What happened?" He looks right at me.

"You don't remember?" I ask. "I immersed with you."

Ben looks confused. "The last thing I remember is eating my dinner... then it was now."

Meyer plops back down on the couch and reaches for his plate. I leap to my feet and grab it from him.

"Hey," he says, somewhat offended. "You said you weren't hungry."

"I'm definitely not anymore. Direction is contaminating the food ink."

Meyer looks at his spaghetti with sudden disgust, and I place the plate on the table beside him.

"What?" Sanda looks to Ben. "Is that what happened to him? You were able to fix it, right?" She swings her attention back to me. "So, *everyone* is now contaminated, but you?"

I bend and grab Ben's hand and help him to his feet. "I wasn't able to completely repair the damage. There's an organic component to the code I can't control. And I think our ability made the reaction that much stronger."

"What does that mean?" Ben sits on the couch across from Meyer again.

"I don't know, yet. We're going to need someone who understands this organic code better. Perhaps Cynthia knows someone from Affinity posted here, in Elore, who can look at Ben and the rest of you."

"This also means any Affinity members in the city still eating printed food are affected too," Aron says.

"Doesn't that girl, Corra, work at GenTech?" Meyer asks. "You knew her, right?"

"Yes, she's a lab chem. It's possible GenTech is partnering with Nutra in creating this. It would make sense since they control all the VacTech. She might be able to think of a solution. Or at least get us some answers."

"But you think I'm okay?" Ben asks.

"I hope so," I say. "The organic portion's energy was much weaker. I think that without the tech component linking the bots, your body may purge the living code."

"Well, test me next," Sanda says, holding her arm out to me.

I clutch her wrist and immerse with her nanos. She's pretty

clean, and I disable what's there without any issues. Immediately, the organic portion disintegrates.

Meyer is clean, but Aron's takes a bit more work to sort out. But, after a few minutes, Aron is clean too. My guess is that both Meyer's and Sanda's nanotech functions differently since their systems didn't originate from Elore.

I immerse with Ben again, and he still has low-level contamination.

"I didn't eat much," Ben says.

"I know," I say. "But it really affected you. And look what happened before. You nearly died at Gabrielle's. Could be your body is still at a disadvantage. You were not completely healed back at the camp."

"Ninety-nine percent seems mostly healed."

I shake my head. "I agree, but our brains and bodies are very different. That one percent could matter."

"Well, I feel okay. I don't want this to stop us." He places his hand on my shoulder. "The ink's effect on me is a little snag in our plans, but we can't get too wrapped up in it. I can keep an eye on the problem myself."

I look over at the plates of pasta on the side tables, and suddenly remember how hungry I am. But I won't be eating any printed meals now.

As if on cue, Sanda walks over to her bag, snatches it from the floor, and pulls out several food bars. "They're apple. Who wants dinner?"

I groan and send a message to Corra.

We have a problem.

❖❖❖

I stare at the top of my bunk, unable to sleep. What if Ben had died?

My Flexx buzzes again, and I grab it from beside me on my bunk. It's Cynthia.

We're working on intel at NutraTech but, so far, it appears the toxin is widespread. Even in Level Three. But, based on ink delivery schedules, the contaminate was only released a few days ago. We have our best teams working on trying to understand what it does. Please hold off on Phase One.

Understood, I send back. As though I hadn't already come up with that plan, but she probably doesn't trust me now.

Sighing, I close the message. Corra will get what we need from GenTech. I have to believe that.

I sit up and throw my legs over the bed's side.

"It's early," Meyer whispers from across the room, "You don't need to be up yet."

I turn toward Meyer, across from my cot, who is lit up by his antique watch while he studies the time and also by one dull auto-light. His hair is tousled, and his sleepy expression makes me smile.

"Cynthia's message woke me," I say, keeping my voice down, not wanting to wake the others. "No way I'm sleeping now so I'm going to go work out there."

"You want company?" He props up on one elbow.

I tip-toe over and touch his cheek. His unshaven face is rough beneath my fingers. I do want his company, but the clearer our minds can be, the fewer mistakes we might make. "Get a couple more hours of sleep."

Meyer kisses my fingertips then plops his head back onto his pillow. His eyes shut, and I stare at his handsome face for a moment. I close my eyes and draw in a long breath. *Please let our plan work,* my heart pleads to the shadows. I want more time with him. I want a life outside of missions and running. Is a regular existence too much to ask?

I scan the room and make out the silhouettes of the others still asleep in their beds. I decide against my boots and, instead, creep out of the already open exit.

A low auto-light flicks on in the hall, and I head down to the main room. Once there, I plunk into a chair in front of a viewer and tap on the screen.

The Alliance of New Adults vids, I think to the system.

A list of vids appears on the screen, each one flanked by a thumbnail image, each thumbnail bearing the face of my former best friend. I remind myself that Kyra was never anything more than a dutiful citizen. Yes, she kept a few of my childhood secrets and did come to me with her own secrets about Ayers. But, in the end, I think those things only made me more of an enemy in her mind. I'm too different and know too much about her.

I reach out to tap a vid released two days ago titled, "New Adults Pairing Responsibilities," but my fingers hover over the screen, repelled. I snap my hand back to my lap and interlace my fingers together. Kyra's face has grown cold, even severe over the last couple of weeks. Her icy-blue eyes stare from the screen as if the vid is only for me.

Tears sting at the corners of my eyes. I wipe them away and

quickly tap the vid before I can stop myself. This is no time for weakness. I watch Kyra calmly inform Elore about how now, more than ever, focus is imperative. Apparently, pairing contracts are taking longer than they were a few years ago.

"This is why we are introducing Direction-chosen pairings," she states. "A new algorithm assembles these connections, and we need your help in testing and perfecting it. I believe in the new system so strongly that I have chosen to be paired by Direction."

She raises her hand away from her body and gestures off-screen. "My pairing contract was signed yesterday and has a 99.98% match for genetic compatibility and for producing children with a Level Two or even Three Intelligence Potential."

The camera pans back and a tall boy with caramel-colored hair appears next to Kyra. My eyes grow wide, and I bring my hand to my mouth.

"No," I whisper.

"I'd like to introduce my Direction-chosen pairing, Daniel Carter."

Daniel nods to the camera. "Kyra and I are pleased to serve our duty to Direction in this age where complete focus is imperative."

Before they can say anything else, I tap the screen, pausing the vid. I stand, unable to tear my gaze from their still-framed images in disbelief.

Kyra can't be paired to Daniel. He's horrible and angry and doesn't possess one ounce of kindness in him. He did nothing but torment me at GenTech. I rub my sweaty palms together and step back from the screen. I whip around to get away from the sight of it all and smack right into Meyer's hard chest.

He's staring at Daniel's name at the bottom of the screen. He may not know Daniel by sight, but I told Meyer about his bullying and how he was the one who turned me in at GenTech after I hacked the Ectopistes project.

Meyer wraps his arms around me. "Avlyn, you need to let Kyra go, or she's going to get you and everyone else killed."

CHAPTER THIRTEEN

"You don't understand her," I say into his chest. "Or know what happened."

"Avlyn, Kyra is a Direction citizen all the way," he whispers. "I know you don't want to believe that, but she is. Most of the Level Two and Three citizens are. They have it good. They're respected and given everything they need. Manning has played on Kyra's ego. She always wanted to be the best, and, since he knows she's your childhood friend, he's using the connection to his advantage. She's the biggest string tying you back to Elore. Manning knows that if you come back into the city, any slip-ups would probably involve her. Now stop watching those propaganda vids, or you're going to prove him right."

I want to tell Meyer all about how I hate Daniel being paired to Kyra and what happened with Ayers, but he's right. I can't save her. Not now. Maybe not ever. I can't put the entire mission in danger and risk the lives of everyone in Elore for Kyra, no matter how much it destroys me.

I pull back from Meyer a few inches. "I told you to stay in bed," I mumble.

Meyer's lips stretch into a sad smile. "Yeah, I woke up again and saw your empty bunk. I didn't want to be alone."

I pull him in tight and run my fingers up his back to his muscular shoulders, closing my eyes and taking in the moment.

When I open them, I look back toward the sleeping quarters. No one else is up.

"I need to talk to you about something."

Nervousness stings my chest. I take Meyer's hand and tug him toward the closest couch.

He gives me a confused look but follows my lead. "Good I hope?"

"Not exactly," I mumble, "But it needs to be said."

I gesture for him to sit down, and he does. I ease onto the couch next to him and fold my hands onto my lap.

"I kissed Aron," I say, not looking up.

"What?" Hurt mixes with a twinge of anger in his voice. "When?"

"Not here," I try to meet his eyes. "Back at Gabrielle's. That night when you and Aron were fighting."

"He kissed you, or you kissed him?" Meyer's fist clenches on his leg.

"He kissed me. But I didn't stop it... not right away."

"But you *did* stop it?" His voice lowers to a thready whisper.

I look up at Meyer, and his brows are deeply furrowed with sadness, but not anger like I had expected.

"I did stop our kiss because I want to only be with you. In the end, he understood. Aron and I were safe for each other. We shared a connection, and it felt comfortable. We're friends. But what I feel for you is so much more. I want to share everything with you. Friendship, love... everything."

Meyer relaxes and sits without speaking for what seems like too long. My stomach churns.

"When I was all by myself on the Philly ship," he finally responds, "all I could think about was getting back to you. I had no idea if I would. It was a million more times likely the ship was going to be discovered and shot down. But Aron's drones helped me get into the ship's computer and turn on the cloaking device. They even tracked down the other drones and found your location, without revealing ours. So, in a sense, Aron brought me back to you."

"I'm sorry I kissed him back." I place my hand on top of his. "I was confused."

His fingers tense and then relax. "I'm sorry too."

I lean into him and lay my head on his shoulder. "I love you, Meyer Quinn."

Meyer slips his hand around my waist and pulls me in close.

"I love you, Avlyn Joy Lark." He touches his lips to my temple and a tingle of electricity jolts through my center and I draw in a sharp breath.

"I think Aron likes Sanda now anyway," he whispers.

I snap back from him. "What?"

"Yeah, you haven't noticed? They're always heading off together."

I had noticed but tried not to think much about it. "Are you okay with that?"

"Not really, but it means he's not after you, anymore." Meyer's lips stretch into a smile and he looks away, as if in thought. "Think I might need to have a talk with him about how no one is good enough for my sister, and, if he does anything to hurt her, I do own a stunner..."

My eyes grow wide.

Meyer chuckles. "No, when I remove the idea that he's more than a friend to you, I can see that Aron is a good guy. And Sanda's eyes sure do light up around him. Listen, on the Philly ship, I had a lot of thinking to do. His drones saved my life. I made a promise to myself that if I got home again, I wasn't going to make something like jealousy tear us apart. It's not worth it."

Meyer leans into me and his soft, warm lips touch mine.

Down the corridor, I hear a muffled beep followed by the elevator doors opening.

"What's that?" I say, startling away from our kiss.

Meyer jumps up and grabs for a stunner lying on the side table. "Stay behind me."

I scan the room for another weapon, but don't find one. We're being sloppy. Too comfortable. This place isn't safe and we're acting like it is.

Clicking footsteps approach. We tuck ourselves against the wall closest to the door. When the intruder is almost upon us, Meyer flings around the corner, stunner first.

"Point that thing someplace else," an incredulous familiar voice snaps.

In the hallway stands Corra with her hands raised chest high and a scowl on her face.

"Fisher told me to come down here and get a few rations. If I'm on a mission at GenTech, she needs me sharp, and I can't eat anything from the printer now."

Meyer lowers his gun. "Why are you down here so early, unannounced?"

Corra rolls her eyes. "If you must know, I'm nervous, and I couldn't sleep. But I figured no one would be up yet, and I wouldn't have to talk with any of you. Guess I was wrong."

"We're just getting a jumpstart on the day," I say.

"You think I could get some of those rations?" Corra asks. "Fisher says they'll be sending more in, but it might take a day or two."

"I'm going to shower," Meyer says. "Avlyn can handle this." And, with a smile, he hands me the stunner and walks down the hall.

"Do you need that?" Corra asks.

"Probably not." I shrug. "But you might try to take too many of our cherry food bars." She doesn't even bother to roll her eyes at my stupid joke. Instead, she pushes past me into the meeting room, arms folded over her chest.

"Corra," I ask, following her into the kitchen. "Why are you doing this?"

"Doing what? Getting breakfast?"

"No. Why are you a part of Affinity?"

Corra stops and hangs near the opening, arms still crossed.

I spot the bag of food rations and angle past her. Riffling through, I pull out two apple-flavored bars and hold them in the air as if they're some kind of prize to be had. They're not, but she doesn't need to know yet.

Corra doesn't budge.

I tip my head to a small table in the corner with two chairs. "You have hours before you need to be at GenTech. Take a seat."

I settle into the seat closest to me and open the wrapper. I break the bar in half and bite a chunk into the smaller half. Instead of complaining, I do my best to make it look like it's delicious. I give her a closed lip smile and swallow the sickly-sweet morsel.

"You know, some of the ingredients are real food."

Corra rolls her eyes and drops her arms. She plunks into the empty seat and holds out her hand. I pull the bar back from her grasp.

"You are a real pain you know that?" she sneers. "And I don't like your blonde hair."

"Payback for all those years at University."

"Point taken." Corra shrugs. "Now, can I have the bar?"

"If you promise not to leave yet." I can hardly believe I'm saying those words to Corra Bradley.

"Fine."

I plop the bar into her hand. "Why did you join Affinity? You don't seem happy about it."

Corra peels off the wrapper and inspects the food bar. She sniffs it and then takes a bite. I guess she likes it enough since she didn't make a funny face.

"I don't like anything these days," she says, still chewing. "But I dislike Direction the most."

"Why do you say that? I mean, aside from all the obvious reasons. What changed *your* mind?"

"When we were at University, I was always trying to get ahead. Bragging to everyone in our class made me feel good, important. In some weird way, it was how I made connections. Even if the students all hated me. They knew me... saw me. But, after Configuration Day, I was alone. I don't speak to my parents. Everyone at GenTech keeps to themselves."

"So, basically, you only liked rubbing people's noses in your success," I scoff. "And you don't have that privilege anymore?"

Corra grabs her bar and pushes from her seat. "I'm leaving. Can I get a few more of these?"

"I'm sorry. I was rude. Please stay."

Corra narrows her eyes. "I knew you wouldn't understand."

"That's because you're not making any sense. None of what you shared is a reason to join Affinity."

Corra huffs back into her seat again. "Before Affinity, the only way I knew how to connect with anyone was by telling them how I was a good citizen. I was ultra-focused and accomplished. When I fought to be top of my class, I was still following the Direction Initiative. I could get away with talking about my accomplishments because we were still at University. After Configuration, interacting with others became much less acceptable."

"Why not accept a pairing? It would have been a good solution."

Corra fiddles with the food bar and takes another small bite. "I can't."

"I didn't want a pairing either growing up. But, when I started to pursue it, albeit for Affinity, the process wasn't bad."

"I'm sure it would've been fine for you. But I still couldn't."

I tip my head. "That still doesn't make sense, Corra. It's a big leap from not wanting a pairing to joining Affinity."

"Trust me... I know. But I couldn't be paired with a man my whole life and produce children with him. I won't do it." Her face tenses and her eyes fill with tears.

Although I don't understand, my heart breaks for her.

"Affinity offers me some fulfillment and a connection to something greater. Even if I can't make changes for me, maybe I can help someone else," Corra says.

It's incredible to me how people can be filled by such deep emotions. Corra was nothing but a girl Kyra and I wanted to shoo away in the University halls, but, all this time, there was a depth to her outward personality, more than we ever knew.

"Well, I'm glad you're here," I say. "I know you're good at what you do and I'm sure you're an asset to Affinity.

Corra sits up in her seat and puffs up a fraction. Same old Corra, loving her validation.

Her lips turn up into a sweet smile. "Thanks, that's nice to hear. And I guess your hair color isn't *that* bad."

I chuckle at her.

Corra checks the handheld attached to her wrist. "I should go. I need to get more information about what I'm looking for at GenTech."

"The code is something organic that works in conjunction with nanotech. Probably making a chemical bond. It's being distributed by NutraTech through the food ink. That's all I know."

"Affinity will get me into the system at GenTech," she says. "I'll let you know if I find anything helpful."

Corra grabs the rest of her food bar from the table and stands. "Can I get a few more of these?"

"Sure." I tip my head toward the bag on the counter. "Take a few and come back for more."

She pockets three bars and walks toward the exit. As she reaches the door, she stops and turns toward me. "Thanks for the talk."

"Anytime." And I mean it.

CHAPTER FOURTEEN

Aron leans over my shoulder and studies my screen. "Fisher send any news?"

"Yeah, I spoke to her this morning on a vid comm." I pause from researching Affinity's intel on SynCorp's latest drone projects and twist in my chair to face him. "They still don't have any solid information on Waters' plans with his beta immersives. But, since he hasn't struck yet, she feels it's not going as well as he had hoped. Personally, I think he's trying to perfect it."

Aron nods. "I'm sending out my drones today so we can get a good look at what's happening up top. I'll need you to alter their coding enough to appear like their ID's come from SynCorp. Their engineers send out tests all the time, so no suspicion should arise. I can alter the code, but I think your process will be more thorough. Affinity sent me all the data to match SynCorp's current ID's."

The last time Aron sent out a drone test in Elore for SynCorp he had used the bot to ask me if I wanted to be his spouse. The thought sends a jittery, embarrassed feeling through my stomach. But I leave the topic unsaid.

"What are you talking about?" Meyer comes up behind us.

I jump in my seat and quickly tuck away the thoughts of Aron's proposal. It means nothing, but I think it must take time to sort through memories that are attached to emotions. It's like the feelings cling to you, unwanted.

"Aron is sending his drones into the city to spy for us," I say.

Aron produces his handheld and folds it out into a tablet. He pokes the screen and swipes a few times. One of his drones rises into the air from his workspace, buzzes around, and then stops alongside him. Holding up his device, Aron shows us the screen. A camera is built into the front of the little drone, and, as it circles us, we can see our faces on Aron's screen.

"I stayed up last night in the lab, installing the camera from a bunch of spare tech parts back there. Sanda and I were checking the lab out. Adding the cameras was her idea first."

Without warning, Meyer clasps Aron on the shoulder. And I hold my breath, afraid he's going to give Aron a brotherly lecture. But, instead, he smiles.

"Well, it sounds like a great idea." Meyer's grip slides off Aron's shoulder. "Good work." He smirks at me and walks toward the kitchen.

Aron leans into me. "You didn't tell him, did you?"

"Actually, I did. He took it pretty well. Better than I had expected." Part of me wants to ask Aron about Sanda, but I stop myself when she comes into the room and walks up to his side.

"Did you see Aron's new drone upgrade?" she says, her voice

chipper. "I couldn't believe what he did with those old parts we found."

Aron looks at her and his lips turn up into a grin that forms the dimple on his cheek. Sanda grins back and then looks down at the concrete floor.

I may not know much about this love thing, but those two are definitely interested in each other. And, to be honest, I kind of like the idea of them together too.

"I'm going to find Ben." My chair makes a sharp, skidding sound on the bare floor as I scoot it back. "He's up, right?"

"I saw him in the bunk room," Sanda says, and returns her attention to Aron and his tablet. "Let me see what else you did."

Ben? I think to him as I start down the hall. But I get no answer.

I round into the sleeping quarters and find him sitting on a bottom bunk, leaning on his knees as if in deep thought.

"Ben," I say from the doorway.

He looks my way.

"Couldn't you hear me when I was mentally calling for you?"

"No, I needed some time to myself, so I blocked you."

I sit on the bed next to him. "Is it what happened last night?"

Ben nods. "I didn't get a lot of sleep. I kept waking up and monitoring my nanos. They're still detecting the intruder. Ruiz told you that something different in your brain allowed for the nanos to bond unnaturally, right? That made the ability emerge."

"Yeah, my best guess is the Intelligence Potential upgrade experiments when we were babies facilitated the bond."

"Well, my body isn't flushing the contaminate, and I think

that might be why. The bond might be too strong."

"Are your symptoms worse?" I reach my hand to check him, but he leans away from me.

"No, not worse," he sighs. "But I feel different."

"I'm worried about it too. But do you think the feeling may be only in your head? Psychosomatic?"

"I don't know," Ben says and shrugs. "I guess that's possible. But I'm concerned I might put this mission at risk."

I shake my head. "I need you on the mission. We're not headed up yet right now, anyway. Aron's working on adding a camera in one of his drones. We're sending it above soon." I stand and turn to him. "So, are you helping or are you just going to sit back here? There's a lot of work to be done you know."

"I'll be out in a few minutes. I need to finish getting ready."

"I have several ideas about getting into the Direction mainframe, and I could use your help."

"Like what?"

"If we're going to block Waters' immersives, we need to scan the Neuro-link system to find obvious vulnerabilities. After we do, we patch them."

"And next?" he asks.

"You won't like this, but I think it's necessary."

A worried look crosses his face and his eyebrows pull together.

"Then I think we need to set a trap... an obvious weakness they won't be able to resist. When the immersives enter the system, we'll be waiting."

"But, Avlyn, if I'm not at one hundred percent, there's no

way that'll work. We don't know how many there'll be immersing or their skill level."

I lock eyes with Ben while projecting calm onto him. "It's a risk for sure. But what choice do we have? We need to get busy working on this. So, don't take long."

His nervousness waves through me. I'll need to be strong for him. I stand and pat him on the shoulder before leaving the room, and then pause in the hallway. Sanda is walking toward me, smiling.

Pulling her aside, I whisper, "Can you help me keep an eye on Ben?"

Her expression grows concerned. "Why? I thought he was okay."

"I think he is. But he's been through a lot, and it might be taking a toll on his mental state. I need him to help me, but I feel bad for possibly pushing him too far."

Sanda wraps her arms around my shoulders and all the stress from the last few days floods me.

"I know we're trying, but I'm not sure any of us are holding it together inside. I slept terribly last night," she says.

I embrace her back. "At least we have each other."

"Always." Sanda smiles once again. "But, right now, Aron needs you back out there." We begin walking toward the work area. "He's got the drones ready for you to program."

Aron looks up from his handheld as we approach. "After the drones go out for a few hours we hold our breath and let the data roll in," Aron says. "I think we should consider asking Fisher if we can go up top tomorrow if everything checks out."

I nod and grab a bot to reprogram its ID sequences. It only takes a few seconds and I move on to the rest.

"There, the drones are ready." I say, sitting down in front of a screen. "I'm logging on to see if I can get access to any more information on the Neuro-link."

"Make sure you're careful not to get caught," Meyer warns.

"I won't do anything stupid, just some peripheral searching."

"Can I help too?" Ben's voice comes from behind.

I spin in my seat. "Are you up for it?"

He pulls a chair over from a few feet away and slumps into it, but with a determined look. I nod and place my hand onto the screen. Ben does the same. I take a deep breath and let my mind connect to the system.

When I open my lids, Ben and I stand in an empty white space, but the energy of possibility seeps through me.

"Let's start with how Direction is planning to use the food contaminate. The link must be Nutra and GenTech, so let's focus there."

"We're only here to look for information," I say, "Don't alter or even download anything at this point. Make a mental note of the information location so we can get back, if necessary. But that's it. We only want the program to see us as part of the system. And, since the information is highly sensitive—and that means highly guarded—we can't trip any alarms."

"Got it," Ben says. "And we're sticking together or performing separate searches?"

"Sticking together this time. Two pairs of eyes are going to be best within each search." I take Ben's hand. "Ready?"

He nods.

I focus on Ben's and the system's energy. Unfortunately, I don't know exactly what I'm looking for and where it might be, so I decide to let the network guide us.

My thoughts and emotions meld with Ben's and become endless strings of broken apart code that flows over the existing bits of information. I'd think the sensation would be more disconcerting than it is, but it's not. In fact, it feels more like home than the real world often does. Zeros and Ones are easy to read, and, despite the complexity of code, it's infinitely more simple than reading people and their emotions and intentions.

"I think this might be something." Ben brings me back to the task.

The code whirlwinds around us and then the experience jolts to a stop. We now stand in a new space teaming with cold energy. Scattered code floats around us, and I can't make any of it out.

"Why did we stop here?" I ask.

"I don't know, something in me told me the information was here," Ben says. "It was a feeling. Could be the signature on my nanos from the contaminate."

"Okay, that makes sense," I say. "But, the data must be encrypted."

Ben smiles at me. "Then, we need to de-encrypt it."

I throw him a grin. "I do love a challenge."

Ben and I touch again, and, as we do, form a duplicate of the data for de-encryption. The code around us vibrates and pulses. I close my eyes and relax my mind. The path should be easy if we let it reveal itself. *Don't overthink and force it*, I remind myself.

Warmth and calm spread throughout my body. I open my lids to the still pulsing code, linked to the beating of mine and Ben's heartbeats, rhythmic and steady. The symbols fade red to orange. Ben and I gradually move our hands from each other, and, in synchronization, direct the code. The symbols swirl around us in a mechanical dance as they find their partner and lock into place. And, as they do, the pulse's volume grows louder. The sway of unpaired symbols becomes increasingly furious, and my own heartbeat roars in my ears as a result. Ben and I guide the stragglers. When the last piece of code clicks into place, the deafening experience goes silent. Silent save for the sound of my and Ben's slowing pulses still beating in time.

The arranged code floats in the space around us. We look at each other, and, without even speaking, we know what to do. Taking a step forward in opposite directions, we envelop ourselves into the code. Somehow, my mind is connected to Ben—as if we are one entity—and I feel everything he is in here, as well as how my own consciousness interacts in this space. The code compacts and draws nearer to our bodies, absorbing the data. My head grows dizzy, and we turn towards one another, touching our palms together. Instantly the fog clears.

Without warning, the code sucks into us. Electricity lights up in my brain and nerves. I grit my teeth against the sensation as it presses in farther. Then nothing. It stops, and I flick my attention to Ben. Within a single heartbeat, the all-consuming feelings returns with a vengeance. A scream scorches our bodies as data explodes from our open mouths and into a white-hot sea of stars.

"Ben," I whisper hoarsely as the intensity wanes. The space

spins into oblivion and everything goes dark.

I gasp, and my eyelids shoot open. Disoriented, I scramble to sit up. All the code is gone, and we're left in a blank room. I shake my head. Ben is beside me, his eyelids just opening.

I twist toward him. "Are you okay?"

Ben blinks several times. "Yes, I think so. But what did the data say?"

"I don't know." I rack my brain to remember, but it's not there.

We both push to a stand, then we blink back into reality.

Sanda looks toward both of us, her jaw is tense and eyes full of worry. "We're glad you're back because Waters just bombed GenTech."

CHAPTER FIFTEEN

Aron connects the camera feed to the MV's big screen. The five of us watch in horror as New Philadelphia ships hover over the city, unleashing their fiery devastation. I can't tell much from the camera on the little drone, but at least two more buildings get hit before the DPF ships appear. The sky flashes into shades of orange as Elore attacks. A Philly ship goes down and explodes. The battle appears to drive off the intruder. For now.

I grab a stunner and holster it to my side. Never know when we'll have to be ready.

Meyer paces, rubbing his hand against his forehead. "We need to get Fisher's orders. Attacks this early were not part of the plan."

"I'm not sure the enemy is ever going to follow the plan," Aron says.

Sanda steps forward. "Especially when you have two enemies who hate each other."

"I'm retrieving the drone. There's so much activity on the

streets, and I don't have the equipment to install another camera right now."

Aron swipes on his tablet, and then the little drone seems to reverse. He flicks off the MV screen, but visions of GenTech getting bombed play in my head, making my stomach clench.

"How bad was the GenTech bombing? Have we heard from Corra?" I ask. Memories of the bombing in Level One on my first day at GenTech reels through my mind. The labs are only about halfway up the building; maybe she got out.

Meyer shakes his head. "We haven't heard anything."

"We should turn on the news." I touch the MV, and it changes from black to the image of Brian Marshall. I stare at the familiar newscaster's face and his salt-and-pepper hair.

"Remain calm," he says, but the words do the opposite for me and anxiety flutters in my chest.

Ben steps up beside me and places his hand on my shoulder. Blue emotion floods me, followed by an instant wave of calm. I breathe a sigh of relief and turn my head to him. He stares at the screen, his gaze blank. He runs a hand through his hair and then looks down at me.

"I don't feel well. Can you fill me in on what they say?"

I narrow my eyes, concerned. "Can I help?" I whisper.

Ben glances at the screen again. "No. I'll be fine." He turns and walks toward the sleeping quarters. I return my attention to the MV. The scene has changed to a live feed by a damaged Level Two building that was hit. Citizens are standing out front, mouths agape and eyes large, but the camera pans from them quickly.

Brian Marshall's unseen voice narrates over the destruction. "Our DPF forces have driven off the invading ships. Check-in stations are available in each sector for those who are unable to reenter their apartment buildings. Guardian drones and members of the DPF will assist each displaced citizen."

"We need to contact Fisher," I say. "The city's Affinity members need instructions."

Just as I say this, Flexxes buzz on our wrists.

I turn mine over, and it's a call for an Affinity meeting in VR. Within seconds, Ben appears in the doorway. "I'm going too," he says.

"But you're not feeling well."

He shrugs. "The feeling went away, and I need to be at the meeting."

I nod, confused why the feeling passed so quickly. I decide not to worry about it right now. "Okay, then we need to go."

After syncing the coordinates to my EP, I look up at the others and say, "I'll see you in there."

I close my eyes and open them to an amphitheater. Rows of stone benches curve around the same grassy area Ruiz had given her speech on after Manning had announced the formation of the DPF. Similar to the first time I was here, a podium waits at the front for Cynthia to address the gathering. Guilt over Ruiz's absence creeps through my gut.

Memories and emotions flood over me. Lena and my mother were still alive, then. Meyer was missing, and I thought he might be dead. The entire experience of being in VR with Affinity members from both inside the city and the Outerbounds was a mystery to me. Overwhelming, actually.

A hand slips over the small of my back, and I glance up at Meyer. A sad smile plays across his lips as he tugs my body closer to him. Then, he gently guides me to sit.

My EP still doesn't detect Corra here and messaging her seems risky with her whereabouts unknown.

New Affinity members blink into existence and fill the arena. But, this time, none of the experience feels as overwhelming. I was a different girl then and I've seen too much.

We need to tell Cynthia exactly what happened to me, Ben speaks in my mind.

My stomach clenches at the thought. I know exactly how that is going to play out.

She'll take you off the mission. I know it. And, without you here, I'm not sure if my ability is strong enough. You saw what happened back at the camp when I had to flip the soldiers on my own.

Ben furrows his eyebrows. I know, but I could put you and the whole team at risk.

I'm not letting that happen. We can handle this together..

Ben gives me a tentative look. *Fine.*

"Members of Affinity," Cynthia's voice fills the air as her face projects onto the sky. I turn my attention from Ben to the podium on the grassy area below.

"It saddens me that my first major announcement is under these circumstances. But, the attack on Elore by New Philadelphia has moved up our timeline. You have already been informed to discontinue eating as much Elorian printed food as possible. We are gaining more intel on this situation as I speak."

Cynthia shifts uncomfortably and clears her throat.

"New Philadelphia is looking to destroy Elore and doesn't want to take the time to integrate Elorian citizens into New Philadelphia's society. Waters was overheard stating 'Take it out. Nothing should stand.' Because of this, a decision has become necessary, one we never thought we would have to make. As Affinity members, we need to consider siding with Elore temporarily. If we don't, everyone here may die."

Horror blankets many of the faces in the arena. Others display anger and shock. If I thought the arena was quiet before, it wasn't. No one moves or breathes in anticipation of what she may say next.

Cynthia looks down, inhales deeply, and then returns her attention to the audience.

"I'm fully aware this isn't the news you wanted to hear, and I'm not the person you wanted at the podium. The death of Adriana Ruiz is a shock to everyone. She was a wonderful person and leader who gave her life to protect the very individuals who may possess the ability to end this war for good."

The words send a mixture of guilt and pride to my core. I glance at Ben and the emotions I'm receiving from him are nearly identical to mine. Ruiz sacrificed herself for us—she sacrificed herself for her people—as a real leader should. And I didn't trust her. Shame works through me like a knife to my stomach. I hate that I failed to see her for the person she was until she was already gone.

"What she did was brave, selfless... and all so each one of you could have the life and freedoms you deserve. The same reasons you joined Affinity. When I left Elore years ago, I believed I was doing the right thing. I wasn't. I should have stayed and fought alongside Ruiz. But, when she spoke with me a year ago, she convinced me to come back. She reminded me of the leader I always intended to be when I took my position on the Direction Council. Ruiz and I wanted to change the world until that goal was taken from us. But, unlike me, she kept on trying to make changes in a new way. I'm back to continue what she started."

The people's energy shifts, not to acceptance, but to interest. Many lean forward in their seats and others uncross their arms. They're willing to listen. Willing to give her a chance.

Cynthia raises her head with an air of authority. "We are doing our best to get more weapons for those in Elore, as well as a new supply of rations. But, everyone will need to be patient."

Will siding with Elore be the death of us all? Can we survive?

I look around at the Affinity members' faces. In here with Ruiz a month ago, the energy was completely different. This time people sit, quietly listening to Cynthia. People had once thought that "Choosing a New Direction" was something on the horizon. Maybe it was. Just not the same direction we're headed in now.

Cynthia grasps the podium's side and leans in toward the audience. "This is no time for division. You don't know or trust me yet. But, Ruiz did. And, each of us has the responsibility to continue what she set in motion. I invite you to join me."

I smile at her words. Cynthia has stopped running and has decided to lead. It's my responsibility to follow in her footsteps and do the same. No matter what that means for my safety.

I thread my hand into the crook of Meyer's arm and pull him close to me. He turns his head my way and locks his eyes onto mine. We hold our gaze for several beats, somehow saying nothing but communicating everything. My old life and self is gone, and this new one is all I now want.

"Thank you for being a part of Affinity," Cynthia's voice interrupts my thoughts. "If you are aware of further information you believe is useful to us, contact your superior. And, finally, please continue to check your Affinity accounts for updates."

I compel a message to Cynthia about what Ben and I found, but I still don't tell her about how it's affecting Ben. I can't have him removed from the mission.

"We need to get back," I say to Ben.

He nods, and I blink hard to release myself from VR. I open my eyes to the bunker as the others open their eyes too.

Aron's spy drone floats in front of him, and he reaches out and grasps it.

"We need to look at the footage further." He twists toward Sanda. "Can you help?"

"Sure," she says and joins him at a screen while Aron links the bot.

"After we finish, we should send the vid to Fisher," Sanda says.

"I have new messages to review that just came into my Affinity account." Meyer holds up his handheld and taps at the screen.

Before he passes by me, he leans in and places a kiss on my forehead, and then he heads toward the sleeping quarters.

As I watch him disappear, an auto-light illuminates down the hall over the elevator's top, and my heart jumps. I raise the device on my wrist to check if I had missed a message from Corra, but there's nothing.

"Someone's coming," I say loud enough for Aron and Sanda to hear across the room.

I grab for the weapon holstered to my hip. Ben does the same with his. Aron and Sanda each grab stunners and then we train our weapons onto the elevator doors.

The chime sounds and my finger rests on the trigger. The door opens and inside the cab stands a wide-eyed Corra. The sleeve of her gray shirt is torn, and ash blackens her cheek. Her short blonde hair contains bits of dirt at the scalp. Her appearance reminds me of when I was blown to the ground in Level One.

She lets out a yelp, throwing her hands in the air.

"Corra," I gasp.

I toss down my weapon and race to her.

"Avlyn," she whispers, shock filling her expression. "It's not safe out there."

Her eyes roll back in her head and I reach for her arm as she collapses to the ground.

Chapter Sixteen

Meyer and Aron carry Corra to the meeting room couch where Sanda uses the med app on her Flexx to scan her. After a moment, Sanda's shoulders sag with relief.

"She's fine. None of her injuries are serious. It was only stress," Sanda says.

Corra's eyelids flutter open. She gasps for a short breath and scrambles to sit up.

"You're okay," I say, crouching beside her. "You're back in your building."

Her eyes flit back and forth between us. "They... they bombed GenTech," she mutters. "Some of the upper floors... I don't even know if those people are alive." Her eyes grow wilder. "We made it outside, and SI drones swarmed in and told us to remain calm, that Direction had the situation under control, and then they sent us home. Everyone was calm—they just accepted what they were told—so I pretended I had too. But, on the way home, another building was hit a block over. I... I saw it." Fear blankets her face as she tries to sit up all the way. "What if they hit this building?"

"Corra," Sanda says, and Corra's eyes cling desperately to hers. "You're in shock right now, and your body is emotionally overloading. Your system isn't used to this fight-or-flight response." Sanda pokes at the screen of her Flexx. "I need to give you something to help calm you down. Otherwise, you're going to pass out again."

Corra nods several times, and Sanda places Corra's hand to the screen of her device. After a moment, the Flexx beeps, and Corra removes her hand. Seconds later, she exhales a long breath and drops back to the sofa, eyelids fluttering shut.

My Flexx buzzes with an alert from Affinity that an auto-broadcast to all of Elore is playing on the MV. But our unit must not be programmed to come on automatically. We can watch it later.

Sanda motions us away from Corra. "I meant it when I said Corra is having difficulty controlling her emotional state. Internally, she's a wreck. Her nanos don't quite know how to respond to the overload. And, my guess is that a lot of people are going to be experiencing the same thing."

Meyer crosses his arms over his chest. "But she said the other people at GenTech were calm. They listened to the SI and went home."

"Maybe they were pretending just like she was," Aron says. "It's kind of what Elorians do best."

Sanda crosses her arms and looks down, as if she's in thought. "What if the food contaminate dulls people's emotions even more? Maybe Manning anticipated some of this? It's basically crowd control. Direction is trying to avoid mass hysteria. No one panics, and Manning still looks as if he's handling the situation."

"But, Corra has been eating food from the printer, right?" Aron asks.

"Yes," I say, "but she told me that she's been stressed and not eating much. Then, I gave her a few food bars. She probably hasn't had any printed food today. So, the effect could be weaker on her."

Corra stirs again, sitting up just enough to rake her ash-smudged fingers through her hair. "Did I really pass out again in front of you all?

Sanda walks to Corra and sits beside her, using her handheld to scan her.

"Your stress chemicals are coming into balance and your blood pressure has normalized. I think you'll be okay. At least, for now. Are you able to give us more details of what happened?"

She takes a long draw of air. "Affinity was able to get me access into the NutraTech project's database. Most of the files were encrypted, so I couldn't get many specifics. But, I was able to find out who worked on the project. When I was copying information, I received an alert. At first, I thought I might've been caught, but it wasn't that. GenTech was telling us to evacuate the building. I released from the VR session, and that's when the first bomb hit. The SI in the building started rounding people up and escorting us down the stairs, playing the same message, 'Remain calm. Direction has the situation under control.

Please return to your dwelling and await further instruction.' And overall, it worked. The bombs were shaking the building, but everyone seemed unnaturally calm and exited GenTech."

"What was it like on the streets?" Meyer asks.

"Bad," she says. "Guardian drones and DPF were everywhere, herding the people along. They were evacuating all of the companies since they seemed to be the targets."

"But New Philly hit an apartment building too, right?" Sanda asks.

Corra nods. "So, I'm not sure home was any safer. A lot of the citizens have no place to go now."

Ben paces. "If all the companies are being evacuated, we might be able to sneak in. But, we aren't going to know if we're stuck down here. A lot of people are on the street, so blending in might be easier."

"Good point," I say. "This *is* a great opportunity to access GenTech for Affinity. We need to know exactly why Manning is contaminating printed food before we can move forward with Phase One. And since that's our mission—"

"Well, they're not going to let us have a tour. And Fisher hasn't approved it anyway," Aron says.

"Fisher will say no. This needs to be done and I know how to get into GenTech the back way," I say.

"You can't be serious, Avlyn." Meyer scoffs.

"On my first VR training session with Affinity, Lena took me through a secret tunnel that led into a storage room on the basement level of GenTech. Meyer was there."

I look to Corra. "I need you to come."

"Why?" Panic sets in her eyes. "No way. I don't want to go out again. Or break into GenTech."

"We need someone who works in the lab and, right now, you're the only one here. Plus, you have a better idea of what we might be looking for." I place my hand on Corra's shoulder. "You've always wanted to be special. Here's your chance. You were the top in our class at University. It's time to prove you are the best at what you do."

Corra narrows her eyes at me but relaxes. "You're not going to get us all killed, are you?"

"I know what just happened out there scared you. But, if we wait too long for Phase One, it will be too late," I say.

Maybe we should leave Corra. She doesn't want to come. Ben thinks to my mind.

I turn to him. "Why would you say that? We need her in the lab."

A quizzical look crosses Corra's face.

It would be easier without her, he thinks to me again.

A small amount of anger builds in my chest. "This mission is most likely to be successful if she comes."

"Wait," Corra says. "What's going on here?"

"Yeah, it's weird," Sanda says. "But the twins can talk to each other in their heads. Maybe we can explain later."

"Wait. What? You're twins?" Corra asks, looking back and forth between Ben and I.

"It's a long story," I say, surprised by how our ability to speak telepathically isn't of more interest to her. "I'll catch you up later. But, yes, Ben is my twin."

Corra rubs at her temples and closes her eyes for a moment. "So, do you have an implant or something?"

I shake my head. "No, there's no implant. We just can do it." I realize at this point that Affinity hadn't explained to Corra about the ability Ben and I share. So, I give her the short version, including a few details of how Ben and I found each other again.

"Really?" she asks when I'm done. "So that's why you were so important to Ruiz."

"You all should go," Aron says. His brown eyes, changed by the CosmoNano tech, peek over the screen where he's been studying footage the drone had captured.

I look to Ben, wrinkling my brow at his comments from a moment ago.

"Fine," he says. "She should come."

I roll my attention back to Corra. "So, you'll come?"

Corra sighs. "Yes."

"The city still seems to be in chaos," Sanda says as she looks at her Flexx. "If we're heading out, we need to do it now. Intel is coming in from Affinity that GenTech is down to a skeleton crew, and the lab remains undamaged."

"What will you do while we're up there?" I ask.

"Aron and I are headed up, too" Sanda says. "Just not with you. We'll scope out security measures around the city."

Aron spins in his seat toward her.

"Good," I say. "The drone footage is great, but we need to get a sense of the atmosphere, how people are really responding. Maybe you can get a few citizens to talk. But, be careful. Aron knows how far you can push without looking out of place." I look to Aron, and he nods.

Meyer, Ben, and I double check our false IDs in the Direction database while Corra returns to her unit to change out of her torn clothes.

Meyer is the same Kian Martin cover he used when we first met, since that identity remains uncompromised. Ben's new name is William Davis and mine is still Alana Miller. I program our new identities to all work at GenTech. Then, I assign our IDs lab access to provide an extra level of security.

Sanda wraps her arms around me and squeezes, then steps back beside Aron. "Please be careful."

"You too," I say to them both.

Before taking the elevator, Meyer, Ben, and I conceal stunners under our coats, including one for Corra. I hold my breath nearly the whole way up to street level. This is it. I'm going back into Elore. A place that wants to see me dead.

The elevator chime startles my held-in breath to free. Slowly, Corra and the apartment building's empty lobby slides into view as the elevator doors glide open. She chose an upgraded unit with her generous GenTech credit salary, just as I had once. The lobby is sleek and modern, displaying simple finishes. And, with no one milling around inside, the space appears typical, calm. But, on the other side of the glass, it's a different story. Groups of citizens crowd the streets. In the middle of the day, the sight is highly unusual as everyone would normally be at their position.

"GenTech is two blocks over," I say under my breath to the others. Everything is programmed into our EPs, but the words just slip out.

Outside, I breathe in the crisp air. From the gray clouds covering the sky above, I get the feeling it could snow soon. The tall buildings of Level Two loom over us, bearing down heavy on my shoulders. I pull my coat in tighter over the dull, uniform-styled clothing Affinity provided us as we weave in and out of people on the street.

"There is no reason to be alarmed," a female voice soothes from the overhead media screens. "Direction has the situation under control, and we are working on preparing shelter for those displaced from their homes."

When we near GenTech, there are DPF stationed out front, blocking the entrance. The adjacent apartment building is unguarded, however. The EP guides me around the back to the service entrance that leads directly to the tunnel and into GenTech. My chest tightens as I remember doing much the same with Lena in the simulation.

I touch my glove-covered hand to the security pad, and the door slides back. "Are you sure this is right?" Corra whispers to me as we enter the building.

"I'm sure." When they're all in, I rearm the security. Just like Lena taught me. *Don't be sloppy,* I repeat her words in my mind. I still miss her. But I push the emotions down and keep focused on the task at hand. I motion for Ben to follow me when my EP flashes.

Service Elevator 16 feet ahead

"The elevator is on the right," Meyer echoes.

I palm the call pad when we get there, and the door opens. "Give me a boost," I say to Meyer.

He quickly moves into the cab's middle while Corra looks on confused. She turns her attention to the elevator's inside palm scanner.

"Wait," I say. "Don't confirm a floor selection. We're going to climb up ourselves."

She and Ben stand back, but I'm still getting excessive nervousness from Ben. And it's making the hair on my arms stand on end.

Are you sure you are okay? I think to Ben as I step onto Meyer's back while he kneels on the ground. I reach for the metal, tiled ceiling in the elevator's ceiling, push a panel up, and then slide it to the side.

I'm fine, my twin's voice comes back to me in my mind. Being out there gave me a weird feeling, that's all.

Still using Meyer as a step, I pull myself up and out of the cab.

But you're going to be alright in here? I think to Ben.

I told you, I'm fine. His voice comes back to me in my head.

My heart wants to believe him.

Reluctantly, I swing my attention to Corra. "You're next."

Corra doesn't have an EP to help her navigate, so Meyer gestures to step onto his back and then I help pull her through the opening.

"Move out of the way," I say to her as soon as she's through. Seconds later, Meyer is pulling himself up, followed by Ben.

Above us is a ladder that climbs to a ledge fifteen-feet above. The EP outlines a hidden panel at the ledge that will lead us into a compact tunnel. We scale the ladder, and, at the top, I use my handheld to activate the hidden panel a foot or so from the rungs.

The panel slides back, and I swing into the opening. I turn and look back to Corra and offer her my hand. Nervously, she clasps it, and I help her in. We start to crawl through the tight space illuminated only by my EP. Ben and Meyer are soon behind, and Meyer secures the panel shut.

We crawl the length of the short tunnel and come to the same dead end as in my sim training, which now seems a lifetime ago. From what I remember, the storage room should be on the other side. I stare at the paneled wall and my EP detects zero signs of life or drone activity.

Gnawing the inside of my lip, I activate the panel and it slides back to reveal an empty storage room, just as I had hoped. I breathe a sigh of relief, and the group exits the secret passage.

"Okay," I look to Meyer. "We've done the next part in the sim too. Now, we just need to get to the lab."

Meyer squares himself. "It's doable."

Ben walks around Meyer and toward the entrance.

Wait a second, Ben, I think. We need to make sure Corra has her bearings before we go.

He doesn't answer and continues forward.

Ben, I think.

He taps the door, and it slides back. He twists towards me, his eyes blank, and then turns and rushes through the opening.

I can't read him. He's mentally blocking me.

I race after him, but he already has his hand on the security panel ten-feet away.

An alarm blares.

Ben! I scream in my mind. *What did you do?*

Ben drops his fingers off the security panel and turns his head toward me. Instantly, I'm flooded with guilt and fear from him. He throws his hand to the panel again, and the alarms stops.

"We have to get out of here, now!" Meyer shouts to us.

Stun me, he says weakly in my mind.

Stun you? I ask.

"I can't be trusted! Something is controlling me!" Ben yells too loudly.

A blast emits from behind me and hits Ben in the chest. He crumples to the ground.

Shocked, I pivot on my heel and find Corra with her stunner trained on Ben, a sudden glint of bravado in her eyes.

CHAPTER SEVENTEEN

I sprint to Ben and throw my hands to his chest, immersing with him. I order his nanos to run a diagnostic. He's fine. Just stunned. My mind races.

Why would Ben set off the security alarm? Was he trying to disable it and made a mistake? I replay the scene frame-by-frame in my mind: Ben walking through the storage room's door; Ben not listening to me; Ben touching the panel. And then it hits me. Ben's betrayal is the effect of the food ink contaminate. Sanda was right. Even after practicing a lifetime of emotion suppression, no one can stay *that* calm after being bombed. Which is why the people on the street are calmer than they should be. The propaganda blaring throughout the city must have affected Ben, and he couldn't hold it together any longer.

There's no way we can get up to the lab now. Guardians will be swarming this place soon.

I need to find a way to disrupt their security response. But we need to get Ben out of the hall first before anyone detects us. I release from my brother's nanos and return to the real world. Meyer and Corra are standing over us.

"What are we going to do?" Corra asks.

I lock eyes with Meyer. "I need you to carry Ben back the way we came. I can't wake him up until we're in a more secure location."

"Do we even want to wake him up?" Meyer asks. "Look at what he just did."

"It wasn't his fault. It's the NutraTech contaminate," I say.

"What?" Corra asks. "I thought you said he was fine."

I stand, my mind reeling. "Look, Corra. I made a mistake. Let's not waste time standing here in the hall and make another one. Now, I need you to help Meyer to get my brother back into the tunnel. I think I can fix his nanos in there, but, if we stay out here, we're going to get caught." I turn to Meyer. "Your orders are to protect both Ben and me. Now do what I'm telling you, soldier."

The look on Meyer's face changes from confusion to determination, and he bends down, grabs Ben and hoists him over his shoulder, letting out a grunt. Meyer then looks at me and clenches his jaw.

"I'll be right behind you two," I assure him. "I have to reprogram the security to throw them off our trail."

"Let's go, Corra," he growls, and she follows him as he walks back into the storage room, Ben limp over his shoulder.

I turn towards the security pad on the wall and touch my palm to it. I order the system to detect an intruder on every level of GenTech in multiple locations. Hopefully, doing so will confuse the guards into thinking that the recent bombing had caused a system malfunction.

I release from the system and immediately throw my hands to my ears to block out the deafening alarms. My EP still shows no Guardians in the vicinity, yet. They must have most of the units on duty outside, dealing with the displaced citizens and bombing victims. I race into the storage room and climb into the still open panel behind the shelving. Once I'm inside, I close the wall and reset the cloaking device to hide the panel from view. My EP lights up the dark area and I find Meyer, Corra, and an unconscious Ben waiting for me in the tunnel.

"There's no way I can get Ben down the ladder without his help, Avlyn," Meyer snaps. "So, you need to fix this, or we're stuck in here for a while. And, don't forget, if he wakes up, he still might be able to alert the guards by yelling. These walls are not completely soundproof."

I crawl in nearer to them. "If, for some reason, what I'm going to try right now doesn't work, I need you and Corra to go back to the bunker," I say.

"I'm not leaving you." Meyer insists. "You're the one who, a minute ago, reminded me of the reason I was here."

I let out a sigh. "I just said that to get you to move."

Meyer scowls at me.

I continue, ignoring his expression. "I'm not leaving him here. I can stay and keep trying. I'll just program his nanotech to sedate him until I can figure it out. No use in all four of us dying or being captured."

Meyer's expression doesn't improve and Corra stands behind

him, shaking her head.

"I know what you're thinking, but it's not going to work," I say. "I'm staying with Ben no matter what."

He opens his mouth to speak.

"Meyer." I cut him off. "If I can't repair Ben, there's no option other than killing him." Revulsion churns in my stomach as I speak the words. "You or Corra can't control him, so neither of you can stay. And, if we leave him here and he wakes up, he'll probably lead Manning straight to the bunker."

Meyer's fully aware of how stubborn I am, and he knits his eyebrows together, saying, "We're not going to kill your brother." Corra remains silent behind him. Typically, she'd have an opinion to throw in, but not this time.

Inhaling deeply, I take Ben's hand and close my eyelids. This has to work.

I open my eyes to a white snowfall of code surrounding me in slow motion. I submerge my hand into the programming and strings of code ripple off the sides of my palm in sheets.

I let calm consume me and any apprehension falls away. I know what I have to do, and it will work. I call up the code affected by the contaminate.

"Ben, you must focus on my voice." He doesn't answer, but the tiniest amount of emotional pull resonates in my mind. He's there. Weak, but there.

"I still don't think I can purge you of the contamination completely, but I do think I can alter it. For it to work, I need you to open yourself up to me."

Still, he doesn't answer.

Everything Direction does is about suppressing emotions. I call up the feelings I had when I first learned Ben was still alive, then when I had met with him in New Philadelphia. The mix of emotions—joy, sadness, loss, elation, and confusion—churns through my mind. And, as it does, the code around me vibrates.

I close my eyes and visualize the force and power of the emotions, reining them in, just as I had with the horse in Thornton. I home in on Ben's affected code again and rush to overtake it. Quickly I sort out where he has been permanently changed and how the code is bonded to the chemical compound still clinging to it. I can't remove the bond, but I can apply another patch to the problem.

If you're still here, I need you to focus on the emotions I shared. Use the feeling to allow me farther into your mind, I think to him.

Heat resonates within my chest, and the feeling spreads from deep inside me, outward, through my arms and into my hands and fingers. The space around me grows thick with excitement and energy, and it's as if I'm not sure of where I begin and end anymore.

It's working, Ben. My mind swirls through the code until my consciousness has mingled with it.

Whack!

An unseen force crashes into me and then twists around my digital form.

I open my mouth to let out a scream, but nothing comes. The relentless pull persists, and I wrestle against the attack, but it continues to call and permeate my mind, bringing me closer to

Ben's thoughts. Closer to safety.

I open my eyes and logic comes back to me with full force. *No, this is not safe!* I compel the code to shift and then throw my hand forward and apply the patch. As if a vacuum activates, the code jolts and I'm tugged backward.

Spinning.

Spinning.

My first instinct is to fight the feeling, make it stop. But, something inside me tells me to relax. To work with it. Through it.

I let myself inhabit the code, the whole system. The sensation is unlike anything I've ever experienced when immersed, and definitely not a feeling found in the real world. It's as if I'm floating, and, not just in one place, but everywhere. All the code is available and within my grasp. I let go of all human thought and become machine. And, against all logic, the space and code begin to push toward me, as if I'm absorbing my surroundings. Faster and faster it moves through me. Eventually, my body resolidifies again.

"Ben!" I shout.

Warm, calming emotions from Ben move through me just like they had before he ate Elore's printed food. So much so, I'm certain the contaminate isn't affecting him anymore. We need to go—now. I release from immersion to the reality of Meyer, Corra, and Ben in the escape tunnel, between GenTech and the apartment building next door.

"How long was I out?" I ask, my panic rising. The experience felt like an eternity, and, yet, not nearly long enough to complete my task.

"Maybe thirty seconds?" Meyer answers.

My mouth falls open. "Thirty seconds?"

"Did it work?" He flicks his attention to my brother. Ben's eyes are still closed.

"I think so," I say and lift his head, "Ben, wake up."

Ben's eyelids fly open and he gasps, and my breath hitches. Fear and anxiety project onto me from him. "Wha... what did I do back there?" He tries to sit up.

I offer support with my hands against his back; even with our healing nanos, the initial effects of a stunner are no fun when you wake up.

"You nearly got us killed," Corra whispers.

Ben whips his attention to me. "I did?" His eyes grow wide, brows creased. "I did! I set off the alarm. Why did I do that?"

"That's what we need to know," Meyer says. "Because, if we can't figure out what happened to you, we're stuck in this tunnel forever."

"You're okay—for now," I say, looking to Ben. "At least, I think."

Ben relaxes a fraction. "I could have killed us," he mutters. "I'm so sorry."

"What do you mean 'you think?,'" Corra asks. "Were you able to fix him or not?"

"Direction is using the contaminate to mix a chemical drug with a trigger in the nanos. I was able to patch the connection point. But I still don't fully understand the compound. Sanda thought it might depress emotions, but the effect seems like more than that, at least for Ben. The drug triggered him to see us as the enemy intent on hurting Direction."

Corra stares at me, deep in thought, her eyes narrowing into slits. "Okay, I've seen a few MedTech projects that could do something similar in the lab recently."

"You mean like a mind control drug?" Meyer asks Corra.

"Well, sort of," Corra says. "More like affecting the emotions to make people more susceptible to suggestion. None of these were my projects. But mind control is possible." She pauses for a moment and blinks. "It makes sense now, why the people on the street were not panicked and still listening to instructions without issue. Except, Ben's reaction was so much greater than I would have expected."

"Ben and I are not like other people," I say.

"Okay," Meyer says, frustration in his voice. "That's all well and good, but, if we go back outside, he could do something crazy again. And, it's not like we can knock him out a second time and carry him through the streets. I think someone will notice."

"Please don't stun me again," Ben mutters and rubs at his chest.

I shake my head. "I told you. I was able to temporarily patch the problem."

"Temporarily?" Corra asks.

"Yes, it's not a permanent solution. The malfunction still exists," I say. "We should get back to the bunker now and figure out how to heal Ben's system permanently."

"Fine," Meyer says. "So, does it mean we can get out of here?"

"I set off all the security in GenTech," I say with a slow, conspiratorial smile. "Hopefully, they'll think it was a glitch from the attack. But, there may be even more Guardians in this area for a while."

"Well, no time like the present." Meyer swings his attention back to Corra. "You first."

Corra takes in a deep breath and heads toward the tunnel exit. Meyer follows her.

"You think you're okay?" I whisper to Ben, not feeling as confident in my patch job as I did a few moments ago.

He pauses for a second, as if in thought. "The whole way here I was anxious. It was like I was torn between you and the team and my uncertainty that Direction was dangerous. I was doing my best to block you from my conflict. That's all gone now. I feel normal."

The tension in my chest falls away, and, without thinking, I wrap my arms around him and squeeze. "I can't lose you, again."

"You coming or staying?" Meyer asks from the now open tunnel exit. Corra is already out of sight.

Keeping my voice down, I answer, "We're coming."

Chapter Eighteen

I lean my back against our bunker's elevator cab as the doors shut. My eyelids droop and my knees buckle, and then I'm sliding to the ground. Guardians were swarming outside GenTech, but there were still enough displaced citizens on the street to keep our small group unnoticed during the short trek to our bunker.

We made it Ben, I think to him, silently thankful he had no issues on the way here.

Do you really think we can use this information about the contaminate in the food ink? His voice comes back to me in my mind.

Right now, it's all we've got. We have to use this info somehow.

I open my eyes and look up to Corra and Meyer who are on opposite sides of the cab, each lost in their own thoughts. Ben stands in the middle, tapping at his Flexx.

"Are you staying with us, Corra?" I ask.

She shakes her head. "No, I'm riding up to my apartment

after you three go below."

The elevator beeps, and the door slides open to the bunker hallway. Corra stretches her hand to the pad to hold it open for us.

"Are you sure?" I ask, concerned for her to be alone after what we just went through.

Meyer looks to me, and I wave him and Ben on.

"I'll be there in a second," I say.

"I'm fine," Corra answers when they've left. "I have a few tasks I need to complete. GenTech sent several messages to my Flexx saying that we need to go online since they're closed. I'm also concerned Direction could spot-check apartments. You never know about these things." She holds out her hand to me, and I allow her to pull me up.

"With everything that's going on, do you think that's likely?"

Corra shrugs. "Probably not. Direction seems busy managing bigger issues. But I guess I need to be alone to think. If I change my mind, I'll come down again."

I can't blame her. Who knows if Corra honestly feels comfortable with me, let alone Meyer, Ben, Aron, and Sanda, whom she had only met. "Well, if you do want to come down, don't let any of us stop you. But, I understand why you'd rather go upstairs right now."

I take a step forward, and Corra grabs my shoulder, keeping me in place. "I'm sorry for how I used to treat you."

"I'm sorry for how I used to think about you."

Corra's lips form a tight smile and she nods twice, releasing me. I walk through the open elevator door and into the corridor without glancing back. The doors shut, and, for a moment, I understand Corra's desire to be alone.

My insides twist as memories of today's already full set of events run through my mind's eye. I could easily see myself hiding in the sleeping quarters, hoping no one would find me. Hoping the dangers and responsibilities would go away. But, it's only the afternoon. Instead of taking a right toward the sleeping quarters, I force myself to go left toward the meeting room. When I get there, Meyer and Ben are waiting for me. One of Aron's drones floats over Meyer's shoulder, making an excited whine as if it's happy to see him again.

"Where are Aron and Sanda?" I ask.

Meyer looks around the room. "Apparently, they're not back yet."

"Did you message Sanda?" I ask, worry tingling in my chest.

"Not yet," he responds. "I was just about to do that."

"Then we need to tell Cynthia what's happening," Ben says. "I already messaged her for a meeting when we were in the elevator."

A sick feeling seeps into my stomach. "She may take you off the mission, and I need your ability to complement mine. I'm not sure I can handle flipping the entire DPF without you. Look what happened with Thompson back at the camp, and that was only one man... not an entire army."

"We can't worry about that right now," Meyer says. "Figuring out what was wrong with Ben and making a permanent solution is the top priority. I know you're good at what you do, Avlyn." Meyer's lips stretch into a tense smile. "Believe me, I do.

But, if Ben stays, we need more guidance. This is too big to risk keep making mistakes. Too many lives are at stake."

"You're right," I say. "I've barely slept this past week, so I'm not even sure how clearly I'm thinking."

"Join the club," Meyer mumbles as his Flexx vibrates in his hand. He holds it up to look at the screen. "Sanda and Aron are on their way back. They're a block over."

I breathe a sigh of relief.

"Cynthia is calling for us. But, she only wants to see Avlyn and me." Ben says, tapping at his Flexx.

I swing my attention to Meyer.

"It's fine, just make sure this gets fixed," he says, as he walks toward the eating area.

"I'm sending the coordinates to your EP," Ben says to me.

"We're meeting with her in VR?" I ask.

"Looks like she has Affinity members from a few different locations she needs in the meeting," Ben says.

I grab Ben's arm and pull him over to the couch. "We should get comfortable, then." Not that informing my grandmother how I had put the whole mission at risk by insisting Ben go with us to GenTech is going to be very comfortable.

The coordinates load into my EP and the text scrolls across the bottom of my vision in green.

"Ok, they're ready," Ben says.

I close my eyes to immerse, and, when I blink them open, we are in what appears to be a stark, gray meeting room. A sizeable oblong table sits in the middle, surrounded by eight black chairs. There are no windows in the room, and the lighting seems to originate from nowhere.

"I guess no one is here yet," I say.

As if on cue, Cynthia appears at the opposite end of the room. Her graying hair is combed straight and brushes the bottom of her shoulders. I open my mouth to speak, but then two more people appear in the space. The first is Melissa Rice, and, to my surprise, Dr. Sloan, dressed neatly in a blue pullover shirt. He runs his hand over his bald head, inhales deeply and then drops his shoulders down from their hunched position.

"It appears we are all here for now," Cynthia says. "Will you all have a seat please?"

I pull out my chair and collapse into it. Ben sits to my right while Cynthia chooses the head of the table and Dr. Sloan sits across from me. Melissa positions herself on my grandmother's right.

"Thank you all for joining me here at this urgent meeting," Cynthia says, placing her hands on the table and leaning in toward us. "I've been told there is news on all fronts, and I would like for each of you to hear it." She looks to Sloan. "Dr. Sloan has requested to speak first."

Sloan pushes his seat backward and rises. The tight expression on his face exhibits more discomfort than the other brief time I had met him in VR. He told me once how he felt more comfortable in virtual reality where he could block out the sensations of the real world. But now, he seems stressed, even in here.

"Thank you for having me, Fisher." Sloan nods to Cynthia and clears his throat. "Ms. Rice, my name is Lennon Sloan, and, until recently, I worked for Waters in New Philadelphia as a technology and virtual reality specialist. I apologize for my nervousness. This past week, I've had more interaction with people than I do in a year. This anxiety is typically eased for me when meeting in a virtual space." He tips his head. "And I suppose it is. But, alas, I'm still finding interaction most arduous."

"You've been extremely helpful, Dr. Sloan," Cynthia interjects. "We appreciate the difficulty you face."

Sloan nods and studies the table. "I have disturbing news, which Fisher already knows. But, we decided not to make this information public until we had gathered as many details as possible." He takes a long breath. "As each of you are aware already, Waters has developed a potential human immersive program based on data he gathered in the short time he had Ms. Lark in custody.

"During that time, he was able to gather enough data on Ms. Lark's ability to begin human trials on how this ability could be used to benefit New Philadelphia. One of these ways, which we discovered recently through the capture of a New Philadelphia hoverpod, is installing technology on the crafts which assists the test subject in immersing with the ship. But, upon further investigation, we've found this is not the program's primary function."

Which I knew. The whole system on the Philly ship seemed like a waste to both Ben and me. I refocus on his briefing.

"It was only an in-field test for Waters to see if his immersion program would work. Since then, he's found adults respond poorly to being altered," Sloan says. "His first round of tests resulted in the deaths of twenty-eight adults, ranging from ages seventeen to thirty-five. For the second round, he lowered the range to as young as twelve years."

A wave of anger and fear from Ben crashes into me. But, knowing what I know, the younger age makes sense. Even though my ability did not show itself until recently, all the groundwork was laid down when I was an infant.

I look to Ben. We can't let our past cloud our thinking. All we can do is keep experimentations from happening more.

Ben raises his hand to his head. *I don't feel right again.*

Panic works its way through my chest. *What do you mean?*

Your being in my head seems to weaken the patch.

Instantly, I pull my thoughts and emotions from him. He closes his eyes and exhales long and slow. Then he nods to me as if he's okay now.

Reluctantly, I bring my attention back to Sloan as he says, "According to our intel, Waters' best results were made using the youngest subjects."

"So, we are looking to virtually battle with an army of twelve-year-olds?" Melissa asks, her face filled with horror. "How do we even justify that?"

"We can't," Fisher says. "It's one of the reasons we're here. As a group, we need to figure out the best method of defeating Waters without harming these children."

My mind spins, knowing it's going to be me and Ben doing the defeating. "Do you know yet how they were able to make the ability work for them?"

"Yes, yes," Sloan says. "I was getting there. From the little I know about you and your brother, Ms. Lark, the genesis of your immersion abilities is quite different. Fisher explained to me how both you and Mr. Porter were subjected to experimentation at a young age."

I swing my attention to Cynthia. How much does she know and hasn't told us? Cynthia doesn't react to my stare.

"Waters found a shortcut based on the changes to your brain, Ms. Lark. During the limited time you were in New Philadelphia, he learned much, but not how to make the physical changes that have organically manifested in your brain and, I'm sure that of, Mr. Porter's. At this time, Waters is using a neural implant device."

"And what can you tell us about the process?" Rice asks.

"Unless Ms. Lark and Mr. Porter's abilities developed much farther ahead of these newly developed immersives, then Elore will probably be crushed. Waters will have the ability to steal any information within the Elorian mainframe, allowing him to shut down the grid and access the Neuro-link controlling the DPF and all Guardian drones. From our Intel, he's very close. But not there yet."

"Then we must beat him to it. We need to create our own army of immersives," Fisher says.

"What do you mean?" Ben says before I get the chance to voice the same thing. "We can't use children against him."

Cynthia shakes her head. "No, I won't risk children. But we were able to secure a sample of the tech Waters is using. It's a slightly outdated model from his latest experiment. But, I'm having it delivered to Avlyn and Ben to study the programming."

She looks to us. "It's already on the way, so please start on this immediately. If you two can figure out exactly how it works and if we might be able to pair this technology with older brains, then it may be the solution we are looking for to stop Waters."

My mind reels. More people who can immerse? What will that mean in the end?

"Is that all we have for this meeting?" Cynthia asks and begins to stand, seeming to forget Ben and I asked for an audience.

"No," I say.

Cynthia looks my way and then falls back into her seat. "Well, please fill us in."

My stomach churns with nervousness, but, instead of holding back, I tell them everything. Everything except the part where the patch apparently falls apart if I communicate directly to Ben's mind. At the end of my admission, Cynthia's face is contemplative but tense. She's definitely mulling around the options, and they must not seem any better to her than they did to me.

She opens her mouth to speak, but Sloan holds up a hand to her. "And how did you repair this?" he asks, with more curiosity than anger.

"Because I couldn't influence the chemical bond the MedTech was reinforcing in Ben, I simply provided a temporary patch. A block from the influence. But it can't last forever, and I need to find a permanent solution."

"How do you feel, Ben?" Sloan asks.

"Better than I did. After Avlyn patched the problem, I

realized I had been fighting my loyalty between Direction and Affinity. I kept trying to push it away, but, eventually, I couldn't. I didn't want to sound the alarm at GenTech, but the thought that we were there to steal from them overcame me. It was as if I was watching another person set off the alarm, and I couldn't stop it. I don't sense that pull toward Direction anymore."

"But you do toward Avlyn?" Melissa asks.

Ben shrugs. "She's my twin. I always want to be loyal to her."

Ben doesn't mention our problem either.

Cynthia purses her lips. "First, I don't want any of you going above again without permission from me. Second, Ben will be staying below until we can resolve this issue fully. I need any additional data you have on the nanos and the chemical compound used in the food supply sent to me immediately. We have people working as we speak on the chemical aspect of the contaminate, but your data would speed up the process."

"Will do," I say, feeling relieved that she's letting Ben stay.

The room becomes quiet, and Sloan leans back in his seat, crossing his arms over his chest, all his earlier discomfort gone. "This is all fascinating information. I'm going to need some time and more data, but I think we may be able to find the weaknesses in both Manning's and Waters' projects and use them against each other."

CHAPTER NINETEEN

I open my eyes in the bunker, flinching at the unexpected grating sound of Manning's voice. I flick my gaze toward the MV and there he is on the screen, leaning into the camera in all his hawk-like glory.

"Citizens of Elore—" he booms.

"Did this just start now?" I ask, swinging my attention around to Sanda, who is back from scoping out the city. Aron stands about a foot away from her while watching the screen intently, his arms crossed over his body.

Sanda nods, "Ayers was on for a moment before—"

My heart clenches at the mention of Ayers' name. And, immediately, Kyra's face flashes in my mind. Ayers continues to climb the ranks, but that disgusting man deserves none of the honor.

"We figured we'd contact you on your EP if he said something important," Sanda continues. "This is an unannounced program."

"Did they say if Kyra will be on?" I ask.

"Avlyn," Meyer says with a scowl. "We need to listen."

I rake my hand through my hair. Meyer is only trying to protect my life and heart, but I just don't want Kyra lost to Direction. Sadness moves through me and Ben narrows his eyes at Meyer.

Ben projects empathy and comfort to me in light blue waves. I look up to the screen, and it's as if I can't even hear Manning anymore. His mouth is moving, but nothing is coming out. My head swirls with dizziness, and I blink. I slowly turn toward Sanda and Aron, but they're only watching the announcement.

I shake off the disorientation, and a strange calm takes its place.

Ben? I think to him. You need to stop.

Ben turns his head toward me and gives me a quizzical look. And, just as he pulls back, the dizziness leaves and the sound of Manning's voice returns at full blast.

What happened? Ben asks in my mind. But, when he looks at me, his eyes widen, realizing that something is wrong.

My stomach drops. I rub my hand over my forehead in frustration. We need to fix this. I stand and motion Ben to follow me out of the meeting area.

"Where are you two going?" Meyer asks. "You really should watch the announcement."

"I know," I answer. "Ben and I need to talk. How about we fill you all in on the meeting with Cynthia and you can tell us about the announcement later?"

Meyer pushes his eyebrows together as his mouth dips into a

frown.

"Please?" I ask.

He shrugs and returns to whatever Manning is saying. "That works."

Ben and I head back to the sleeping quarters. I close the door behind us. Heaviness weighs across my entire body about what I am about to say. "We need to disconnect our mental link."

"What?" Ben asks. "We can't do that. We need our ability to work together."

"Not permanently. But, like you said, it seems as if the patch is breaking down if we're connected. I think you might even be able to spread the contaminate to me, like a virus."

Horror washes over his face.

"You know how to block my thoughts and emotions. I need you to teach me how to do it too."

Ben slowly walks to the nearest bed and flops onto the bottom bunk, face down, muffling, "This whole thing is a mess. All because of the stupid food ink."

"Be grateful I suddenly wasn't in the mood to eat. Who knows how the organic properties would have affected me. We both could've died. Then where would we be?"

"I guess we'd be dead and wouldn't care," he mutters into the mattress.

"Ben," I reply in a low tone.

"You know I don't mean that, but you and I need to remain a team. Nothing seems to work right when one of us is on our own."

I sigh and sit on the end of his bed. "We're short on a lot of options, Ben. Separating will give us more time to solve the problem. Right now, it seems like the patch I used on your nanos is only solid as long as we don't communicate through our minds."

Ben slowly twists to prop up on his elbows. "But, if we connect now for me to teach you, won't that be a risk?"

"We need to try something," I say. "What else can we do other than send you back to the Sub with Melissa Rice for more testing?"

Ben furrows his brow. "That's not what I want, either."

"Then we need to do this."

He swings his legs toward the floor, then sits up. He brings out his Flexx. "I think I can program a VR space, showing you what to do without us needing a direct mind connection." He taps on his device for a few moments. "There. I don't think you are going to like what happens, but don't fight it. It's the only way I know how to make the disconnect work."

I nod. "Okay. Let's give it a try."

The coordinates appear on the bottom of my vision, and a whirlwind of white takes me away. Nothing materializes, and a barrage of crushing emotions weigh down on me. The white fades to gray then black. Fear wells in me before transforming into a stabbing pain in my limbs and core. I want to fight it, but Ben told me not too. What if he was wrong? Panic travels up my body, and I want to scream and tell him to stop. Just when I fear these feelings will consume me, a hand grabs mine and yanks me forward, ending the horrible sensations with a snap.

But, what I see next is barely better. Two babies—Ben and

me—lie in incubators, screaming after a Medic injected us with something painful. The sound is like a knife in my eardrums, and I throw my hands up to block the noise. But, it's no use. The memory is embedded into my brain, and there's no way to dull the images.

Someone grabs me by the arm again, and I spin toward them. When I do, the vision vanishes, and I gasp. Grown Ben is now in front of me. His eyes are wide, and pupils dilated. His chest heaves for breath as the two of us stand in an open field, with deep blue skies and tall green grasses blowing in a gentle wind.

"What was that?" I manage to get out while trying to steady myself.

Ben closes his eyes and inhales deeply.

"Those are the kind of emotions that nearly killed me after Dad—Devan died. All my horrible memories, starting with the experiments. They changed who we are, Avlyn. All the way down to our DNA. I decided that if I was able to train myself to block and control those memories, I could hide any feeling. I would never allow myself to be so affected emotionally again. I would do everything I could to control the pain. When I found you, I'll admit it was difficult to block your emotions and thoughts. But, opening up completely and without reservation, wasn't an option for me. I had too much to hide, with Devan's death and the memories of the experiments. I didn't want to release those vulnerable moments until I was ready. If I ever was."

"But it doesn't always work, does it?" I say, thinking of how I accessed Ben's memories about Devan's death.

"Like I said, it takes a lot of effort to block you. There's no way this is going to be foolproof. But I think you're right. Severing our mind connection will keep us both safer."

"So, what do I have to do?" I ask, nervous about what the answer might be after perceiving his intensity of pain.

"You need to confront your worst memories and fears and then control whether you experience them or not. When I figured out how to block memories, I could also emotionally close off almost anything at will."

The thought of doing what Ben suggests sends a shiver down my spine. But controlling my memories and emotions is what needs to happen to keep us all safe.

"Are you able to complete the process with me?" I ask.

Ben shakes his head. "This will have to be your journey. But I'll be waiting when you're done." Concern brews in Ben's eyes, but no emotion radiates from him, and I know that he's already blocking me.

Ben touches me on the shoulder and gives me a tight smile. Then, he vanishes from the scene and leaves me all alone in the field. Before I do anything, I drink in the breeze and the blue sky above, knowing in a moment my emotional state will no longer know this peace.

I close my eyes and invite the emotions and memories haunting the back of my mind to creep toward the forefront. My eyelids droop when the heavy thoughts slowly consume me. As they take hold, flashes of experiences I never wanted to happen burst into my mind from the experiments, Mother's death, Jayson and Lena's capture and execution, my inability to help Kyra, to the city of Thornton going up in flames. Pain stabs at my core, but I allow it all.

A sharp sensation jabs at my arm, and it's as if acid fills my veins. I scream, and the vision and pain twist into something new. I'm back in the tunnel, escaping Elore with Father, Mother, and Meyer. Debris shakes from the ceiling and showers over us, but a shove throws me into the wall. I turn back and know what is waiting for me this time: Mother. Crushed and dying. She saved me; sacrificed herself for me. The weight of grief punches me in the gut, and I'm thrust back into Thornton. An explosion roars in my ears and, without looking, I know what happens: New Philly ships blow up one of the small buildings, the one where Ruiz is standing with the mothers and children of Thornton. Ruiz is dead. The little boy Ash is gone. They're all dead because of me.

Me.

"Get out of my head," I half scream, half growl.

But these memories will never leave me. Instead, I must lock them away. This thought pierces through me. I spent my entire life controlling and stuffing down my emotions, and it's not something I want to return to. But, suppressing the memories must be done, so that Ben, or anyone else, can't find them.

I square myself, gritting my teeth together. I inhale deeply through my nose and let the memories rush through me like a massive wave as I exhale. I allow the pain and ingest the grief. I don't fight the sensation of drowning despite the fears that bubble to the surface of my consciousness.

With a snap, it stops. I'm left in a bright, white space. A space of nothing. Then, something in my mind shifts. Ben's presence is here. His consciousness is attempting to infiltrate my mind. To test me.

I raise my hand and propelling energy radiates from me, pushing away my connection to Ben—like magnetic opposites facing off. I fall to my knees, still holding out my hand, and resist the urge to reverse the polarity of the feeling. This is not forever; it's okay to let Ben go.

I collapse to the ground and cover my face. I'm empty. So empty.

My eyelids open to the bunk room and Ben sits beside me on the bed, just as I left him.

But now the loss on his face is palpable.

Ben! I think to him. But there's nothing.

Only emptiness. Darkness. Our mind connection is gone.

CHAPTER TWENTY

"It's done, isn't it?" Ben asks.

I nod, not wanting to voice the answer. I had thirteen years without Ben, thinking he was dead. I'm grateful he's still here in body, more than anything. He's my twin, and I love him. But, being able to connect with him in our minds helped me fill the loss of years. Now, our nexus is missing, and, with it, the telepathic comfort my brother gave me.

"What if our disconnection severs the mental link permanently?" I ask.

He shrugs. "I don't know. I guess we have to take that chance for everyone."

I let out a deep breath and push my feelings of loss away, not as far back as the memories, but I can't let the grief affect me. Nor will I allow the disconnection to ruin the sacrifice Ben and I are making.

"We can't tell them about this, you know," Ben says.

"Tell who?"

"Anyone. Meyer, Sanda, Aron... Cynthia. They won't understand, and it'll just add problems. We were able to take care of the issue and move on. Then, when the war is all done, we can work on getting the ability back."

"Cynthia needs to know something," I say.

"We'll just tell her we have it under control. She doesn't need to know the details."

I shake my head. I hate not being able to confide in Meyer, but Ben is right. I have no idea how any of them will react, and there are enough complications. All they need to know is that Ben and I are fine.

Ben straightens his shoulders. "Let's go and figure out what we need to do. Maybe we should take different tasks while we're preparing."

"What do you suggest?"

"How about you look for information on the DPF and other ways we might be able to turn off their kill switches," he says. "And figure out how the Neuro-link works. I'll scour the mainframe for weaknesses and start patching them while also preparing a trap for Waters. But don't set anything into major motion until we tell Cynthia about what we're doing."

I force myself to stand and walk to the door. Ben follows.

"It's going to be okay, you know," he says.

"No, I don't know that. But, it's something I have to accept." I tap the pad, and the door slides back.

My breath hitches when I step into the corridor and find a sterling Aerrx drone entering the elevator, its tentacles retracted into its body. The door slides shut.

I look at Ben, and he shrugs. In the meeting room, Aron and Sanda sit at one of the screens, studying more of the footage taken by our drone, and Meyer is sprawled across the couch with his Flexx folded out into a tablet, swiping at the screen.

"What was that?" I ask.

Sanda points to a small, tan box. "It's a package addressed to you and Ben from Fisher."

I snatch the box. On top the label reads:

To be opened by A and/or B only.

"What did Manning say on the vid?" Ben asks.

Meyer looks up from his handheld. "Nothing much we don't already know, except for curfew has been lifted. There are too many displaced citizens to adequately enforce it."

"Well, no curfew should work in our favor," I say.

"Yes." A look of concern brews in Meyer's dark eyes. "Are you two okay?"

I nod. But it's a lie. I'm not okay.

Ben walks to my side. "Open it."

I motion Ben away and pry open the box. Inside rests what appears to be an EP.

"Why would they send us an EP?" I ask as our Flexxes both vibrate at the same time.

Ben turns over his wrist and taps the screen on his device, and I pull mine from my pocket.

Instructions for immersion device: The device functions similarly to a standard EP except it has the additional upgrade of allowing the wearer's nanotech to form a link to their brain by a virtual connection to a computer device. As far as we can tell, the user slowly learns how to control the environment and to locate and download information as well as plant viruses and Trojans.

This information is as far as our research has uncovered in the short amount of time Waters' immersion tech has been in our hands. And, because time is limited, we need to pass this investigation off to you. Please be cautious in both accessing the technology's information and testing it.

C.F.

Ben looks up from his screen at nearly the same time as I do. My heart flips with the impulse to speak to him in my mind, and then it drops when I remember how I can't.

"You take the device and figure it out," I say to Ben. "Download any information you can get and learn how to replicate it."

"I'll head to the lab, so I can focus." He takes the box containing the immersive device from my hands. "I'll let you know what I find."

"What was it?" Meyer says, after Ben leaves.

I realize Meyer and the others still don't know anything about the meeting with Fisher. "Remember Dr. Sloan?"

Meyer furrows his brows. "How could I forget him? He's the reason I never got to eat my lunch in Philly. That burrito cart probably doesn't even exist anymore."

I can't help but chuckle. "After all this, you're still worried about a burrito?"

Meyer scowls. "Those were good burritos." He pauses for a beat and then softly laughs. "Let me start over. Yes, I remember Sloan, he's odd."

"He *is* a bit odd," I reply. "But he just likes the virtual world better than the real one. Sometimes, I understand where he's coming from. Anyway, he figured out what Waters was doing in Thornton and alerted Ruiz, and then he arranged to get my father out of New Philly. Without Sloan, Father would be dead. And, now, he helped Cynthia get her hands on an immersion device."

"An immersion device?"

"Whatever they were using to allow the immersive tech to function on the New Philly ship." I stop for a second and consider my words, remembering what Sloan said in the meeting. "Was the person in the chair a child?"

Meyer's face grows serious. "Yes. And part of what I told you when I got back to the camp wasn't true. Aron's drones didn't kill her. The pilot did, right in front of me. As soon as he did, the drones swarmed and took him down. There was nothing I could do."

"Why didn't you tell me this before?" I ask, taking his hand in mine.

"Because I wanted to forget. It didn't change the fact that Waters had the tech, either, no matter if he's using children to make it function or not."

"Cynthia's intel shows that the initial trials worked best on children."

"So how does this affect us?" Meyer says, trouble brewing in his eyes. "There's no way I'll be a part of using children to fight back."

I shake my head. "She wants Ben and I to study the tech and see if we can modify it to work for adults. It's based off EP tech, so we may be able to make adjustments to Affinity's existing units."

Meyer looks around. "Why aren't you working on the project with Ben?"

"We need to be working on this *and* the DPF." I shift on my feet. Everything in me wants to share what just happened to Ben and me, and the loss I now feel. Instead, I say, "So, we decided to split up. Both are important for the mission's success."

"I've been in communication with a few Affinity members in the city," Meyer says. "I have a few old contacts. Some of them are stuck in these displacement centers because their buildings were bombed. Since they're aware of the printed food issue, they're not eating much. But, unfortunately, it's the only thing available in the centers. I received a message from Affinity. I may need to go out later to get my own sense of how people are being affected."

"On your own?"

He nods. "Looks like it. Sanda and Aron are both tasked to the drones, and you and Ben aren't available. Plus, being up there on my own is easier. I don't need to worry about anyone but me. But, I haven't been assigned yet."

I know Meyer is more than capable of completing missions on his own. But, that doesn't make me any less apprehensive when thinking about him exposed to the city.

Boom!

We all instinctively duck as the muffled sound comes from above. I glance at the ceiling as it shakes, my heart in my throat.

"What was that?" Meyer yells to Aron and Sanda.

Aron is already typing on the system in front of them.

"Was our building hit or was it a nearby one?" I ask as Meyer and I race toward Aron's screens.

I look around to check if Ben is out here and start to think to him. But, I shake off the urge and quickly compel a message to my Flexx and send it to my brother, instead.

"Reports are coming in," Sanda says. "Three buildings in this area were hit."

My EP lights up with information, but I have no idea if the details are complete.

The ceiling rumbles again, and I hear Ben's footsteps from the hall.

"What's going on?" he asks.

"We're trying to find out if this building might be hit," I say.

My Flexx buzzes in my pocket, and I pull it out to look at the message. It's Corra. My heart jumps when I realize she's upstairs in her unit. If we've been hit, she'll know.

The building next to us has been struck. GenTech requires its employees in this building and a few others to evacuate to a satellite location. I'm assigned to Station 2b. It's one of the most heavily guarded by the DPF. I have no idea when I'll be back. If I'm back.

I show the message to everyone before I send a reply.

"Well, it's good to know this building hasn't been hit," Aron says. "Maybe Fisher will assign us a new contact. There might be another Affinity member in a unit above who doesn't work for GenTech."

I don't like the thought of it, but there's nothing I can do for

Corra. I step away from the group, who continue to read the updates.

What time do you have to report? I message back to Corra.

Seconds later the handheld buzzes.

9:00 AM Tomorrow.

I tuck the Flexx back into my pocket, trying to figure out what to do with this information. Nothing. I have my own responsibilities to attend to.

The Flexx buzzes again, and I pull it out, expecting another message from Corra. But it's not. It's Cynthia.

The recent bombings and evacuations created a rare opportunity to put Phase One into action. GenTech is working at a satellite directly at Neuro-link's source access site. I hate to send you into the city, but, at this point, we are running out of time. We need information. Several Affinity members who work for GenTech are being evacuated to Station 2b. The station is located directly beside the primary Neuro-link offices in Level Two. We need for you to get into that building. Stand by for further instructions.

Chapter Twenty-One

Corra and I walk side by side out of her building, our boots stuffed with food bars so we can avoid eating printed food at the satellite station. Our breaths puff in front of our faces and the cold stings at my nose. I squint against the morning sun, assessing the damage to a few surrounding buildings. Several display charred surfaces. And, a few of the buildings are missing front walls, exposing the dwellings inside. The drones have not even begun to repair the damage, but several zip above us on their way to who knows where. A larger DPF hover ship patrols the sky, making a growling sound as it floats along.

"Remind me, why do you need to do this again?" Corra asks in a whisper. "There's no way they'll think you work at GenTech."

"Affinity rearranged everything in the GenTech database to appear as if I started a few days before the attacks. Since there were no other hires in the InfoSec department that day, no one will put it together how I hadn't attended any training sessions yet." I cross my arms over my chest, avoiding eye contact with a few passing citizens and one DPF soldier armed with a large gun. "The InfoSec department is different than the lab too. Typically, we kept our heads down and worked in VR by ourselves. I'm not even sure I could identify half the people who worked there when I did."

Corra shrugs. "You're probably right, but it's a huge risk. And, I thought you needed Ben to complete Phase One?"

"I do. But sending us both in just for information is too high a risk. If plans change, Cynthia will let us know."

Up ahead sits the gray building we're looking for. Despite my confident words, nervousness twists in my stomach as I see one human guardian with dark, curly hair patrolling the front. At least, there are not as many guards as I thought there would be. My EP doesn't detect any others close by, either.

I fuss with my blonde hair nervously and stare at the sidewalk. Will he recognize me as Avlyn Lark?

He passes by where we stand, then keeps going toward the back of the building and away from us. I look up at Corra with a shaky smile. "You go ahead first."

She picks up speed. I slow my walk and casually watch as she approaches the building's entrance. The glass door at the front slides back, and she enters. I allow another person to go in before I pick up the pace and follow.

When I arrive at the front of the building, the large door slides back, revealing a line four people deep and a check-in station manned by a floating SI, shaped as if it were a torso and head with two retractable, tentacle-like arms.

Corra takes her place as the fifth in line, and I hold my head up and walk to line's end. She plays her part well and doesn't look back at me but only straight ahead. The SI allows the man in front of her to pass, and Corra steps forward.

As I wait for my turn, panic jabs at my stomach. What if Daniel is here? Even with my altered appearance, he has noticed me enough in the past to recognize me.

"Next?" The robotic voice of the SI breaks my thoughts, and I look over to see Corra is gone, as well as the other in front of me, and it's now my turn for check-in.

I place my palm on the hand scanner and wait for alarms to blare.

"Avlyn Joy Lark, Traitor. Traitor of the Elorian people," sounds the mechanical voice of the SI unit. But it's all in my mind.

"Please proceed to the door ahead," is what it actually says, tone flat.

The screen in front of me displays my false name and GenTech position.

Alana Miller/Information Security

My image appears next to the details, displaying my altered blonde hair and blue eyes. Seeing it sends a chill down my spine. How is this ever going to work?

The stabbing in my gut stops, and I move to step through the door. Can't change my mind now.

I send a message to Affinity through my EP.

Made it past security.

An MV mounted on the wall directs me to the left, and I

follow the hall to a large, open room. Inside, around fifty GenTech employees sit around various tables. Another large MV is affixed at the head of the room, displaying the GenTech slogan: "Making Life Better."

I spot Corra and my first instinct is to take a seat at her table, but I resist the urge and join a group across from her. Even though it hasn't been that long since I worked at GenTech, no one in this room looks familiar, giving me a measure of security. Still, it would be best not to make eye contact with any employee.

A few more citizens come in and take their seats and the MV flickers. Margo Yates, the president of GenTech, appears on the screen. She's a regal woman with short red hair, and, I'd guess, in her late fifties or so. I never actually saw her when I worked at GenTech. The closest I came was when we broke into her office, though she wasn't physically there.

"Greetings, Genesis Technologies employees," she says in a low, serious voice. "You have the privilege of being among the chosen few to perform several essential duties. Direction needs our expert assistance in maintaining the integrity of the Neurolink technology, ensuring the DPF remain in top working order so they may continue to protect our great city of Elore."

She means to control the DPF's minds against their will, of course. But, no one thinks about it like that. Level Ones have little value, and, according to Direction, they should be grateful to be used at all.

"We've invited the best and the brightest in many of Genesis Technologies' departments, including research, the chemistry lab, and information security. We are tasked with the privilege of maintaining the integrity of Elore's way of life."

Yates continues speaking for another five minutes or so, but I barely hear her. My mind reels with the knowledge that even if I'm able to obtain the information allowing us to flip the DPF and remove Manning from power, we'll still have the problem of Waters.

A muffled boom thunders and the building rattles. I almost flinch but remember to act calm. Not a thing from this mission will be easy.

Before I know it, Yates is gone from the MV. The chosen GenTech employees are now standing and filing back out the door. I look for Corra, but she's not paying attention to me. My Flexx buzzes on my wrist.

Information Security personnel proceed to 305.

I have no idea what I'm doing yet, but at least I know where to go. I follow the rest of the employees out to the main lobby and take the elevator up to three. Corra stands at the back of the cab, and I'm near the front. I'd prefer to use the stairs, but it's better to stick with the crowd.

The cab chimes at floor three and I exit alongside two other employees, leaving Corra behind.

I follow the markers on the wall to 305b. Inside, the room appears much like InfoSec back at GenTech—rows of drab cubicles where we can all be together and utterly alone simultaneously. Dread seeps through me. Before I joined Affinity, I would have been stuck here for a lifetime. How do these people live like this? Why is this a life worth fighting and preserving for them? I exhale a deep breath.

There are five employees that I can see in here, and another two follow behind me. I find an empty cubicle and have a seat. My Flexx buzzes as the device pairs to the computer system.

Welcome, Alana Miller.

Affix your headset and follow the directions in your vision.

I remove the headset from below the screen and place it over my head and across my eyes. The dull workspace disappears only to be replaced with a lower-quality digital one where I'm now all alone. Nice... the good old days.

My instructions appear, and I quickly read through them. Nothing out of the ordinary, basically monitoring for possible intrusions in the Neuro-link. The same dull routine I had at my old job.

But, today, I have a purpose. To find a backdoor into the Neuro-link system that is so small no one, but me, would notice it. And, all this boring work will help me accomplish my goal.

❧ ❧ ❧

Hours later, my enthusiasm has waned considerably. But, I have learned that the Neuro-link is broken out into segments. The access I'm granted right now, however, doesn't allow me to view the other sections—not yet. But, it's enough for my first day.

Incoming message, scrolls across my vision, and a new avatar enters my space.

My breath hitches as I immediately recognize its owner, despite the simulation's low quality.

"My name is Daniel Carter, and I am your remote Information Security supervisor," says Daniel's avatar.

All I want to do is run and hide from him. What if he

recognizes me? I shake off the thought. Daniel has no reason to believe I'd be in Elore, let alone at the GenTech satellite. Plus, both my real-life appearance and that of my company avatar has changed. But, if anyone could sniff me out, it would be him, especially if he comes into our real-life workspace.

My mind files through everything I did over the past few hours. I know I was careful, but was I careful enough?

"Today was a testing round," Daniel announces. "And, I am pleased to say that each of you passed. Our algorithms in choosing you for service were correct, and your work for Genesis Technologies is exceptional."

So, that's why I couldn't get in. We were inside a dummy program. Frustrated in how I hadn't realized this before now, I curse under my breath. But it's a lesson learned. I need to stay aware and make no assumptions about what Direction is doing.

"Tomorrow morning you will each have genuine access to the Neuro-link system," he says. "But, as of now, you are dismissed as we bring in another team of employees."

Daniel's avatar dips his head. "Genesis Technologies thanks you for your service. Maintain forward focus." And then he blinks out.

CHAPTER TWENTY-TWO

After a night of tossing and turning in the sleeping space I was assigned, my nanos wake me at precisely 5:00 AM. I roll away from the white wall I'm facing. The room is filled with twenty cots, and, interestingly, Corra was given the same room too.

Those in charge mixed the different departments together in each sleeping space. This arrangement is just another way to keep employees from the same departments unfamiliar with each other—duty over relationships in Elore. I wouldn't be surprised if they even rotate our room assignments should we stay here for more than a few days.

Though her cot is right beside mine, Corra and I still have not spoken since before we arrived. Rustling comes from behind me as she stirs from her sleep. Several of the other women wake, and two of them are already on their feet, changing into the fresh clothing Direction issued to us last night after our meal.

The dull, rumbling sound of another explosion thunders from outside of the building. The common noise doesn't even make me flinch anymore.

I glance over at Corra, dying to speak with her about whatever project GenTech has assigned to her. But the women here are exceptionally fond of keeping to themselves, like good Elorian citizens, so talking to Corra would be a poor choice. Last night, I sent Affinity a report of how I had worked on a dummy program all day. I considered sending Corra an encrypted message on our Affinity accounts as well. But, I should only do so for an emergency affecting my mission, not just to find out how she's doing.

My stomach groans and I find myself longing for the two squished food bars hidden in the boots beside my bed. I haven't eaten since before we arrived yesterday. The nasty bars are starting to sound pretty good. Last night, when they provided us dinner, I pushed my food around to make it look as if I had eaten some. I could've eaten one of the bars before bed, but that would have only given me a full belly while I slept. Having one this morning was more important since I'll need to focus today.

During dinner, I noticed how several other workers hadn't eaten much, either. I think the stress from the bombings and unfamiliar environment is wearing on people, despite their calm facades.

I throw off my blanket and swing my legs to the floor, the cot squeaking quietly as I do. In one swoop, I grab my clothing and boots then head to the restroom, leaving Corra behind. After washing my face and changing, I stuff down one of the cherry food bars and save the other for later. I've no idea what I'm going to do after that for food. Hopefully, I won't be here long. Today

I'll get what I need and go back to the bunker with a plan.

My EP lights up across the bottom of my vision.

Provide a data feed of your work in the Neuro-link for us to analyze.

I roll my eyes. Great. Now more people are watching over my shoulder. That doesn't add to the pressure at all.

My Flexx buzzes on my wrist alerting me that it's nearly time to start work. By any luck, Daniel won't appear in VR today, but knowing he's monitoring our progress makes me hyper-aware of how I need to be extra cautious. I wipe any evidence of the bar from my lips and stuff the wrapper into the side of my boot. I exit the restroom along with a few other women and find my group of InfoSec workers down the hall, all waiting to be led to our suite.

A silver assistant drone escorts us, and I settle into my chair and affix my headset. I link the data feed to Affinity through my EP. The room replaces with a virtual reality one, and my new instructions scroll in front of my vision. I quickly read through them and activate the code I'm to monitor. Unlike yesterday, I do a complete sweep of today's code right away, and, sure enough, it's not a testing system. My mind wavers between the option to immerse to go deeper or stay on the outskirts where they have me assigned. Anxiety swirls around in my belly. But I inhale deeply and settle myself.

I should wait. We are being watched and taking risks could be stupid. And Affinity only wants information before we make our move. Yet, the last thing I want is to be here forever. The longer I am, the higher the risk of being exposed. But, I've also seen people die at the hands of Elore and New Philadelphia. If

Affinity fails— if I fail—it's likely humanity will not survive.

Who needs a virus like the Collapse to exterminate the population when there's fundamental human nature and the desire for power?

I spend the next few hours working on my project, fixing a few errors and weak spots just as I'm supposed to do. The task is tedious and easy, so my mind is only half in it. My knee bounces with anticipation, and I can't wait any longer. I'll test the waters. I don't need to go entirely in; I can check it out and then come back to what I was doing here. And then an idea coalesces.

I scroll through the code and quickly find a handful of weaknesses but leave them in place. For anyone else, the project would have taken all day, but, for me, it's like picking out black dots on a white wall. The errors are completely obvious. In my mind, I code a program to run in the background while I'm immersed inside a deeper security level of the Neuro-link. I set it to run over the next six hours, re-find and repair the bugs at a pretty slow pace. Not too slow, so it doesn't make me look incompetent, but not so fast that I give away any of my ability. And while it works, I can navigate other areas without suspicion. They'll never notice I'm gone.

That's the hope, at least.

I recheck my program three times to make sure it's functioning correctly, adding an alert feature to pull me back if anything goes wrong or if any messages come through. Then, I activate the loop and take a deep breath. This is it.

I close my eyes and let Neuro-link's code join with my mind.

"Take me to the core," I order the system.

The project code whirls around me and whisks me to my ordered location. But, when it stops, a sound like a thousand bees consumes my mind. I throw my hands up to cover my ears from the unexpected noise. However, my efforts don't work, and I drop to my knees, burying my head between my elbows.

Then, something shifts, and, from the buzzing, a faint voice emerges. It grows louder but still unintelligible. Muffled sound travels past me, knocking me completely over. It dissipates, but then another round of muffled sound does the same, and another. As each round adds to the others, the jumble of noise becomes clearer. It's not buzzing. They're words—thoughts.

Maintain forward focus...

Direction has your best interests in mind...

The phrases swirl around in my thoughts, melding with my own. At the Neuro-link's core, the minds of the DPF congregate, both separate and together. They pull at my consciousness to join them. The invitation is not so much in their words. Warmth fills my entire body, making me feel safe, whole, a part of something. Without my permission, my arm reaches toward the sound. Part of me wants to allow this collective in, to embrace it. But the other part of me, a small part albeit, wants nothing to do with these voices.

A child version of Ben's face flashes through my mind as he hands me the heart necklace. "Hide it," he whispers.

The memory jolts me from my near trance, and I throw up a wall in my mind, just like the one I used to block Ben's thoughts and feelings.

The voices suck away, as though caught up in a vacuum.

Then, I'm left alone in a white space, alone in my mind. I scramble to my feet, and my mental state struggles to orient itself. Loneliness slithers through me.

How in the world am I going to be able to flip the DPF if their minds are so interlinked? I rack my brain to figure it out, but nothing comes. Complete deactivation of the Neuro-link might work, but, with the DPF's kill switch implant, the risk is too high. Individually, we seem to have a chance to succeed. At the core, however, the collective effect appears to be at its strongest.

If the effect on me was that powerful for just those few seconds, what will happen to Ben if he's exposed? Will he be able to fight it with the contaminate still in his system? What if it breaks down the patch I made?

I open the blockage in my mind to learn more about how the Neuro-link works. Maybe I can figure out a backdoor or introduce a slower moving virus that transitions the linked minds way of thinking gradually enough and without triggering the kill switch.

Warning

I flinch, and a nervous twinge of energy travels through me as the word blinks across the bottom of my vision.

All InfoSec workers, please disengage from your virtual reality program within the next 5 minutes. A countdown timer displays next to the words.

I relax, and the tingling in my chest dissipates. Then I blink down hard and release from the Neuro-link system.

I quickly disable my bug-finding program, shocked when realizing how long I've been in. It's nearly quitting time. I shouldn't be surprised since VR almost always alters the perception of time for me. The Neuro-link made that even more pronounced. Disappointment by how I hadn't delved farther in seeps through my stomach. My idea of a virus might work, though. But, I'll have to be here for another day to try it.

I release to the real world just as a far-off explosion rattles the room and my desk.

"Thank you for your service," a drone assistant announces behind me in its robotic voice. I twist in my seat toward it as several other workers do the same.

"There are four of you who have displayed exemplary work today," it says.

Can't be me. I was barely paying attention to my work, and it's not as if I set the program to find the bugs at a pace that should have attracted attention.

The drone continues, "In the morning, due to safety issues, the following four GenTech workers will be transferred from this location to a more secure area in Level Three. Each will be tasked with Information Security in an undisclosed building for Direction and Director Manning. Please stand when your name is called."

My heart nearly skips a beat, and I glance at the other people in the room. There are at least twenty-five InfoSec employees.

"Alana Miller..." The drone says, and I don't even hear the other names because it doesn't matter. I stand as all the eyes in the room are on me. This was our last opportunity to get into the Neuro-link, and I blew it somehow. There's little chance I can get away with another identity change too, now that everyone in this room has peered my way while I stand.

Abort mission, blinks at the bottom of my vision. Await instructions for removal.

CHAPTER TWENTY-THREE

The building rattles as a bomb explodes closer than before. The sound resonates through my body, causing my chest to tighten.

"Please remain calm," the drone says in its dull, robotic voice as it ushers us into the same meeting area as our orientation meeting. "In a few moments, an important broadcast will be aired. When you've finished eating, you may work on the new project sent to your Flexx."

I spot Corra across the room, grab an already prepared meal and a set of utensils from a long table to my right, and then sit one table away from her. Is Affinity going to pull her out of here too? I can't see why they would risk doing so. I look down at my food and sigh. Savory slices of chicken topped with green flecks of seasoning, a swirl of mashed potatoes, and a pile of green beans crowd the plate. The warm meal's salty smell wafts to my nose, and I instantly regret not being able to eat it. But, worries about tomorrow and how I managed to screw this up on the second day effectively deactivate my appetite.

I disconnect my Affinity data feed from my EP and wait. While most everyone but Corra and I eat, I push my food around on my plate. Lucky for us, a few others don't seem to be very hungry either and have left most of their food uneaten. Every so often, Corra's attention wanders over to me as if she wants to tell me something. I feel the same. Before I go, I want to inform her of my transfer.

Instead, I look down at my Flexx and poke at the screen, like the other employees in this dark room. Half-heartedly, I work on the extra security project assigned to me, which is, unfortunately, not related to the Neuro-link.

The Direction logo—a spinning earth with the arrow pointed up—appears on the MV located at the head of the room. I find myself watching it way too much. Something about the spinning almost relaxes me.

As I stare, the logo disappears and is replaced by Brian Marshall. I've seen this man's face so many times now, he somehow feels like an old friend. But I know he is most definitely not. At the sight of him, the others in here stop eating or working and pay attention to whatever Brian's about to say.

"Up next, we have a special announcement by the Representative of The Alliance of New Adults, Kyra Carter," Brian booms.

My chest clenches, not only at the mention of Kyra's name, but at her new last name. *Daniel's* last name. The initial shock turns to anger. There's no way it was a coincidence that they were paired. It seems too much like a punishment for Kyra, and, perhaps, even a punishment for me. Kyra would never be happy with him. She always wanted to be paired with the best, and yes, Daniel is capable. But he's also angry and bitter. My childhood friend was never those things. Maybe she is now. If I were in her position, I might be.

I disconnect from my thoughts and find Kyra's face already on the screen. Her chin-length blonde hair is combed neatly, and her blue eyes are set against her naturally tan skin. As usual, she looks beautiful. But her tense expression makes her otherwise soft appearance harsh, strained. Stressed.

Although I know she betrayed me, my heart still breaks for her.

"Greetings, citizens of Elore," she says. "I've been asked by Director Manning to speak to you today. Direction would like to commend you for your forward focus despite our current difficult circumstances. Outside forces have come against us with the intent to destroy the lives we lead. Direction maintains that its highest goals are the protection and—" She pauses briefly and clears her throat. "Excuse me—protection and safety of its citizens. These outside forces intend to destroy everything we've worked so hard to build our great city into."

I can't take my eyes from her as the camera pans back just enough to show her hands. They grip the podium's sides tightly, causing her knuckles to go white. As if the slightly raised camera angle notices too, it slowly raises higher, blocking her fingers from view.

What if Kyra knows what she's saying is wrong? What if it's not safe for her? Or she's being forced? *Stop it, Avlyn. Of course, it's*

213

not safe for her, I think to myself. It's not safe for *anyone* right now. I'm sure Kyra is just concerned that our city is under attack, same as others.

But I scan the room and the people in this room are calm, probably from the food ink contaminate they just filled their bellies with. They're not completely controlled like the DPF, but enough to take off the edge.

I return my attention to Kyra on the screen and watch as a tiny bead of sweat trickles underneath her hairline. She's not been nervous in any of the other vids I've watched, just this one. So, what's different?

"Director Manning has Representative Ayers and I working closely together again after he returns from the Level Three representatives' office tomorrow—"

I don't even hear the rest of her words but watch as any light she held in her eyes dull as the camera pans back and shows Ayers to her left, standing tall with a haughty smile. And then it hits me. Taking the Alliance of New Adults job must have removed her from working with *that* man—her opportunity to escape him. Maybe even her pairing to Daniel was to accomplish this too.

Revulsion wells up inside of me. I can't leave Kyra to suffer. Someone has to care about her. Someone has to save her. If I give her another out, a permanent one, I know she'll take it. My fist tightens on my lap as I will away my feelings of disgust for how she's been treated— pushed aside and abused and with no one to listen.

I grab for my Flexx and pull it onto my lap underneath the table. Despite the risk, I enter the Elorian mainframe.

The world around me partially dulls as I fight to keep my mind halfway between reality and immersion.

"*Data on Kyra Carter. Security pad check in for the last four days,*" I think to the system. The information I seek is secure, but not nearly as much as the Neuro-link.

Almost immediately, the data downloads and my brain sorts through it, following the patterns, creating a map of her habits. It should be simple, but it's less so than I thought. She must have multiple responsibilities while meeting with people all over Elore. There's obviously no regard for her safety as Manning isn't keeping her in a secure location. Apparently, she's expendable—likely replaceable. Though, I'm sure in Manning's mind everyone is replaceable.

But one thing stands out: she's at work early, very early, and alone in the Level Two Representatives' building. Maybe I can convince Affinity to capture her. I make a note of all the security near her building and then release completely to the real world.

My surroundings take shape and I look up to the MV, now displaying the spinning Direction logo again. Everyone in the room is back to work on their tablets, so I guess I may not have looked as out of place as I had feared. Just a good citizen who couldn't wait to get back to work. Even Corra, busy on her Flexx, doesn't appear to notice what I'd been doing.

I lean back in my seat, tension building at my temples as I wonder when and how Affinity plans to get me out of here. They had better do it soon too. Since I'm not waiting around to see where I'll be transferred to tomorrow.

My EP wakes me at 4:00 AM, earlier than the girls rise in our shared sleeping space. Instructions from Affinity to leave the building show in my EP.

Your assessment has been altered in the GenTech database. It will appear you transferred early, and then sent home.

Okay, so no one will question my being gone? It's never going to work.

But, instead of worrying about potential problems, Kyra immediately comes to my mind again. She tends to arrive at her office by this time daily, sometimes even spending the night. She could be there right now.

I sit up, and my EP illuminates the room, casting a green glow across the floor and over the walls. The cots are still filled with sleeping women. Corra is in the space right behind me, still asleep too. The heat sensors in my EP don't detect any extra guards outside of the room right now. Here's my chance.

Quickly, I pull my blanket over my head and compel an encrypted message to Corra's Flexx. Hopefully, she'll figure it out rather than worry if Direction took me away. Not that I'm convinced they still won't.

They transferred me out.

I swing my legs to the floor and slip my toes into my boot, a little disappointed that I had eaten the remaining food bar last night before going to sleep. My foot pushes into the boot and then abruptly stops when my toes touch something solid, and cold. Removing the shoe, I reach inside. My heart leaps as I pull out a small stunner. Quickly, I look around to check if anyone is awake, but no one stirs. Someone must have slipped this in during the night. I tuck the stunner into the back of my pants' waistband.

Gingerly, I pull out the coat I've been using as an extra pillow and slip my arms inside, then rise, and tiptoe through the room. At the door, I palm the security pad, ordering it not only to open but also to erase the system's activity log for leaving the room before waking hours. While I'm in, I also download the building's schematic, showing me the best route for escape—down the staircase in the back and out a rarely used service door.

And, if for some reason I get caught outside the room, I'll tell them I needed to use the restroom and got lost. Although, the coat might tip them off to the lie. But I push all those possibilities from my mind and make my way down the dimly lit corridor toward the building's back exit.

The door is locked, but the security is a simple bypass, and, within seconds, I'm striding along a dark street, heading south. Brisk air hits my lungs, making it difficult to breathe. There are no sounds of bombs or attacks, and, if it weren't for the risk I'm taking, I'd call the night a peaceful one. I scan the area for Guardians, but my EP doesn't detect that many and none are close enough to be dangerous. I guess protecting the city from New Philadelphia has taken precedence over safeguarding Elore from the people inside of it. I'm sure they stationed most of the Guardians in Level Three, and for the most valuable citizens. The idea normally would have bothered me, but today it works to my advantage.

Directions back to the bunker show in my EP. My way is amply lit by the moon and streetlights. Only a few times do I need to hide in the shadows to avoid being spotted by an occasional Guardian drone or DPF soldier. Across from me, dim light spills over a displacement center, and, surprisingly, a few people walk out and onto the street. I keep my head down and avoid eye contact. This must be how Kyra is allowed into her office at all hours so easily.

Up ahead and to my left is the Representatives' building where she works. I shudder, thinking of the terrible things Ayers did to her in there.

My chest tightens, and I exhale a quick puff of air that blows out like smoke. I pull my coat tight around me, suddenly chilled to the bone. The clouds above threaten snow.

I can't leave her. I make a beeline for the entrance.

And, if I'm wrong about my best friend again? No. This is going to work. Kyra *will* come with me, and we'll figure out the rest later.

CHAPTER TWENTY-FOUR

I palm the security pad and immerse with the building's system, obfuscating any incoming or outgoing communication. I want to speak to Kyra, but I'm not stupid. The behavior I observed during the announcement could've been all in my mind and not what's really in her heart. But, I have to find out.

I touch my fingers to the stunner tucked inside of my waistband, under my coat. If she turns on me, I do have a plan. It's not as if I've done this before, but it should work. I'll stun her first, then immerse with her nano-tech and overload her system. It should be enough to cause short-term memory loss. She won't even remember I was here.

At least I hope this idea works. But, I can't handle knowing there's a chance she was innocent, just a person dragged along in Manning's and Ayers' bigger plans. Or fearing how she couldn't escape without getting herself killed.

My body shakes as I walk down the empty hall toward her office. To be honest, part of me hopes Kyra might not be there.

But I'm confident she is.

I pass a gray door that reads "Mitchell Ayers," and a shiver runs down my spine. I want to block out the memory of how it was here—this exact office—where Manning had me taken after I was caught breaking into GenTech. The place where he offered me a deal to sell out Affinity. The place he took my parents to be tortured, and where everything horrible had happened to Kyra, setting her on a path against me. I force my feet forward. Kyra's office door is up ahead on the left, and I grab my stunner from under my coat. Once I arrive, I touch the pad before I can change my mind and the door slides back.

Immediately, my eyes are drawn to the girl with blonde hair, whose face is so familiar to me. We were friends since age ten. Seeing her now wells up feelings of hope and terror in me. Her rounded eyes lock onto mine, and the slack-jawed expression on her face screams recognition despite my changed appearance.

Kyra Carter, lights up on the bottom of my EP.

I thrust myself through the opening and slam my hand to the inside pad, closing the door, all the while training my weapon on her.

"Don't move or you're dead," I threaten, both entirely meaning it and not at the same time.

Her eyes grow wider, her lips still parted in shock.

"How... how did you get in here?" she stutters, her right hand reaching for the Flexx attached to her left wrist.

"You touch that Flexx, and you die," I growl.

"Avlyn, you can't be here. If Guardians catch you, they'll arrest you."

"You think I don't know? You're the one who announced on those vids that I was Elore's number one enemy."

Kyra knits her eyebrows together.

I walk closer to her desk and wave her toward the two chairs sitting in front of it. "I want you out from behind there and where I can fully see you. We need to talk."

"Isn't that what we're doing?" she whispers.

The comm out of her office should be blocked, but I don't want to take any chances that she'll secretly alert someone. Gesturing to the chairs with my stunner, I say, "Keep your hands off your Flexx."

Kyra raises her hands up to shoulder level and slowly rises behind her desk. I motion the weapon again toward the chair facing away from the door. She inches around and lowers herself into it, back straight, her gaze fastened to mine.

I pull out the other chair and sit down, still pointing my stunner in her direction. Now I can keep an eye on the exit and her at the same time.

Kyra's expression changes from one of shock into one of fear. Within seconds, her eyes become glassy. Seeing this new response catches me somewhat off guard.

It could be anything, Avlyn. She might only be afraid that you're going to actually kill her.

"Start talking, Kyra. And I want the real you, not the person you present in the vids."

Kyra looses a trembling breath, and, once again, her expression changes—hardens. Looking me square in the eye, she says, "Affinity will lose, Avlyn. They were always going to lose.

You should have taken Manning's deal. You'd be a Level Three and none of this would have happened."

"Everything would have happened. You have no idea what is going on outside of Elore, do you?" I inquire. "Look around you. The city is being bombed, crushed by New Philadelphia. We are all going to lose if something isn't done. It's time for you to stand up for yourself."

"I did stand up for myself," she snaps. "I saw an opportunity and I took it."

The words shoot anger into my core like bolts of fire. "You're a liar."

She laughs. "A liar? And what are you? A traitor?"

I lean closer to her. "Yes. A traitor to an ideology that makes people believe they don't matter. That they can't fight the system when taken advantage of because no one cares. And, the only way to survive in this world is to play along no matter the consequences to themselves or to others. So, yes. I am a traitor and proud of it."

I bore my heated gaze into hers. Wordlessly, she breaks away and stares at the floor.

"Kyra, you were my best friend," I soften my voice. "We trusted each other. I know you did because you came to me... after what happened with Ayers."

Kyra exhales as if she's had the wind knocked from her and raises her head again. Tears stream down her face. "I... was so scared. Those Guardians came to the unit across the hall, and I just knew they were there for me too. That night I couldn't sleep at all. I even took the MedTech, and all night I dreamed of the

Guardians bursting down your door. Taking us both away. I couldn't risk it, so I decided to cut contact."

"If you were worried about both of us, then why did you give me that Flexx with the tracker in it? I almost died, and a lot of people did, my mother for one."

Kyra brushes at the tears. "I didn't know. The entire thing was a setup. Manning wanted to discover the location of Ruiz and figured you would go straight to her. I know that now, but I had no idea at the time. When I saw you on the security vid, I couldn't resist helping you."

Kyra's Flexx buzzes on her wrist, but she glances at my stunner and ignores it.

"Then why are you part of ANA?"

"Avlyn, I wasn't given a choice. After I helped you, Ayers and Manning threatened to expose me as a traitor, saying that I helped you escape if I didn't play along. Ayers knew it would keep me close to him and—" She looks away and lets out a breath through her nose. "He... he has information on Manning."

"And that's why Ayers is in Manning's shadow all the time now?"

"Yes." Kyra rubs her face. "I never meant for this to happen. All the speeches are written for me. I only said it all to stay alive. And I figured the accusations would make you never come back."

"And Daniel?"

She scoffs. "Daniel is a pig. He's no better than Ayers or Manning, except for the fact that he hasn't touched me. I won't let him. At least I have a choice in that, but he's a pawn too. You and Daniel have a past. They figured they'd up the stakes to lure

223

you back into the city by bringing him in. And look... it worked."

I clench my teeth against Kyra's words. "I'm back for much bigger things than Daniel. Affinity needs to claim the city, so we can fight against Waters."

"Affinity should let the city be destroyed and get away. Elore is a horrible place," she says.

"Not everyone here is, though. It's the same for New Philadelphia. Leadership needs to change, and then the people will follow."

Kyra shakes her head. "You were always so naive."

"No. I'm not naive, not anymore. You can't imagine what I've seen—what I know."

"You can't imagine what *I've* been through," she shoots back, flicking a glance at my stunner, still pointed at her.

"No, I can't. You're right. But I do know that we're at a place in time where we're going to collapse or thrive. Only one of them can happen. You need to stop being afraid, Kyra. You know what side to take. You just have to do it."

I lower my weapon and place it on the desk. How can I ask Kyra to stop being afraid with a gun pointed at her? "Work with us. We could use an insider in the government sector."

She looks at me, stunned by my request. "Why do you trust me?"

"Because I know your heart. I always have." I reach my hand to her and she takes it.

"I don't think I can stay here anymore. I can't hold it together."

I grip her tighter. "Then, I'll get you out. I know I can

arrange for it."

Kyra looks at me, her eyes full of tears, and then she nods in agreement.

I smile as my own eyes well up with tears at the thought of her being safe.

Warning: Human Detected

Click.

The office door whooshes open. I jump to my feet as a face I could have stood to never see again waits in the opening.

Daniel Carter

I grab for my stunner on my hip, but it's not there.

"So, this is why you were not answering your messages, Kyra," Daniel seethes, never taking his eyes—or his stunner—off me. Suddenly recognition lights his eyes. "Hanging out with traitors again, Kyra?"

"Shut up, Daniel," she growls.

"Don't you tell me to shut up." He switches his attention to me and narrows his eyes. "You've done something to your hair... and your eyes. But I'd know you, Avlyn Lark."

"Then why don't you kill me?" I grit between clenched teeth.

"Because I think you might be more valuable to Manning alive than dead."

"You are so stupid, Daniel," Kyra says, punctuating each word for emphasis. "We're all going to be dead soon and you're still trying to get promoted."

Kyra's words shock me. She meant everything she admitted.

"And here I was trying to protect you, Kyra," Daniel says. "I picked up a data request for information on you from the

GenTech satellite location. I didn't think much of it until an unknown person tripped the security system I installed in your office." He looks at me and narrows his eyes again. "And look what trash I found?"

Daniel slides his finger to the trigger, and Kyra growls like a wild animal. Every bit of rage, every injustice she's lived, all of it bottled up in her tiny body, suddenly explodes onto him.

I one-eighty to my stunner on the desk and grab for it.

Pop!

A stunner discharges and I twist to the sound only to watch Kyra crumple to the office floor. Daniel stands in momentary shock of what he's done.

Those things don't just stun at that distance, Aron's words echo in my mind.

My rage bubbles to the surface, and I instantly compel the setting to activate on my weapon and shoot Daniel straight in the chest. His eyes go wide, and the blast blows him back against the door with a crack. His body slides to the floor.

Daniel Carter: Deceased.

I kneel next to Kyra, my tears flowing as I grab for my friend's body. "No, no, no," I whisper. "Not now, not when things were going to be okay."

A labored breath comes from her mouth and, for a split second, I think she might live. But, there's no way her nanos can repair something like a blast to the chest. The damage is too extensive.

My tears fall onto her face, and everything in me says to run. I've got to get out of here.

"Avlyn," Kyra hoarsely whispers.

"Kyra," I sob. "You'll be fine." But I know it's not true.

"No, no, I'm not." Kyra groans against the pain. "I know what information Ayers has on Manning. Affinity should know in case Ayers tries to use it somehow."

"Shh," I soothe, holding her. "It doesn't matter. None of that matters now."

She groans again, clutching her chest. "Ayers may try to stage a coup in the middle of a war." She grits her teeth and gasps for an elusive breath. "The new leader of Affinity..."

"Fisher?"

"Yes. Over thirty years ago, Manning forced her and Ruiz out," Kyra says, so softly I can barely hear her. "Fisher was pregnant. The baby was... Manning's."

My mind races at her words. Manning's?

I refocus on Kyra. I can't think about what she just said. I need to help my friend. But, as I struggle to come up with a solution, the life leaves her body.

Kyra Carter: Deceased.

CHAPTER TWENTY-FIVE

"No, no, no!" I throw my hands under Kyra's shoulders and try to will her body to work again. To fix her nanos. But, her energy is gone.

My chest tenses and I lower Kyra's body to the ground and scan the room, my mind spinning. I take one last look at my childhood friend and hold back the tears and emotions threatening to destroy me. Her face is lovely, even in death.

Is Bess Manning's child? That can't be true. But, after what just happened, I don't understand why Kyra would lie to me. Maybe she got it wrong. My heart pounds, knowing that isn't true. Cynthia lied to me. Or, at least hid information.

From my brain's fog, I realize that I shouldn't be here; citizens will be in the building soon, if they're not already. Blocking the door lies Daniel's body, dead from my stunner. A horrifying mixture of satisfaction and guilt resonates through me as I stare into his vacant eyes. He was a horrible person, but maybe he didn't have much choice in the matter, either.

I grip my stunner and reduce the setting. No more killing today. There's been enough.

I race for the quickest exit and skid out onto the ice-slicked street in less than thirty seconds. I nearly topple over but catch myself. Somehow, I conjure up the mental power to pull my thoughts together while blending in with the mix of displaced citizens as well as those who are heading to their positions. The majority of the several-block trek toward the bunker is a blur. If it weren't for my EP guiding the way, I'm not sure I'd have found my way back here.

Before I know it, I'm in the elevator and on the way down to the bunker. I hurl my fist into the back of the cab. Pain shoots down my arm and increases the rage building from inside my core.

The elevator chimes. I charge out of the barely open doors. Meyer meets me in the hall, stunner in hand, lowering his weapon when he sees me.

"Why didn't you message?" he asks.

I don't even acknowledge him. Instead, I turn the other way and bolt down the hall toward the sleeping quarters. I slam my palm on the pad and stumble into the room the moment the door activates to slide open.

"What's going on?" Meyer's deep voice comes from behind.

I flinch and spin toward him. "Get out!"

His eyes widen, and he steps toward me, but I inch back.

"I told you to leave!"

Meyer raises his hands shoulder high and shakes his head. "I'll leave, but you need to give me some information. You're safe, right? We're safe for now?"

"We're safe," I hiss. "But Kyra's dead."

"Kyra?" Meyer steps toward me again, and I move away from him. He stops. "Why would you know if Kyra is dead?"

"Because I was with her when she died," I admit with a growl in my throat.

Meyer's jaw stiffens. "Why were you with Kyra? There's no way those were your orders, and don't you try to tell me they were."

"I did it for me," I spit back. "For Kyra. And you know what? I was right about her all along. Yes... I risked everything. I risked it to try to go back for a friend I left behind. One that everyone wrote off and abandoned." Tears burn at the corners of my eyes, and I fight to keep them back. I refuse to let them out. "Now she's dead, and you don't need to worry about her anymore. So, get out and leave me alone."

"You could be dead too," Meyer whispers, some of his anger falling away.

"Just leave me alone." I fling myself away from him. "Give me space, okay?"

"Okay. But you need to tell Fisher about Kyra." His footsteps clomp across the concrete floor as he *finally* exits the room.

"Oh, believe me," I mumble. "I'll be speaking to Cynthia."

I turn back toward the closed door and let out a long breath. After throwing my stunner onto my bunk, I visualize a message in my mind to Cynthia.

I need to speak to you in person. Now. Don't ask questions.

I attach the coordinates for the VR meeting and send. Then I sit on my bed, blink down hard and open my eyes to the meeting place I envisioned in my mind. There's not one interesting thing about it, just a white room, no doors, no windows.

I fall to my knees and let out a primal scream, throwing my hands out from my sides. The sound echoes in the room and comes back to me, and I fall flat on my back, feeling none of it.

"Avlyn?" Cynthia's voice echoes in the space, sending a jolt of electricity through my chest.

I scramble to stand and find her about ten feet from me. I study the lines on her face, the dusting of freckles over her skin. Very much like mine. Except she's not like me. I don't want her to be like me.

"Kyra's dead," I finally say.

Cynthia opens her mouth to speak, and I raise my hand to stop her.

"She's dead. That's all you need to know right now. We have other things to talk about."

"It sounds like we need to discuss what you just told me. I need to understand how you are aware of this fact."

I cross my arms over my chest. "Kyra's dead and so is Daniel. You won't need to worry about them anymore."

Her expression grows tight and concerned. "Avlyn, what is going on? I deserve the right to know."

I let out a low growl and step toward her. "Just like I had the right to know that Manning is my grandfather?"

Cynthia's eyes widen, and her pupils enlarge. After a beat, she inches closer to me, but I hold out my palm, stopping her from moving closer again.

"Your grandfather?" she asks, a nervous smile crossing her lips.

"Don't lie to me, Cynthia."

She closes her mouth and crosses her arms over her chest. First, she looks me in the eye and then away. "It's true. But what good does it do for me to tell you? Does it somehow make the situation better?"

"It's the truth!" I yell. "This isn't some little thing. Does Bess know?"

Cynthia flicks her attention back to me. "Bess knows. She didn't want me to tell you, either."

"Why? Because I'm weak? Can't handle it?"

"*Can* you handle it? You're not doing very well with the information right now."

"That's because my best friend told me right before she died in my arms." My hands curl into fists. "Ayers is holding the information against Manning. He's planning on staging a coup."

Panic takes hold of Cynthia's face. "I need to know everything."

I rub my hand over my face, not wanting to relive Kyra's death again.

"Tell me, Avlyn."

"When I was at the GenTech satellite, they showed a vid of Kyra."

Cynthia places her hands on her hips and paces slowly, listening to me.

"I don't know if anyone else noticed it, but what she was saying didn't match the story she was telling with her eyes. I don't even know if she was doing it on purpose. Her tense expression and something in the tone of her voice told me she was lying. That she was doing something she was forced into. So, I took a risk."

I tell Cynthia everything. How Kyra was set up and then how it was used against her. How she was willing to come with me and couldn't bear what she was being forced into anymore. And, when I get to the part about Daniel finding Kyra and her attacking him, I break down.

"If she hadn't attacked Daniel, maybe she'd be alive," I sob.

Cynthia's arms wrap around me and, despite my anger, I accept the embrace. "But you might not have been. Daniel would have either shot you or brought you to Manning. If what you told me about Kyra is true, then she loved you. Everything she did was her attempt to save you. And this last time? It was no different."

Cynthia pulls away from me. "You must believe the details I kept from Bess all those years and from you now are also no different. Everything I did for my family was to protect them."

The burn of anger returns to my chest. "But I had a right to know."

She nods her head. "Of course, you did. But keeping you safe was my priority. Your DNA was masked, so it was unlikely you'd find out accidentally. The information would only be a burden to you."

"But, Bess knows now?"

"Yes. She was suspicious and pressed me to tell her. So, I did. We both agreed this was information we could share later."

My mind reels with thoughts of how cruel Manning is and

how he craves power over everyone. And, I can't help thinking about what Ayers had done to Kyra. "Did Manning hurt you? Force you?"

Cynthia blinks slowly and lets out a long breath, and then turns from me. "No," she admits. "That was a lifetime ago, and Colin Manning was a different person. At least, the young and stupid me thought he was. I had chosen to focus on my career rather than have a child, and Manning was the same. We were both lonely. Our affair should have never happened. We both knew it. And, when he had the chance to get rid of both Ruiz and me? He took it."

I soften my stance to her.

"Then the threats began," she continues. "Both Adriana and I agreed that we needed to escape the city. Then I discovered I was pregnant, and I knew it was even more imperative to get away. If Manning ever found out, he would have had both me and our baby killed. Still, after Bess was born, it became increasingly difficult for me to hide who she was. People, even in the Outerbounds, recognized me and I had no idea what information would reach Manning. Sending Bess back into Elore was not a good option, but this plan had advantages the Outerbounds couldn't offer me."

"Like what?"

Cynthia shrugs. "I'd always know where she was since very few people could get in or out of the city. Letting someone raise her in the Outerbounds meant she might be lost to me for good. It wasn't a risk I was willing to take. The DNA masker had worked, and so I took the chance."

She twists toward me again. "Look, we all make choices we regret. But the reality? Each of us only have one chance in our lives, then the moment is gone. We must live with that choice and whatever the consequences may be. I'm sorry that I kept secrets from you. But, I'm only human." She lifts a trembling, sad smile. "That's all I could ever be."

For so long, I've wanted to be angry with who I am, where I came from. But, when it came down to the answers I sought, I didn't understand what it all meant. And, I wanted to hate Bess just because she was a lower status than me. As if that very fact somehow made me less. Cynthia, Bess, Kyra... Me. We made mistakes, every single one of us. But we were only trying to survive.

I still want to be furious with Cynthia. But I can't anymore.

Studying my grandmother, I see more than our family resemblance. Beyond the once dark hair and pale, freckled skin. Cynthia is me in fifty years. A woman with a life full of regrets mixed with happiness, sorrow, and contentment.

"When this is over, please make sure people know that Kyra wasn't at fault and only doing the best she could too." I can't give Kyra much, but at least I can make this request for her.

Cynthia's lips form into a small, sad smile. "Yes. But, right now, I need for you to focus. Because if we don't win this war. I'm not entirely sure humanity will survive."

Chapter Twenty-Six

"I need some time to consider our next course of action," Cynthia says. "We're currently evaluating the data you were able to obtain on the Neuro-link."

"I was nearly in," I say. "I just needed more time."

"The problem is we are short on time, Avlyn. You should return to the bunker."

Disappointment in myself fills me. I nod and blink down hard to release from VR. In an instant, I find myself back in the bunk room, alone. Reality weighs down on me, and I throw my head into my hands.

Kyra is gone.

Tears soak my face and I rub them away, wishing I was able to go back into the VR world and make everything okay. But, I can't. I can't let Kyra's last actions be a waste. Cynthia is right: if Kyra wouldn't have sacrificed herself, I might be dead too. I must honor what she did by making it count.

I pull myself up straight, wipe away any remaining tears, and head out toward the meeting area. But, in the hall, Meyer leans against the wall, waiting. A concerned look washes over his face when he sees me. I stare at him for a moment and then wrap my arms around his waist. I lean my head on his chest, and the beating of his heart thrums in my ear. Relief from his presence settles over me.

"Are you all right?" he asks.

"Not really, but I will be someday."

"Is Corra still safe?" he mumbles.

"She was when I left." I should have asked Cynthia. "There's no word from her?"

"None. But that doesn't mean anything," he says as he gently pushes me back to see my face.

The muscles in my stomach tense and push down any fear for Corra. I've seen that she's quite capable when she wants to be, so I have to believe her ability to survive will continue. Corra has orders, and she's good at following them.

"I'm sorry about Kyra," Meyer says. "I know she was your friend."

I squeeze and release him. From our position, I can see everyone else huddled around one of the screens. "What's going on?"

Meyer's dark eyes twinkle with excitement. "Ben figured out the immersive tech and Aron is putting the last touches on linking the program to the EP." He leans into me. "Don't tell him I said so, but you were right. I think Aron really is a genius."

I let out a chuckle. "Maybe you like him better than you like me." It's no time for a joke. But, teasing Meyer feels good and even gives me a little hope that life could somehow be normal again. If life ever was normal.

A smile overtakes Meyer's lips. "He does have that dimple on his cheek." I glare briefly at him, but it doesn't last long when he places his warm hands on my upper arms. "Come see."

"The dimple or the project?"

Meyer's lips form a wide smile, but he doesn't answer. I follow him toward the group and Ben turns to me, concerned. "You okay?"

I nod, but guilt swirls around in my stomach. It's not a good time to share our lineage with Ben. We have enough problems.

"I'll be fine," I say.

Ben accepts my answer, but his furrowed brow indicates he knows it's not exactly true.

"Show Avlyn what you've done," Meyer says to Aron, and both Ben and I turn our attention back to the group.

"What Sanda, Ben, and I did," Aron corrects as he continues swiping over the data on a tablet. Sanda stands behind him and swipes on her own tablet screen, one displaying similar information.

"Yes, yes," Meyer says with impatience.

The fact that Meyer is so interested in Aron's work lifts my spirits. Not a lot, but it's nice to see them making a connection.

Aron pokes the screen. "There." He turns his head and looks up at Sanda. "You think that did it?"

She nods. "I double-checked your work, and I believe it will. But you're the expert."

Aron turns his attention to me. "You're just in time for the beta test."

"Beta test?" I ask. "Who's going to test it?"

"Me," he says.

I tap the screen and scroll through the data, double-checking the code.

"I already did that," Ben says. "Everything looks clean. Immersion should work. But you should go in with him and test it out."

The coding *is* clean. "But it didn't work on the older test subjects in New Philadelphia."

"They didn't have either of us to help develop their assisted tech," Ben insists. "And, if it doesn't work, we'll need to start over."

I look to Aron. "Let's do this."

Aron nods enthusiastically and unpairs the EP box from the system. He opens the top and removes the transparent EP, balancing it on the end of his index finger.

I hold my breath as he places the device onto his eye and watch as the tech nearly vanishes. Aron blinks down hard to activate it and, in my mind, I envision a meeting place and develop the coordinates, slap my hand down on his shoulder to immerse with his tech, taking us both to that location.

My eyelids shoot open in a vacant room, and Aron stands before me looking as he naturally does without the CosmoNano tech changes. Blond-haired and-blue eyed.

"Where are we?" he asks.

"Nowhere. I wanted to give you a blank slate. The test is going to be if you can control the VR space."

"How am I supposed to do that?"

"To be honest, I can't tell you exactly. But, controlling the virtual environment worked for me in the past when I focused on a place I wanted to be. Something meaningful or even a place connected to someone I love. If you can modify our surroundings with your thoughts, it's probably a good start."

Aron raises his eyebrows.

"Some of the best advice I've received was to not overthink things," I continue. "When you do, it blocks you from doing what you already know works. Let the tech lead your mind."

Aron inhales deeply and closes his eyes. His face tenses, but nothing happens. The space remains static.

"It's a feeling," I whisper. "You can't force it. Imagine something that makes you feel happy. A place or time you want to go back to."

It might be a pointless thought. Aron didn't have much to live for inside of Elore. And, most of the time we spent in the Outerbounds wasn't great, either. But as my thought fades, the energy shifts, and the ground jolts. Then, without warning, code cyclones around us, breaking our bodies apart while rebuilding a new reality.

Bam!

Scratchy tan grass crunches under my feet. Off in the distance are mountains and, past the clearing, are evergreens. We're back at the Affinity camp. I let the wind blow through my hair as the sunrise peeks over the mountains, painting the sky in pinks and oranges. Not seeing Aron, I break from the calm scene and turn in the opposite direction.

Behind me is the New Philadelphia ship Meyer had stolen. Why would Aron bring us here? And then nervous electricity tingles in my chest, because I see why. To the hovercraft's right, I spot them.

Sanda has her arms wrapped around Aron's neck, and they're kissing. He's holding her around the waist, tight to his body. This is not just any little kiss but a real one. Heat shoots up my neck at the sight of them, and I turn away. So, I guess Meyer was right.

"Avlyn!" Aron calls, his voice thick with embarrassment.

I turn my attention back to him. Sanda is gone, vanished.

"I... I didn't mean to bring us here," he says, eyes wide and cheeks flushed. "You told me to go with a feeling, and I guess that was the first thing that popped into my mind."

I chuckle and clear my throat. "So... this kiss really happened?"

Aron's lips quirk into a shy smile, forming the dimple on his cheek. "It did," he says softly. "I really like her."

The tension in my chest dissipates. I like Sanda too. If she paired up with Aron, I think it would be a perfect match. Better than he and I ever would have been. "Meyer thought you did. I hadn't completely decided yet."

Aron's eyes go wide again. "*Meyer* knows?"

"Don't worry. Just be good to Sanda. Meyer *is* her brother and all." I laugh and turn in a slow circle. "But, look at this." I gesture around to the view "You did it. You controlled the setting using your mind."

"I did, didn't I?" His eyes light up with excitement.

"I think now we simply need to work on being more

deliberate. Less... spontaneous. Do you think you can control the environment again?"

"Maybe." Aron closes his eyes and relaxes his shoulders.

The scene around us remains as he concentrates. I study the grass below, and suddenly something shifts. The blades morph into code and I know whatever he's doing is working. I bend down, letting my fingers graze over the grass. My hand passes through and the blades disappear, as does everything else.

I look up at Aron as he slowly opens his eyes. My heart sinks. Maybe that was it; perhaps he can't make it happen again. I start to open my mouth, but, before I do, he raises his hand, palm up. The space above his palm shimmers and one of his micro drones materializes. Aron's lips curl up into a smile, and, behind him, twenty more drones come into existence.

Aron lowers his hand to his side and twists to look at the tech floating behind him. "If only they were this fast to make in real life."

I let out a belly laugh, amazed at what he was able to do so quickly, how intricately he can manipulate the code.

"We can make more of these immersive EPs, right?" I ask.

Aron waves his hand and all but one drone, now floating over his shoulder, vanishes. "Yes, Affinity will simply need to convert existing EPs. The process is fairly straightforward."

"If the five of us can use modified EPs to keep Waters' immersives out of the mainframe, then I think we have a real chance," I say.

"Were you able to figure out the Neuro-link?"

His question takes all the wind out of my sails. "No, the

mission was a failure all the way around." My shoulders tense as images of Kyra dying in my arms flashes in my mind. I want to be able to share that pain with Aron, but don't. Instead, I shake off the emotions. "The DPF tech works slightly differently in each person. So, what will work on one individual doesn't seem to work on another. If I had enough time…"

"Then there may only be one option," Aron says. "Because the intel coming in from New Philadelphia is Waters' immersives are nearly running at full capacity. When that happens, he'll launch a full-fledged attack. And, since Manning is unaware Philly will be coming at him in two different directions, he's probably overconfident. We also risk Direction seeing us as a threat to the system, even if we're only trying to protect the Neuro-link." Aron tilts his head at the little drone hovering above his palm. "It's time for Fisher to make good on her willingness to make a truce with Manning."

Panic rushes through me as I stand still, like a stone. A truce means Ben and I will have to be exposed. Up to this point, Manning hasn't fully understood what we can do. It's like the rescue from the Elorian bunker all over again. To get New Philadelphia to attack Elore, Ruiz had to tell Waters about my ability. *And look where that confession led*, I remind myself.

"Without Manning's help, I'm not sure there'll be any way to win this. There's not enough time for anything else."

I push away the anxiety forming in my core. "Let's get these EPs ready so you, Meyer, and Sanda can practice. Ben can help you perfect the tech while we plan a strategy for holding off the immersives. Our goal will be to shut them down, but not kill them."

"You think if we kill them in here they'll die in the real world?"

I shake my head. "I don't know, yet. But the virus Ben downloaded from the Trojan nearly killed him."

"Well, I'm not into killing children," Aron mumbles.

"You and me both." I cross my arms over my chest and pace a few steps. "I must speak with Cynthia again."

CHAPTER TWENTY-SEVEN

"Did it work?" Sanda asks when we've blinked back into reality.

I smile at her knowing that she holds a secret about her and Aron.

"What?" she insists.

"Oh, it worked." I slide a glance to Aron whose cheeks are lightly flushed with embarrassment. Amused, I continue, "Now you just need to upgrade your EPs. With Ben's help, it shouldn't take long. But I need to meet Cynthia again."

"Should I be a part of that?" Ben asks.

"No, they need you here. I'll fill you in later."

Ben nods, and I immediately feel guilty for keeping information from him. Like me, he deserves to know about our relation to Manning. But, my brother needs to focus on this current task first.

I tap Meyer on the shoulder and motion him away. His eyes sparkle, unable to control the excitement on his face.

"It worked?" he asks.

"From our preliminary tests, it seems so. Aron was able to control the environment using only his thoughts. I'm not yet sure how far he can manipulate the code, but, if nothing else, you all could function as our Guardians while Ben and I do what we need to keep the enemy's immersives out." I give him a nervous smile and turn to the hallway. "Once the EPs are fully upgraded, training will begin. Ben will help guide you."

He places his hand on my shoulder to stop me. "Why aren't you joining the training sessions?"

"It's best if Ben and I keep our distance for the time being, and I need to discuss something with Cynthia."

"Discuss what?" he asks.

"The truce with Manning she talked about."

Meyer leans in closer to me. "I guess I didn't think our fight would really end in a truce. Sounds risky to me."

"Of course, it's risky, but, if we don't, all this work on the immersive tech will be a waste. If Affinity and Direction join together, we may actually have a chance against Waters."

"Well, keep me filled in. I feel like I don't know anything going on around here anymore, and I don't like it."

I raise on my toes and kiss his cheek. "Go work on the EPs with the others. You'll enjoy immersing."

Meyer smiles and walks back to the meeting room. I head around the corner and immediately lean my back to the wall, then slide to the floor. I send a message to Cynthia along with coordinates.

We need to meet again.

Without another thought, I blink down hard to activate my EP and open my eyes to my chosen space. I look down at the sand and my now bare feet. This time I'm wearing the same green dress Meyer programmed for me the first time we came here. The fabric whips around my legs. Frothy waves lap against the shoreline a few feet away while larger ones crash farther in the distance. The ocean's briny scent fills my nose.

"This is an interesting location," Cynthia says from behind me.

"Meyer and I come here sometimes." I turn to find her dressed in a pair of tan pants and a black shirt, the ensemble completed with boots. Not beachwear. But it doesn't matter today.

Cynthia crosses her arms over her chest. "Why did you call me again?"

"Aron is making progress on the immersive EPs. He believes we'll be ready to go shortly."

Cynthia raises her eyebrows. "So quickly?"

"Aron is very good at what he does, and, with Ben's help on getting the software right, the tech works. Aron and I immersed together. Didn't take long before he was getting the hang of it. Hopefully, Meyer and Sanda will perform the same. But, if Ben and I can't both get into the Neuro-link to flip the DPF, our only other option is to make a truce with Manning."

Her jaw clenches. "I know. It's already in the works. And I'm glad you messaged me to meet again."

"Why?" I ask, not sure I want to hear the answer.

"Because you need to be there."

Panic rises in me. "I... I don't want to see Manning."

"And you think I do? But, we have to reveal the plan on how to fight the immersives. The only way he's going to believe we can do it is if we completely disclose your ability to him."

I already knew this was coming, but the reality of it doesn't make me feel any better about the situation. There are so many things that could go wrong.

"And will Ben come too?" I ask.

"To Direction's knowledge, Ben is dead. So, there's no reason to associate him with you. It would only open the door for more questions we don't want. All Direction needs to know is that you'll have virtual Guardians who will be assisting you. And one of those Guardians will happen to be Ben."

"When is the meeting happening?" I ask.

"A vehicle will arrive for you shortly. So, go ahead and make your way to the Sub tunnel when we're done."

I square myself. "Do I need to know anything else?"

Cynthia places her hand on my shoulder. "Just that anything could happen. To be honest, I'm not sure if we're going to come out alive." She nods and vanishes.

I take one last look around at the beach scene and inhale deeply. Maybe we'll live, and I'll visit someplace this beautiful for real one day.

I release from VR and find myself back in the dimly lit hall. I rise, and, with tentative steps, return to the meeting room to find the whole group has immersed. They each sit on a chair, eyes closed. I approach Meyer and run my hands through his thick, dark hair.

"I love you, be back soon," I murmur. But I have no idea if the last words are true. I make a mental note to message Meyer when I'm already below.

I take the elevator down under the bunker and walk the short distance to where the vehicle dropped us off upon arrival. In the distance, a two-seat vehicle moves through the dimly lit tunnel with a passenger inside.

Corra Bradley illuminates along the bottom of my vision and relief overtakes me. She's still alive.

"How'd you get down here?" I ask as the open-topped vehicle pulls up.

"Affinity arranged for me to get out of the GenTech satellite, and I followed orders," she says in a low tone. "I went to a safe house, and they escorted me down here. Apparently, you took a detour again."

"You know I'm not that great at following orders," I say.

Corra raises her eyebrow at me. "Yes, so I've heard. Get in."

I walk to the other side of the vehicle and climb in next to Corra. The car slowly turns around and then drives away from the bunker.

"Why are you escorting me to the Sub?" I ask.

"Just like last time, they wanted you to see a face you know."

The breeze blows our hair back slightly as we travel.

"Do you know anything about my next mission?

Corra shakes her head. "No, and I don't want to. All I know is that I need to bring you to Melissa Rice, and then I go back into the research lab in the Sub."

So much of me wants to tell her about Manning, to tell

someone. But I know it's best if I don't, especially as I haven't told Ben yet. "Kyra's dead," I say instead.

She glances over at me, her expression flat. "They piped in new propaganda, and they already have a new guy lined up to take her place."

"So, you knew?"

Corra shrugs. "Direction played it off as she was killed in a bombing, but there were whispers after the vid aired." She pauses for a moment. "You were there, weren't you?"

"Why would you think that?" I ask as if I'm shocked.

"Because it all happened right after you left the GenTech satellite. I put it together." Corra crosses her arms over her chest and leans back in her seat. "You watched the vid of her broadcast, it upset you, and so you went to find her."

"If you knew as much, why didn't you try and stop me?"

"Avlyn, sometimes we have to face up to things in our lives," she says. "I figured it wouldn't matter what I said. Kind of like when you made the stop with me at your bio mother's apartment instead of going straight to Ruiz in the bunker."

"But that was stupid. I could've gotten both you and me killed."

Corra chuckles dryly. "Well, I just need to accept that you can be stupid sometimes."

I furrow my brows at her. "And you did agree to go with us into GenTech."

"Yeah, that was a bad choice on my part. But sometimes stupid is worth the risk. It's why I joined Affinity." She leans forward, placing her hands on her knees. "Why is she dead?"

"Because *she* was stupid... and she saved me." Tears burn in the corners of my eyes at the memory.

"Then she thought stupid was worth the risk too." Corra stretches her hand out and takes mine.

"She was my friend, despite everything." I squeeze Corra's fingers, not wanting to let go. I've already lost two friends on this journey, and I have no wish to lose Corra too.

The tunnel widens into a larger hangar and the temperature drops. The cold air blasts my face. Affinity soldiers bustle around, preparing hover pods for what is likely to come, and my chest tightens at the sight of all the war preparations.

Corra releases my hand. "Before Affinity pulled me from the satellite, I was able to get some information on the food ink contaminate."

My breath hitches at her words. Ben can hopefully be healed now. "What did you find?"

"Don't get too excited. We don't know much yet. But we do know the drug affects the limbic system. As we thought, the purpose is to make people more submissive. Manning had been using this drug on the DPF, and, then, must have realized its potential for controlling the general population. The effect should be mild. Once people stop eating the food, the drug should flush from their system."

"But that hasn't happened for Ben," I say.

Corra looks down. "I know. I'm afraid it could have affected his limbic system permanently. We're almost at our location." The vehicle slows, then halts.

"Does Ben know?"

Corra shakes her head and we both exit the vehicle. I look around, but no one is waiting for me.

"Fisher will meet you in private," Corra says as if she reads my mind. "She didn't want to create any extra attention by meeting you here." She gestures me ahead.

I follow her past several groups of people who don't give us a second glance as they busy with their duties. We travel down a corridor to a private room. Once there, Corra palms the security panel and a door slides back. Inside, Cynthia speaks with a group of people I don't recognize. Corra and I enter, gaining Cynthia's attention who, then, motions me over.

"Bye, Avlyn," Corra says from my side.

I want to tell her not to go. But I don't. "Thank you."

Corra gives me a lopsided smile. "You can do this."

The door slides shut behind Corra, and I walk toward Cynthia. She bids the others goodbye and walks straight for me.

"It's time for us to leave," she whispers in my ear and guides me to the exit.

"What about an update? I don't even know what we're doing other than meeting with Manning."

The doors slide back, and Cynthia pilots me into the hall. "I'll fill you in on the way," she says.

"What if Manning changes his mind once we get there."

Cynthia shakes her head. "There's too much benefit in this partnership for him to do that."

"But you don't trust him, right?"

Cynthia pauses and grabs my arm. "Of course not. We have to play our cards right."

I give her a quizzical look because I'm not sure what she's talking about. But she doesn't seem to notice.

"We need to give just enough information to satisfy him and then get out together *and* alive," she says and starts walking again.

"Guardians are accompanying us, right?" I catch up with her.

"This trip is just you and me," she answers. "Soldiers will escort us, but, once inside the city, we're on our own. And again, not a word about Ben other than he's one of the people on your team. In Manning's eyes, Ben is dead, so he shouldn't suspect anything. Dr. Sloan will be joining us via hologram and add in his support for a takeover in New Philly. He's nearly pinpointed Waters location, and, from the intel, it should also lead us to the immersives. So, if you and Ben can't shut them down, we may be able to manually."

"Manually?" I ask.

"They may need to die, Avlyn."

I gulp down the guilt that builds in my throat. "And does Manning know about me?"

"Know what? About your ability?" she asks. "He doesn't fully understand yet, but we told him we had a weapon that could safeguard Elore. He knows that involves you."

"That's not what I'm asking. Are you positive Manning doesn't know who Bess is, who I am?"

We arrive at a white, medium-sized enclosed vehicle and Cynthia activates the door.

"Get in," she says.

I obey as she rounds to the other side, opens her door and slides in next to me. The doors click shut.

"I'm almost completely certain Manning doesn't know, and I don't intend for him to find out," she says.

The vehicle moves forward, and the panel in front of us lights up.

Destination: Level Three: Direction Headquarters.

I've seen the Direction Headquarters on vids before, but I've never been there. Since there are few reasons for most Level Twos to visit Level Three, I've only entered Three a couple of times. The Headquarters, however, is where Manning makes his announcements.

Our transport works its way up a long ramp, and a metal shield slides open ahead of us, revealing the bright sun outside of the Sub. As the light hits us, the windows darken slightly.

"Manning specifically instructed us to use tinted windows. He doesn't want the general population to know we're meeting with him yet," Cynthia says.

I peer out the side window and spot drones in the sky as well as two other vehicles now flanking us. I have no idea where they came from.

"Those are ours. Don't worry. They'll take us to the city limits. Then, we're on our own."

I bring out my Flexx to message Meyer. It's not as if I can tell him anything specific.

I love you is all I type and send.

Without speaking, we travel for twenty-two minutes as a few flurries of snow wisp at the windshield. The minutes seem to fly by, though, and soon we are met by Elorian escort drones.

Cynthia taps the panel to speak into the comm. "We're fine.

But you should wait for us here."

The two vehicles on each side of ours fall back as we enter Elore.

The next leg of the trip doesn't take long as our entry point was near Level Three. I lean back in my seat and take deliberate breaths in a half-hearted attempt to distract my imagination from envisioning all the horrible things that could happen minutes from now.

The car stops and my eyelids pop open. Cynthia lays her hand on my arm. "Let me guide the conversation."

I nod, and my door slides back. A drone floats next to the opening, its tentacles retracted.

"Greetings," it says in a robotic voice, and a beam emits from the front of its body, scanning me. The beam clicks off. "Please follow me." I guess it didn't find anything it thought dangerous, since it didn't stun me. So, that's something.

Cynthia and I follow the SI into the building, and another trails behind. Neither of the drones appear aggressive, but I'm well aware they could kill us at will. Inside, the building seems empty of any other humans.

The SI moves us into the glass elevator. Cynthia and I both take turns placing our palms on the pad. Once positively identified, the doors shut, and the cab rises. At the thirty-fifth floor, the elevator halts and the doors slide back. Another Guardian drone greets us, and we follow it to an unmarked white door.

"Please step inside," says the drone.

CHAPTER TWENTY-EIGHT

The room is thick with tension and anticipation. My lungs struggle to take in the air that suddenly feels too dense.

Manning wears a charcoal-gray shirt and slim-fitting black pants instead of his usual white lab coat. Does knowing he's my grandfather change anything for me? Maybe Ben and I are part monsters too.

He stares at Cynthia, boring into her.

Manning now knows Cynthia was pregnant with his child when she fled from Elore, no thanks to Ayers. But hopefully, he's unaware I share in the secret. And I highly doubt he'll mention it in this setting, or any other. It's information he'd most likely take to his death, if he could.

Cynthia is unrelenting under his stare.

SI Guardians line the windowless room, and a large rectangular table is positioned in the middle of the space, surrounded by a dozen shiny, silver metal chairs.

"Ms. Lark." Manning's voice makes me flinch. "Your

appearance has changed since we last met."

Before I get the chance to answer—not that I wanted to anyway—the door behind us opens.

Mitchell Ayers shows in my EP.

He stands in the doorway with a haughty expression on his face, looking every bit his middle age. As Ayers steps into the room, another SI Guardian follows behind him and enters.

"It appears we have all arrived," Manning says.

I follow Ayers with my eyes, as, without a word, he makes his way around Cynthia and me and toward a chair. Hatred boils in my chest. I watch his face for any sign he's been affected by Kyra's death, but, of course, he's like a stone. A true Elorian.

"We haven't all arrived," Cynthia says, producing her handheld. "My colleague, Dr. Sloan, will be joining us via hologram."

Manning has already taken a seat at the head of the table, and Ayers sits to his right. Manning nods to Cynthia, and she proceeds to tap on her handheld to bring up the program. As she does this, I move to pull out the chair on Manning's left, but he tips his head toward the chair beside Ayers. The exact place I have no desire to be. But, this is no time to make waves.

Cynthia places the handheld in the center of the table between us. I begrudgingly walk around the table to the right side. Purposefully, I pull out the seat next to Ayers and drag it a few extra inches from him, then slump down and unzip my coat, leaving it on. No sense making myself at home.

A blue light emits from the device, and a transparent version of Dr. Sloan flickers into existence. His expression is tense, and he appears no more comfortable to be taking part in the meeting as a hologram than he probably would in person. This time, however, I have the same feeling he probably does. Almost anywhere would be better than here.

Manning gives Cynthia a gesture for her to begin. She straightens and pushes back her shoulders, lifting her chin a notch.

"Affinity would like to propose a truce," Cynthia says.

Ayers chuckles, but Manning's expression remains hawk-like.

"And why do you suppose that would be something in Direction's best interest?" Manning asks, folding his hands on top of the table.

Because if you don't, everyone in Elore is going to die? These are the words caught in my throat, but I voice none of them. Manning is too arrogant to care about the citizens of Elore, caring only for satisfying his need for power over others.

"Affinity and Direction want the same thing," Cynthia says. "What *is* best for the Elorian people? We've always had differing opinions on how this should be accomplished. But, right now, that is inconsequential. If there's no Elore, then our opinions don't matter."

"Elore is a strong city," Ayers interjects. "So far we have been able to fight off New Philadelphia with the DPF and SI."

Cynthia slowly turns her attention to Ayers. "These strikes are nothing," she growls. "Waters is playing with you, weakening your defenses. All these years, Direction has focused on keeping Elore isolated. The citizens aren't prepared, and neither are you. Waters wants control, and if that means destroying Elore, then he will."

Manning leans back in his seat, silent, his jaw clenched tight.

"You spent years lying to Elore about how a pandemic could resurface in the Outerbounds," Cynthia says. "You should have been aware of what was *really* out there instead of creating a scenario. It made you weak. It made Affinity weak, too, something I'm willing to admit."

Cynthia stares at Manning, whose face is still devoid of emotion.

Sloan's hologram clears his throat, breaking the tension a fraction. "Director Manning, Representative Ayers, Fisher is quite correct in how New Philadelphia is soon to gain the upper hand. You are also correct that you are fairly equally matched in ships and soldiers, both SI and human."

"Then inform us why they will have the upper hand," Manning finally speaks.

"Yes, yes," Sloan says. "Give me a moment." He pauses and stares at both Manning and Ayers to ensure they won't interrupt him again.

"Waters has developed a new technology allowing the human mind to enter into any technology it wishes," Sloan says. "This would include the Elore mainframe and the Neuro-link controlling the DPF. When this weapon becomes fully operational, New Philadelphia will have the capability to take down Elore from the inside out. And, from my intel, Waters considers this a 'take no prisoners' war. In other words, he'll kill most everyone off and take the city's spoils for himself. We need for an official truce between Affinity and Elore."

Ayers scoffs. "It's an Affinity trick. There's no way New Philadelphia can breach our mainframe. Security is too high."

I think about the times Ben and I entered the mainframe from Gabrielle's without detection, and I know he's wrong. Not if the immersives share my gift to discover weaknesses in code. Everything in me fights to keep silent about my abilities, but that's not why we're here.

"I've been in the mainframe multiple times without detection." I make no mention of Ben, even when Manning twists his attention to me. "You are correct, however, that without direct access to the source it's more difficult, but it's not impossible. And, at this point, Waters may not be interested in flying under the radar. He may use brute force, instead."

Narrowing his eyes, Manning says, "*You* again, Ms. Lark. Why did you come back to Elore? You had your chance to leave, but here you are again." He leans back in his seat and crosses his arms over his chest. "Did you find that the Outerbounds were not all you hoped it would be?"

The question punches me in the gut. I did believe the Outerbounds would bring the sort of freedom I craved. Even Meyer, who'd lived there most of his life, thought it was better than it was. "Yes, Director Manning," I admit, "The Outerbounds is imperfect. But it simply means I can't expect others to make my life what I want it to be. That part is up to me."

Manning smiles, showing off a row of perfectly aligned teeth, and the action sends a shiver down my spine because it's not a friendly expression. "Well then... we have more in common than I might have thought."

Unfortunately, yes. We do, Director Manning. Every part of me burns with hate that this man and I are related by blood.

Cynthia clears her throat, breaking my concentration. "Avlyn, please inform Director Manning of your abilities."

Nausea twinges in my stomach. Cynthia's face is stern, determined, but there's still softness in her eyes.

This is not a time to cloud my mind with heavy emotions. To stand up to Manning, I need to maintain a clear head. I spent years pushing down emotion, hiding each feeling. This is a skill I know how to perform. Briefly, I close my eyes and inhale from my core. With this action, I offer up an homage to Michael, my father, wherever he is.

"Director Manning, while I was in Elore, you had the impression that my system hacking skills were more advanced than an average hacker. My skills have been for a long time—you were right. But, something happened to increase these skills even more."

"And what might that be, Ms. Lark?" Manning sneers.

"We're not entirely sure." It's partially true since we don't have all the details yet. But, I won't reveal the experimentation because this knowledge could lead to Ben. "It appears that the last VacTech update triggered a shift in my nanotech, giving me more of an upgrade than was intended."

Manning's face tenses. "Would you please get to the point?"

"Somehow the shift made it possible for me to... immerse with technology. I can control it, modify it. And without detection."

"Immerse?" Manning asks, a growl in his voice.

"Through touch," I say, "My mind connects to a technology's system and then my nanos integrate with the program. My thoughts and actions can move through the data almost as if it were as real as this." I raise my hand and gesture to the room.

Manning squints at Cynthia.

"She is lying, Director," Ayers voices. "You should have Fisher and Lark taken into custody immediately."

My throat constricts at his words.

"If this were possible, Direction would have already discovered this ability," Ayers continues. "We employ the best minds in Elore."

"I assure you, Director Manning," Cynthia says, ignoring Ayers and keeping a cool expression, "We are not deceiving you. Avlyn's ability is amazing for sure, and we came here with a truce in mind as well as the offer to use her exceptional skills to protect Elore by coupling her upgrade with similar technology smuggled out of New Philadelphia. By implanting this immersive ability into a few key people, led by Avlyn, we can block Waters from destroying the mainframe and taking out all of the systems and data in Elore."

Manning's eyes are trained on Cynthia. I can almost see the thoughts running through his head, none of which involves freedom for his citizens, I'm sure.

Next to me, the heat of Ayers' anger is palatable. I glance over at him and note how his jaw is tense and nostrils flared.

Manning locks eyes with me. "So, what do you need?"

"We need your assurance of a truce and that we also have full access to the mainframe. This includes the Neuro-link to the DPF. They need to no longer view Affinity as the enemy, only New Philadelphia. Affinity will fight by their side to protect the city."

I hate how forming a truce will out many Affinity members in Elore as well as reveal our underground base outside of the city. There'll be no going back after this.

"Dr. Sloan is leading the rebellion in New Philadelphia," I say, "and they're working to remove Waters from power. If all three aspects of the plan are successful, a truce between the cities is possible and we can go from there."

Manning's chair screeches over the floor as he pushes from the table and stands. "I'll need a demonstration of this ability, but, barring a deception, I agree to a truce."

Cynthia flicks her attention to me. I suppose we should have discussed what a demonstration of my ability might be before we arrived. I don't want to give him too much, too soon. I bring my hand up and run my fingers through my hair.

And then an idea comes to me.

I order my CosmoNano tech to revert. All three set of eyes swing to me as my hair returns to its natural brown.

"This is a conspiracy," Ayers growls.

But a greedy smile crosses Manning's lips, and he reaches out his hand to Cynthia. She exhales quickly and motions to take it.

Like a flash, Ayers is on his feet.

Wham!

His hand slams onto the Flexx in the table's middle, disabling Sloan's hologram. "You will regret this, Manning." He points at Cynthia. "I warned you about your past relations with this woman coming to light. Your secrets have made you soft."

I freeze in my seat, my mind reeling with what to do next. I'm weaponless. I could take over one of the Sis, but, then, what about the rest? They could kill Cynthia or I before I move onto the next.

"Guardians, take Representative Ayers into custody," Manning booms to the SI in the meeting room. But not one of the bots move.

I glance at Cynthia, who hasn't made a move either.

"While you've been distracted with worry over scandals arising from your many secrets, I've been working to slowly build a group of citizens who are unhappy with your leadership skills." Ayers pulls at his shirt, straightening it, before regaining his composure. "The SI joining us today are reprogrammed to follow my orders. They've also recorded the entire meeting, including your agreement to work with this rebel group," he sneers. "A few modifications and cuts to the vid and people won't question the change in leadership. Now, don't make me kill you right here for your traitorous activities against the citizens of Elore. It'll be so much easier if you simply admit your mistakes to the people and step down."

"Ayers, you are making a mistake," Manning says.

"No, Director—" He looks from Manning to Cynthia. "Excuse me, *former* Directors. I'm taking my opportunity." Then he rounds toward me. "Oh, and I'm taking Ms. Lark as well, just in case she isn't lying."

"No!" Cynthia yells, panic in her voice.

"Don't worry, Ms. Fisher. You won't be around," Ayers sneers and turns to the SI. "Arrest her."

I leap from my seat, but I'm not fast enough and he snatches my arm. Terror races through my body as everything I hate about Ayers whirls through my mind. But it all comes to a screeching halt when an image of Kyra's beautiful dead face burns bright in my memories. Anger rises from the ashes of my grief and my mind claws for the nanos implanted in his body. Like some wild beast, I force my hate into him, ripping and shredding, and overloading the tech.

Order your SI to stand down! I scream into his mind. Or I'll kill you!

My consciousness waffles from the immersive world to the real one, and I wait to hear the words I'm looking for.

"Stand down," Ayers groans.

But, when I do hear the words, my rage only increases. This man doesn't deserve mercy. He gave Kyra none. I release to the real world and thrust my hands flat onto his chest.

"Die, you monster!" I scream, flipping his nanotech's programming from preserving life to ending it.

Ayers crumbles to the floor.

Chapter Twenty-Nine

My breath comes out in quick puffs, and the situation's reality jolts me. I killed a man with my bare hands, with my mind. I murdered Ayers. Heat rakes up my neck and my palms go sweaty. I whirl my attention around the room. The SI is still standing down, and Cynthia waits slightly wide-eyed and stunned. Manning emits a calm demeanor, but my actions appear to hold great interest for him by the way he stares at me.

"Ms. Lark, if that was a demonstration of your ability, then your skills are quite useful. That man has been a thorn in my side for some time now." He crosses his arms over his chest and scans around the room. "Now, where were we?"

"I killed him." My voice comes out in a barely audible squeak.

The look of shock falls from Cynthia's face, and she races to me. The room twists as her arms fold around me, making my knees buckle. The gesture instantly clears my mind. But, what if her compassion for me gives away our connection?

I push up and center myself. "I'm fine, Fisher."

Cynthia's arms loosen as she backs away a few inches. She straightens her shirt and raises her chin, then returns her attention to Manning.

"Do we have a truce, Director?" Cynthia asks. "And assurance that the DPF will not attack Affinity members?"

Manning nods. "And Ms. Lark and her team will have access to protect the mainframe without resistance. We'll need DNA scans of each person on her team, so any existing security systems already in place do not view them as a threat."

I don't like the sound of that, but then I remember how Ben's encounter with the Trojan had nearly killed him.

"And," Cynthia says, emphasizing the single word, "you will need to make an official announcement to the people of Elore about how a truce with Affinity is called upon to defeat our common enemy."

"Agreed." Manning holds out his hand, and Cynthia takes it. They lock gazes and part of me wonders what unspoken secrets are exchanged.

I walk over to the nearest SI and place my hand on its metallic body and quickly alter its programming to ensure it doesn't attempt to attack any of us. I do the same to all the others.

"Ayers' programming is disabled, and I deleted the self-contained vid he created," I say. "Looks like he didn't want an information leak before editing was complete."

"Or never intended to use the vid, only threaten to do so," Manning sneers. "Ayers was a coward and a sneak."

I glance down at the dead man on the floor. Although what I

did could be considered self-defense, I know all too well what it was—revenge. And it leaves a bitter taste in my mouth.

Cynthia grabs my arm. "We need to prepare our forces."

Manning retrieves his Flexx from his wrist and folds the thin material out into a tablet. After swiping a few times at the screen, he nods to himself. "You have my assurance of safe passage. We'll remain in contact and confirm our strategy." He walks to the table and picks up Cynthia's Flexx and hands it to her. "You should also contact Dr. Sloan. I'm sure he'll be concerned."

"You know they followed us," I say to Cynthia as we exit the vehicle, our transport now surrounded by several other cars, each Affinity member armed with at least one gun. Several drones hover in the sky above us. But not ours.

"Of course, they did," she says. "By offering a truce, we played all our cards."

I give her a confused look, still not understanding what she means by the phrase.

Her lips stretch into a tense smile. "After today, Affinity is no more. This either means unity with Elore or death. We won't find out until all is said and done." Cynthia urges me forward, and we enter the Sub.

It takes a few moments for my eyes to adjust to the lower light, but, once they do, I see Corra coming toward us.

"Go with her," Cynthia says. "She has her orders and will take you to the proper place."

I turn toward my grandmother and grasp for her hand. "Thank you for what you did."

She chuckles. "For what? Encouraging you to put you and your brother in danger? Which is exactly what I have been trying my best to avoid."

"No," I say. "For doing what it took to protect those you love. You protected Bess the only way you knew how. And that brought us to this crossroad—trying to protect a whole lot of people we care about, even if they don't know it yet."

Cynthia pulls me into an embrace, and I don't fight the affection. Warmth spreads over me despite how the cold, dark situation surrounds us.

"If for some reason you see Bess again," I whisper into her ear, "pass a hug onto her, please?"

Cynthia pulls from me and shakes her head. "No, that's your job."

"Ma'am—" A guard comes up from behind and diverts Cynthia's attention. My grandmother turns her head back to me, smiles, and then follows him.

"Avlyn," Corra says from off to the side, and I turn toward her. "I need to escort you to the rest."

"The rest of what?" I say as tears sting at the corners of my eyes.

"The rest of your team."

"Meyer's here?" I ask.

Corra nods. "Yes, they evacuated the bunker and came here. We were waiting on finding out if the truce was happening. Your pairing has been a mess the whole time you were gone."

Embarrassment flushes my cheeks. "Meyer's not my pairing... we're—" I try to remember the word Meyer used before.

"We're dating."

Corra tweaks her eyebrow at me. "Whatever. He's waiting for you."

The thought of Meyer fills me with happiness. But, the momentary bliss quickly fades to fear. Affinity members bustle around in preparations for what could end up becoming a massacre involving New Philadelphia.

Announcements of unfamiliar codes and instructions through a speaker echo off the walls and floors. I attempt to block it all out as Corra leads me through a series of gray corridors. Auto-lights flash near the floor, but I keep my eyes straight ahead and glued to her back.

"Down here," Corra hastens and then stops at an unmarked door.

Without a moment to waste, I hustle inside and immediately spot Meyer, Ben, Sanda, Aron, and a few other faces I've never seen. From how the strangers are dressed in Affinity uniforms, I decide that they must be soldiers. The knots in my stomach ease a little. The room is set up with several rows of reclining chairs designed for immersion, similar to the one in the New Philadelphia ship.

Meyer turns toward the creaking sound of the door, and, upon seeing me, his eyes light up with relief. "You made it back," he says, reaching for my upper arms and squeezing them gently.

I let out a happy sigh and touch his face, glad to see it again. "Yes." There are a million more things I want to share with him, but I don't, and I'm not entirely sure I'll ever be able to. "Now, get me up to speed."

Sanda jogs over a few steps and tugs me away from Meyer, but not before he presses his lips to my forehead. "We've been waiting for you. We're all ready to go."

Ben holds up a device that looks like an external VR headset, resembling one I used at GenTech a lifetime ago. "The three of us—" He nods to Aron and Sanda. "—combined the immersive tech with the hardware from the Philly ship, still available to us in the Sub. Aron and I ripped the thing apart."

"We've been able to modify and test ten EPs," Sanda continues. "So, we can immerse alongside you and Ben and function as a small army of bodyguards. You can do what you need to do within the system, and we are there to make sure you *can* do it."

"Do we know yet what happens if you're hurt or die in the system?" I ask.

"It's not something we've been able to test, of course," Ben says. "If what happened to me at Gabrielle's is any indication, then what happens in VR immersion has real-world consequences. But to combat that, we've arranged for a team of Medics to be in the room with us when we link and immerse. They can wake us up at any time and stabilize the injured if need be." A wrinkle appears between her brother's brows. "We've practiced, at least."

I study Ben's face, still feeling a bit lost without our mental connection. His tense expression tells me that he's stressed, but that's about it. I want to know exactly what he's feeling right now. Is he confident? Nervous? Does he think this is going to work? When this is all over, I long to have our connection restored.

Without it, I don't feel entirely whole.

"And this is the rest of our team?" I gesture to the unfamiliar soldiers.

Aron nods. "A few more are still on the way."

Behind me, a man I recognize approaches us. Carver, the DPF I flipped before I came back to Elore. He's also dressed in an Affinity soldier uniform. My eyes widen when I see him. And right behind him is Barrett.

I jog toward them. "You both are here," I say, peering behind them to see if anyone else is coming. "What about Thompson?" And the second the question leaves my mouth I regret it.

"He's here," Carver says. "But they placed him in a secure room. He's still in a coma. That's why Barrett and I volunteered for the job. We figure the three of us are in this together. We believe you and your brother can succeed, and I want to help Thompson get back to his family."

I smile at them and their bravery. "Well, I'm honored to have you both on our team."

"Elore is our home and we don't want to lose it," Barrett says.

"You should get your EPs and then get hooked into the system," I say.

Carver gives me a little salute, and then the two of them join the medics and the other soldiers.

I notice Ben watching us and I gesture him over. "Do you think this is going to work?" I ask as he reaches my side.

Ben sighs. "We simply need to focus on the task at hand. While you were at the GenTech satellite, I was able to access the mainframe and find weak spots. I fortified each one, then I set up a point for an obvious exploit. Hopefully, the new immersives are inexperienced and will take the easy way in. And, the point of entry should be tempting," he says with a big smile. "It's hooked to the Neuro-link. We may not even need to connect our minds."

I clasp him on the shoulder. "Let's do this, then."

The two of us walk over to Aron. His companion drone floats above his shoulder, letting out a series of worried buzzing sounds.

"Okay," Aron says. "We've set up a comm from Fisher. So, you'll be able to stay in contact with her and know what's going on up top, if need be. You'll be able to activate and deactivate the comm at will. We've also received the go-ahead from Direction. Everyone's DNA signatures are now entered into the system, granting the Neuro-link access we need to avoid any possible attacks."

"Ben and I will go in now to double-check any other possible points of entry and also to ready the false backdoor," I say.

"Good idea," Aron says. "Take two of the chairs, and I'll load in the coordinates Ben programmed."

I look to Ben and we take our seats. Sanda hits a button on the arm and the seats' backs recline.

"The chairs are hooked into the system. The two of you should be able to get in without anything special," Sanda says. "Just lay your hands on the arms and do your thing. Good luck. The rest of us will be in soon."

I give her a tight smile, my heart pounding. Nervously, I touch the heart pendant under my shirt. "Thanks."

I lean my head back and close my eyes. As I do, the sharp

sound of an alarm pierces my ears, and everything turns white.

My eyelids shoot open to the digital world, and Ben materializes beside me.

100 or more New Philadelphia ships near the city limits. Brace for attack, scrolls across my vision in green, glowing letters.

I look to Ben. "I sure hope you did a good job of securing the mainframe, because we don't have time to check."

CHAPTER THIRTY

Ben and I fly into action as soldiers blink into existence around us. He calls up the false backdoor's location he had programmed, and the coding materializes and morphs into a gigantic towering gate made up of millions of tiny glowing symbols. A thick lever locks the two doors together. None of it is real; it's only the visualization of code from Ben's mind to help everyone concretely see what we're fighting.

My pulse races as we furiously manipulate the coding to program an illusion of easy entry. Everything in me wishes I could mentally connect with my twin as we work. Still, we have a good working rhythm. Ben clicks the last piece of code into place, and the gate groans and snaps. The lever securing the two doors slides back in a deafening roar. I flinch, anticipating how New Philly's immersives might come straight through the opening at any second.

Almost as if the doors release a breath, they puff open. Then nothing. Complete silence overtakes the virtual space, almost like a vacuum. The scene seems to take on slow motion, and I glance behind me. My soldiers are ready. Aron has wasted no time in calling up a cluster of micro drones. One buzzes over his shoulder as he readies a large, black gun. Sanda flanks him, waiting to fight, a ball of aqua, glowing light hovers in front of her hand, poised toward the gate, her face fierce and teeth bared.

Meyer barrels in our direction, weapon trained to protect us from whatever may come in the gate. The rest of the soldiers—including Carver and Barrett—remain ready.

Maybe the immersives won't come. Maybe Waters failed, and we won't have to do this at all. Guilt permeates me as I think of all the children Waters is using to fight his war. But they do come. Mourning shifts to awareness when tingling starts in my limbs.

Energy pushes against my chest, and the hairs on my arms stand. My world kicks into high speed, and, with a thud, the gates fly open. Like an electric ball of power, light surrounds me and knocks me back, slamming me onto the ground. I quickly scramble to my feet and grab for Ben's hand, pulling him upright.

Streaks of light hurtle past us and out the gate opening, Aron's drones are on the attack. Four additional golden orbs flank the two of us and project a dome of transparent light in front of our bodies.

"I gave you a shield," Aron's voice yells in my comm.

The pairs of drones follow every one of mine and Ben's moves. Protecting us.

"Pull back, soldiers!" I yell. "Let the enemy come, so we know what we're dealing with."

Our group steps back a few feet. Aron's drone army retreats backward as well, but while still targeting blasts to the sides of the opening, their shots echoing in my ears.

A buzzing tickle attacks my thoughts, throwing me off balance, disorienting me further when my surroundings change. Code falls around me in a blizzard. I can't make anything out.

Ms. Lark, President Waters speaks to my mind. I anticipated running into you.

I push him from my consciousness and the space resolidifies. I whip towards Ben. "Did you hear him?" I yell, looking toward the gate where the immersives still haven't entered.

"Hear who?" Ben has his hands raised, ready to fight.

"Waters, I heard him."

"You think *he's* immersive now?" Ben yells over the noise of drones.

I steel myself for what's to come. "No clue. But he was trying to get into my head."

"Report status," Cynthia says through my comm, breaking my thoughts.

"We don't know, yet," I yell. "We're still waiting."

But that doesn't last long. I click off my comm as the gates vibrate and glow, and I receive my first glimpse of the immersives. They're not fully formed like in the real world. Their human shapes are made up of code, almost iridescent. Their energy waves against me and pulses through my body, though diffused by my shield. I glance at Ben and he's planted firmly, teeth gritted.

Data scrolls across the bottom of my vision, and my brain evaluates the code, checking for weakness—and strengths. So far, twenty immersives have entered.

Odds of success: Unknown.

Well, *that's* comforting. Out of the corner of my eye, I see Meyer and two others flank me while shooting at the immersive army. The beams absorb into the environment before the blasts can hit any of the intended targets. Apparently, Waters' soldiers have a type of shielding too.

Avlyn, Waters' voice enters my head again, and my mind spins as I watch a swarm of Aron's micro drones fly forward. A wave of nausea ripples through me. *Why are you doing this? I don't have an interest in killing you. It would be so much easier if you would simply join me.*

I try to push out his thoughts, but he digs in farther.

You know this truce with Elore isn't going to work. Help me take over the DPF and defeat Manning, and I'll grant you and your friends sanctuary.

"You're a liar," I scream, and then force his thoughts from my head. The battle comes back full volume as our group advances to protect the mainframe's entry point.

Sanda flies past Ben and me, throwing a ball of light forward, and a blast of energy from the enemy blows her back, slamming her to the ground. A group of Aron's drones swarm to her front for added protection as she rises, shaking off the effect. And then she resumes her attack, her face full of grit.

Meyer leads several soldiers forward, but, as he does, the immersives come together and emit a bright light. When the light dims, the enemy group has doubled in size, and no longer in human form. Only a mass of energy and code remains. A deep rumble comes from the monstrosity and fear clenches my chest. The mass lurches forward. Ben and I throw our hands out and send energy toward the mass, holding the immersives steady.

In retaliation, a burst of lightning shoots from the mass' center and blasts several of our soldiers, including Barrett and Carver. They stumble to the ground and don't move. I wait, silently urging them up. And then I gasp, loud and full of terror. Their bodies disappear, and I have no idea if they're dead or only called back to the real world.

Focus, I command my mind, homing in on the immersives' code. In response, they draw back and grow brighter, doubling in size again. While the transformation happens, however, the code flickers, as if it's unstable.

And then it hits me. This is all a show. Waters had planted information that the immersives were children so we wouldn't fight back as hard, breaking us down until we revealed a weakness, and all so he could slip past and gain entry. These immersives are probably nothing more than a program he created.

"We need to stop trying to hold him off," I yell to Ben. "That's what Waters wants. He's hoping we will slip up. We need to join directly with the fake immersives and destroy them."

"But our orders are not to harm the immersives."

"I have the feeling they aren't real people. They're just a program."

"Are you sure?" Ben calls back to me.

I shake my head. "Not really, but this isn't working. Waters' goal is to tire us out and to discover weaknesses. We need to do what we do best."

"Offense," Ben says.

I nod and tap my comm. "I need you all to fall back. Ben and I are going in."

"No way," Meyer's voice returns. "Not with the enemy replicating like that."

"You have your orders, soldier." I twist around, and Meyer is racing toward my position. "Fall back!" I yell as a burst of energy emits from the immersive soldiers. In a flash, Aron tackles Meyer, and the light absorbs into Aron instead, throwing them both to the ground.

"No!" I scream.

Ben grabs my shoulder. "If we're doing this, it has to be now."

I tear my gaze from Meyer and Aron. At the center of the immersive group, the code flickers more. The older strings are breaking down. But, if they continue replacing dysfunctional code, the immersives have a chance to overpower us.

I nod and disable my shield. I wave the drone aside, slamming it to the ground. Ben does the same. We race full speed toward the core of the enemy's code. In front of us, the replication stops and the immersives change from iridescent to a glowing red. Their energy punches toward us, stinging every nerve ending in my body. But, I will the pain away as my brother and I both lean into the immersives, absorbing the intensity of energy they give off.

Nearly synchronized, Ben and I launch into the air, as if we can fly, and come down in the center of the code cluster. I throw out my hands. Ben mirrors my actions. And, despite our lack of mental connection, it's as if we know what the other will do before they do it.

I call out to the code in my mind, and, at first, it resists. I sense Waters trying to enter my mind again. My first instinct is to pull away. But something in me tells me not to. I open up and allow him.

I barely sense him begin to speak when I grab hold of his consciousness, silencing him, trapping him.

The code whirlwinds around Ben and as if it were air on fire. I reach for him and grasp his hand, holding on tight while willing the code's energy toward us.

Although I risk transferring the contaminate in Ben's body to me, I dig deep into myself and locate the mechanism that allows me to block Ben's thoughts from my mind. I throw away the mental guards and let my consciousness seep into his.

Immediately, Ben whips his attention to me. *Why are you in my head? You need to get out.*

"The Neuro-link shouldn't see me as an enemy anymore," I say. "We need to combine our ability to force Waters' program from the mainframe. We need a virus!"

Without another word, Ben's awareness floods into mine. Immediately, the two of us call up the immersive software code in our minds, making it appear. We form a virus and hold out our hands in front of us. Glowing white-hot, a ball of twisting code materializes in our palms. We throw our hands forward and slam our coded-weapon into the immersives.

The program's gleaming light of energy flickers and vanishes. But, as soon as it does, the remaining immersives rush us in a last-ditch attempt.

I plant my feet on the ground, standing back-to-back with Ben, and, in unison, we send our virus into their energy. Ravenous, our bug tears into them. Ben and I drop to our knees and throw out a shield to surround our bodies.

The false immersives let out a roar and, in an instant, they're gone.

Chapter Thirty-One

Silence fills the space as we all stand in shock.

"New Philly is retreating, Waters surrendered, and Sloan's team is closing in on the enemy," comes an unfamiliar voice in my ear. A chorus of cheers sounds from behind me and from the comm's background.

My heart leaps as I lean my hands down to my knees, panting.

My EP lights up.

Please remain immersed and repair any damaged code at the Neuro-link.

Meyer jogs up beside me and touches my back, his eyes wild with panic. "What happened to Aron?"

"He's not here?"

Meyer shakes his head. "He was still conscious and controlling the drones after taking a hit for me. I dragged him off to the side, but he vanished right before the explosion."

"Did you comm in to find out?" I ask, torn between the urge

to blink out of here and find him and knowing the Neuro-link's security is wide open.

"No one's answering."

I search for Sanda as several of our army blink out of existence. She stands about thirty feet away, obviously looking for Aron, her forehead tight with tension.

"Then go and take Sanda," I say. "Comm me as soon as you know something."

I go to Ben, sitting on the ground, his knees pulled up to his chest. He stares into the space where the gate once was.

"Are you okay?" I whisper, kneeling down next to him.

He looks up with a blank sheen to his eyes. "We did it, right?"

I nod, but not knowing what happened to Aron is killing me. I hold my hand out to him. He takes it, and I pull him up.

"We need to finish up in here and get back to reality," I say.

I start to call up the coding when words scroll across the bottom of my vision. My pulse picks up speed, worried the news is about Aron. But it's worse.

Emergency: The Neuro-link needs to be locked down. Stat. Manning turned.

My chest tightens. Energy courses through my body as the Neuro-link's coding changes. And I know what's going to happen. Manning has re-flipped the DPF and is going to kill everyone in Affinity.

I whirl toward Ben and open my mouth to speak. But, like a bird of prey, he's in the air, lunging straight for me. His frame plows into mine. Our bodies tangle and hit the ground. Pain shoots through my back and arm.

"Ben, stop!"

But he doesn't stop. When we relinked our minds, it must have destroyed the patch to his damaged system. Fire rages in his eyes as I struggle to free myself from his grasp. I loosen my right arm, tighten my fist, pull back, and punch him in the jaw. The blow barely fazes him. In a flash, his hands are around my neck. I choke and gasp for air as he squeezes.

I blink down hard to release myself from VR. Nothing happens. I reopen my eyes to silently plead with Ben as he works to kill me.

Then I understand—he's blocking me from leaving.

I grapple for his arms and try to kick him to get loose—it's futile. *Ben!* I scream to him in my mind. But I hit a black nothing. *You can't do this.*

He pulls me to my feet and forces me toward the Neuro-link's code.

"What are you doing?" I scream. My body seizes as we draw closer, as if something unseen wraps around my mind, tightening. Squeezing. Forcing foreign thoughts to trickle in.

I could use my ability for better gain.

What is Affinity? Nothing but a small band of people who are weak.

Ruiz and Waters could have used our ability for great power and what did they try to do, instead? Make peace? Look how that has turned out. It's a massive failure.

Direction wants what is best for the survival of the Elorian people. I must maintain my forward focus.

As the thoughts consume me, my body relaxes. *Yes, this feels right.* It's what has always been right. The darkness dissipates from my mind, and everything's so obvious now.

Avlyn? Ben thinks in my consciousness. You're with me. I sense it. Director Manning wants the best for us. We can help Elore and her people become stronger than ever. This is what we were born to do. I know it.

His voice drones as if he's in a trance. My mind spins. Something isn't right, but I love Ben. I trust him. And the words sound true. Why would he lie to me? Ben and I were born to make the world a better place. We are special.

Yes, Ben thinks to me. We are unique, and Direction values us. We must do what it takes to protect Elore.

Yes, I agree. Every ounce of my body means the words too. I've never been so sure about anything in my life.

Relaxation fills me, and I become aware of Ben releasing his grasp on my throat since I'm no longer a threat. The VR world solidifies around me again and Ben backs away.

"Come with me." Ben nods toward the Neuro-link.

I stand and reach for his grasp, but, using my free hand, I touch my neck where Ben's hands used to be. My fingers graze over the chain, slip down to the heart charm, and then, as if lightning struck, a flash of memories and feelings consumes my body and mind...

...Ben gifting the necklace to me when we were four. "Hide it," he whispers in his childish voice and thrusts the chain into my tiny hands.

...Meyer's smile the first time I met him.

... Lena twisting toward me, mouthing the words *go* as she and Jayson were captured by Guardians.

... Mother dying, and, with her last breath, letting me know she cared for me.

... Finding out Ben was alive.

... Meyer's lips on mine when I kissed him for the first time. His hands wrapping around the small of my back.

... Ruiz dying in the Thornton explosion... finding out Aron cares for Sanda... Kyra sacrificing herself for me...

These memories, intertwined with many others, rip through my mind and clear away the thoughts Ben had impressed upon me. I look at my twin, and a rainbow of emotions floods my senses. Yellow like sunshine, blue despair, red of passion, a deep orange of safety. I want it all. I never want to go back to before all these feelings and experiences were not allowed. And, no matter what, I can't let Manning continue to take from the people of Elore.

Ben lowers his chin and furrows his brow. He launches toward me, hands extended, his mind still controlled by the Neuro-link. I brace myself as he crashes into me. But, this time, I stand firm and grapple for his shoulders. Clenching my jaw, I focus all my emotional energy on him.

Ben bares his teeth at me. "I won't let you through," he growls.

"Love means everything to you, Ben. It's what allowed you to survive. It's what brought you back to me. You never lost hope of us finding each other. Your love saved me. It gave me a reason to fight and a reason to look beyond myself. I know you feel this way too. Fight Direction's control. I know you can."

I continue pushing every memory I can into his mind, but it's only met with equal resistance. Ben throws me off and I slam into the ground. But I don't stay down. Launching back to my feet, I tackle him, forcing both of our bodies into the Neuro-link's code.

"I will not let Manning take us!" I scream.

Everything turns silent, and Ben suddenly goes limp. My body and consciousness settle for a beat. Then a scintillating light of emotional energy from inside of me explodes. I direct the blast toward Ben and into the whole of the Neuro-link. White, hot light consumes everything.

The minds of hundreds—no, thousands—of voices join with mine. Mingling. Most of the DPF Level Ones are confused... scared. Some are angry. I invoke the thought of a deep sigh and tell them it's okay. They're free now. Manning can't harm them again, not the way he did before. I also show them what freedom is. That now all they have to do is reach out and take it.

"Cynthia Fisher will help you. Trust her. Trust Affinity."

Happiness warms me and the voices quiet until they're gone. I gasp and fall to my knees.

Everything is gone.

"Ben, you need to go," I whisper, and, gathering the little strength I have left, I cast his mind from my presence.

The second he leaves, the explosion I created reverses, like a vacuum, and collides into my body, absorbing me. I look down and watch as my body dissipates. I shimmer and break into code and then wisp away, starting at my feet and moving up. But, something about this destruction feels peaceful. Feels right. As if the world will be okay, even without me.

I smile, close my eyes, and let my body disperse.

Lose your life, and you will find it, I think to myself.

It was all worth it.

I let go.

CHAPTER THIRTY-TWO

"Avlyn... Avlyn..." a muffled voice meets my ears.

I open my eyelids to a blurry scene and blink several times to clear my vision, noting a sterile room with white walls. I can only guess that I'm in a med facility. My hand is connected to tubing, which leads to a bag of clear liquid hanging on a metal hook. Ben's grinning face is over mine. With a laugh, he grabs for my shoulders and wraps his arms around me, pulling me up from my lying down position. "We didn't know if you were going to wake up."

"Wait," I say. "I was dead."

Ben carefully releases me. "You pretty much were, but your nanos kept trying to heal you. Your body wanted to give up, which made the tech only work harder. Nobody has seen anything like it before. It was like your nanos were alive and wanted to keep you that way, too."

My breath hitches and I sit up on my own. "Wait, are you okay?" My mind reels, thinking about the battle. "What about

Aron?"

"Whatever you did destroyed the effect of the food ink contaminate in my system. It's completely gone," Ben says.

My heart races at what he hasn't said. "Is Aron alive?"

Ben nods slowly. "He's still in a coma, Avlyn. That blast from the immersive program did a number on him. Luckily, one of the medics put him into immediate stasis when he released. If Meyer wasn't here looking after you, he was checking up on Aron. That's where both he and Sanda are now."

Tears sting at the corners of my eyes. "But he *is* going to live, right?"

"The medics think so, but his entire nervous system was damaged. His nanotech tried to repair the injuries too quickly and his whole body went into shock. It could take months before he's even close to normal, even after waking him. The medics are also concerned about permanent memory loss."

Relief fills my chest that he's alive.

What about Barrett and Carver?

Sadness washes over Ben's face. Barrett's fine. Carver didn't make it. The blast hit him too hard.

Guilt tightens my chest. "I want to see Aron." I try to push up, but Ben stretches out his hand and clasps my shoulder.

"Soon. We need the medic to okay it."

I scowl at him.

" And your complete merger with the Neuro-link also permanently flipped all of the DPF. So, Thompson woke up and is okay, too," he says, ignoring my displeasure and probably trying to distract me. "You neutralized their kill switch functions. When the soldiers realized what was happening, they turned around and stormed Direction Headquarters."

"They captured Manning?"

Ben looks down. "I guess he decided he didn't want to live, if he couldn't be the leader."

I don't even know what to say to those words. Part of me is glad he's dead, but the other part wishes he could've seen the light too.

"Manning was our grandfather," I admit.

Ben nods his head. "Cynthia told me a few days ago. Affinity is in charge of Elore now and helping the citizens transition."

"A few days ago? How long have I been unconscious?"

"Five."

Five *days?* I think to Ben, sitting all the way up. But he doesn't answer. In fact, I get nothing from him. "Why are you still blocking me?"

Ben looks down and away. "That's the bad news of this whole thing."

"What are you talking about?" Panic burns in my chest.

"It's gone," he whispers.

"What's gone?"

"Everything. Our mind connection. The ability. It's over."

I wildly scan around the room and find there's a Flexx on the table beside my bed. I snatch it and try to immerse. But nothing happens.

"Avlyn, it's gone. All of it."

I look up at him, tears pricking the back of my eyes. And I know it's all true.

"It can't be gone! We were going to stop Direction and Waters and then we would find our connection again. That's what we agreed on. We were special. It made us special." Tears now stream down my face and I don't even try to stop them.

Ben exhales through his nose and shakes his head. "Avlyn, this ability was never what made you special. Your willingness to give up everything for the people you loved, the people you knew deserved better, *that* made you special. Immersing allowed you to accomplish that." He reaches out and gently takes the device and places it on the table again. "Our ability served its purpose."

I lean back onto my pillow and look away from him at the wall. "So, I just have to be me now?" I ask, not entirely sure how that makes me feel.

❖ ❖ ❖

"What are you going to do today?" I ask.

Sanda shrugs. "Aron has an appointment for rehabilitation later, but I noticed a few cafes are open."

"Are they serving fresh food, yet?"

"No," she says. "It's not real food, but I'm tired of food bars. But I thought he and I might stop by a cafe for lunch."

I smile at her. "You mean like an appointment for a pairing contract."

She laughs and waves me off. "I mean a date, Avlyn. I like Aron." She pauses to think for a beat. "I like him a lot. But I feel like I'm a little young for a pairing. I want to get to know the guy when we don't have to worry about getting killed or killing anyone. I think I'm also just starting to process that my parents aren't coming back. Meyer and I had a long talk last night."

I stare at her for a few seconds, not knowing what to say.

"How about you?" she asks.

"I have a promise to keep, a debt to repay."

"A debt?" She raises her eyebrow. "Don't you think you paid any debt you might owe?"

"Not exactly." I grab my bag off the sofa and head for the door of our apartment in Level One—the place we've stayed at for the past three weeks. Cynthia offered us an apartment in Level Three, but, for some reason, I felt more comfortable over the thought of a Level One unit. Closer to Bess. Closer to Devan. Closer to the place I came from. I feel like I'm digging up buried treasure by being here. It's a dirty job but satisfying.

Bess still hasn't arrived in Elore, but I've spoken to her several times on a personal vid. I'm not sure if Michael will come back. He hasn't expressed interest, but at least I've talked with him twice as well.

I reach out and turn the ancient looking door handle; I'm still not entirely used to these old-style doors.

"Have fun today," I call over my shoulder, pausing to study Sanda's beautiful, sepia-colored skin and the way her smile lights up against it. In the back of my mind is the far-off memory of the first time I saw her, when she had graffitied the side of a building to warn the people of Elore. She smiled at me that day, too, probably never being able to imagine the event would somehow lead us to today. To being nearly sisters.

"Bye, Corra," I yell and hear her groan from the bedroom. Corra has changed. I would never have pegged her for someone who'd sleep until nearly noon every day. But I guess when you stop trying to prove you're someone you're not, your habits change. I'm sure a little rest never hurt anyone, though, so I haven't given her a hard time.

I flick my attention back to Sanda. "Don't let her sleep all day."

"I'll try not to." She laughs.

I leave the unit and walk next door to where Meyer, Ben, and Aron are staying. It was one thing for the girls and me to share an apartment, but the guys deciding to stay together by choice was a bit of a shock. They all keep saying it's a temporary arrangement, and, in the end, it probably will be. But, I've watched how they've settled into a routine with each other. We all share a bond I'm not sure will ever really break.

I place my hand on the visitor alert when thumping footfalls near the door. It slides back, and Ben's smiling face greets me.

"He's almost ready," he says as I enter.

I scan the room and find a few pieces of clothing scattered about and dirty dishes stacked on the table and piled beside the couch's closest side.

"You should clean up in here," I say.

"You sound like Aron," Ben chuckles.

"Well, I think Aron is right."

Ben waves his hand in my direction, dismissing me, just as Meyer walks from his room, followed by the pet drone Aron had gifted him. Meyer's hair is still wet and disheveled, and he wears a fresh, long-sleeved white shirt and a pair of blue pants. What did he call them again? Jeans, I think. We never had those in Elore before. But things are already changing. I even saw a food cart the other day while on one of my walks through the city. Maybe they have burritos and I can make up for the one Meyer lost in New Philadelphia. I make a mental note to try to swing by that spot on the way home this afternoon.

Meyer smiles widely when he sees me, and internally I melt just a little bit, forgetting all about the mess in the living room.

"You sure you want me to go?" Meyer asks.

I nod. "This is a promise I've carried, and I want someone I love to be with me when I fulfill it."

"Then, let's get to it," he says, pulling on a dark puffy jacket and stretching a hat over his head.

"Good luck," Ben says from the kitchen.

Part of me longs for the ability and connection we shared before. But, I'm starting to consider our mental telepathy as a gift we were given for a while. A gift that brought our family back together. A gift that helped bring peace to Elore, New Philadelphia, and the Outerbounds. A gift that saved both of our lives. Ben and I experienced something no one else had, even if it was only for a short amount of time. I'm grateful and look forward to just being brother and sister. Being normal—whatever normal is.

"Thanks," I call back. I'm pretty sure I don't need any luck in this situation, but nervousness still flutters in my stomach.

"You have the package, right?" Ben calls.

I pat at the right pocket of my coat and feel the crinkly paper. "Yes."

As we walk to the door, Meyer's drone follows us.

"You need to stay here," Meyer turns and addresses the bot.

The poor little thing makes a disappointed whine and floats back to Meyer's room.

I chuckle and turn the handle on the door. "Let's go."

Minutes later, Meyer and I find ourselves on the street below.

"Auto taxi or walk?" Meyer asks as he peers toward the sidewalk. There are noticeably more groups of citizens out and about than before, some chatting quietly, others are more animated despite the cold air and sprinkling of snow on the ground. Some still stare at handhelds, however, probably not knowing what else to do.

I pull my coat in tight to my body, and the fabric does a sufficient job of staying the chill. "Walk. It's not very far," I answer, looking up at the sky. Once again, the spectacular dance of bustling drones amazes me as they zip to and fro, loaded with deliveries or on their way to help with rebuilding efforts. No longer do the SI feel like jailors. Elorians are free to leave the city if they wish now. Although, most have stayed. Elore is their home.

Cynthia's face flickers on the gigantic media screen attached to a building up ahead. Her graying hair is combed straight, and her expression is serious, though tempered by kindness. My grandmother cares for these people and has stepped up to a position of power she never intended to have again. I find it suits her.

"The Elorian council will be meeting with New Philadelphia under the temporary leadership of Dr. Lennon Sloan," Cynthia says.

The screen flips to another scene of Sloan appearing tense, undeniably uncomfortable, and surrounded by unfamiliar people. I'm sure he wishes all this could take place in VR, but, unfortunately for him, not all of it can. Words scroll across the bottom of the vid.

Waters is awaiting trial and Sloan signs peace treaty with Elore. Talks of reconciliation between New Philadelphia and Elore continue.

Part of me still wonders if I could've lived with myself had my instinct proved wrong and Waters immersive army—the one Ben and I had attacked and destroyed— was truly made up of children. But, since it was a program, I guess I never really have to confront the shame or grief. Sloan had evidence for the immersion program entirely wiped out, as well as the research notes for using weaponized tech on children. I hope no one will ever attempt to dig that up again. Cynthia also had all the modified EPs and all of Aron's research destroyed.

My grandmother's face overtakes the screen again, and, as I stare at her, she begins to speak. But I don't hear what she says until she gets to the words, "Thank you for the part you all are playing in creating The Unity of States. With your help, we will choose a *new* direction. One where we are all equal, all free."

The screen goes dark and I return my attention to Meyer. I wait a beat for the Direction logo I knew for so long to appear and, thankfully, it never does.

On the way, we pass by the park where he and I first really met, and I reach for his hand as we explore the streets of what used to be Level One. I'm sure it will take some time for citizens not to think of it as that way anymore. With Intelligence Potential now outlawed, and corporations experiencing breakdown and restructuring, positions are open to anyone. It's not a perfect system as most of the Level Ones need new training, but we have to start somewhere.

A few more blocks and we arrive at a simple brown, brick building, standing five floors high. There should be nothing intimidating or unique about this place. But the nervousness in my stomach returns.

"You sure you want to do this today?" Meyer asks.

"I told them I was coming." We enter the building's front and a sign directs us toward the stairs. Three floors up, we exit into a corridor.

"Three hundred twenty-one," I say and find the correct unit. I stand silently, hoping this meeting proves a positive one. Letting out a slow breath, I press my finger to the visitor's alert and look up to Meyer.

"No turning back," I say.

Meyer slips his hand around my waist. "I love a girl who sets her mind to something and does it."

I smile and lean into him.

Click.

The door cracks open and a woman with shoulder-length, light blonde hair stands in front of us. My breath hitches at the sight of her. She looks so much like a vision of the woman who, so long ago on the streets of Level One, tried to protect her child from losing both of his parents to the DPF draft.

"Good morning," the woman says, interrupting my thoughts.

"Please come in." She smiles and opens the door wider so we can enter into her modest apartment.

She gestures us to the sofa and Meyer and I take a seat.

"I'm Rae, Naomi's older sister." Rae holds out her hand, and we each take turns shaking it. "Naomi and I only met a few times, but I feel as if I've gotten to know her through Ethan. She and Liam would have loved what was happening in Elore now. I'm sad they don't get the chance to see it."

Liam was Jensen's first name. Memories of his sacrifice at Gabrielle's to help Ben whirl through my mind. I open my mouth to speak, to tell Rae I'm so sorry that I couldn't save her nephew's parents, but she speaks first.

"I'll get Ethan," she says, and disappears into one of the bedrooms.

A moment later, she reappears with a small boy, around age seven.

Relief floods me at the sight of him. Of course, I knew he was still alive. But seeing him in person makes the whole situation more real for me.

Ethan stands close to his aunt's leg, not moving toward us.

I rise, leaving Meyer on the couch, and slip my hand into my coat pocket, feeling for the package Bess had delivered to Ben. Both she and Ben agreed this was the place it belonged, and all of us wanted to give a gift—one that meant something special to our family—to a boy who has endured so much.

I pull the present out, clutching the object in my palm. I slowly walk to the boy and kneel to be at his eye level and present the package. At first, he doesn't move. But, eventually, he reaches out and takes the offered gift. He methodically yanks and tugs at the strips of adhesive sealing the wrap, and then pulls out the small stuffed rabbit.

Ben's rabbit.

"It's not much," I whisper. "But my family and I wanted to give you a gift."

Ethan nods and hands his aunt the wrapping paper while clutching the rabbit to his chest. Once his aunt takes the paper, he holds his hand out to me and I take it.

"I'm Ethan," he says.

"Yes. I met your parents, and I wanted you to know how courageous they were. If it wasn't for your father's love for you, I'm not sure my brother Ben or I would be alive today. I'm not sure if any of us would be, actually."

Ethan's lips stretch into a sad smile.

"Would you like to hear more about why?" I ask.

He nods, and I gesture for both him and his aunt to sit.

Then I tell them the story of how it wasn't Intelligence Potential or extraordinary abilities that changed the world.

In the end, it was love that had saved us all.

Epilogue

I close my eyes as long blades of grass dance around my ankles in a gentle breeze. Occasionally, a small part of me misses the ability I had for a while; But, on days like this, I never do. Being completely human again is comforting. Real.

Somewhere off behind me, a high-pitched sound of bird calls echo on the wind. The earthy scent in the air fills my lungs and awakens my senses. I'm glad I notice these sensations. I notice a lot of things these days, more than I used to.

A soft cry comes from my arms, and I open my eyes and glance down. I pull the blanket swaddled around my newborn infant just a little tighter.

"Shh, shh," I soothe. "I know, I'm a little nervous too." But it's not exactly true. The feelings inside of me are indescribable. I think it's a mix of sadness, anger, and happiness, even though that sounds strange. But all those emotions are there, twisting and turning into one, and I've learned its okay.

I sigh and walk toward marked stones in the earth.

Two memorials sit a few feet apart from each other, and my gaze caresses the names inscribed on each stone.

Kyra Lewis

Darlene Lark

Neither are buried beneath the stones. My mother's body was never recovered after my escape from Elore. And Kyra? Her body was cremated, per custom. But I couldn't stand to completely let them go, and so a few years ago I decided to build a memorial on our land to honor both women. I've made plans to add one for Lena in a few months, too.

Neither Meyer nor I wanted to live in the city after everything. So, Cynthia arranged for us to take ownership of twenty acres outside the city. I've discovered how having a grandmother who helps run the country makes it far easier to achieve requests like owning land.

I touch my fingertips to my friend's carved name.

Not everyone sees Kyra as a hero, but, in my heart, she'll always be. Life takes us down roads we don't always want to travel, and that's what happened to her. In the end, however, her heart was pure, just like I had always known. She had saved me. I owe her my respect, my love. She was my friend.

"Mother?" I turn my attention to the other stone. I don't cry anymore when I talk to her. For a while there, that's all I did. Our relationship was cut much too short. Growing up, I wanted Mother and Father to be proud of me. To deem me a good citizen. Only in that final moment with her— when she died in the tunnel—did I understand that she was proud of me and always had been. She even loved me in her own way. It's all I have of her now, so I must believe it's true.

"Father's well," I share with her. "He just received a promotion with the New City Project's tech team. The project was the latest decision made by the Unity of States Council. The people of Elore, New Philly, and all small-scattered cities in the Outerbounds voted to build a brand-new city in-between the larger two. Kind of a fresh start for those who feel as if they fit in neither. Father is living on location now."

My child stirs again in my arms. I look down as her eyelids open, revealing her hazel eyes. The sight of them quirks my lips into a smile. I rock my body back and forth to calm her. Her lids shut again as she drifts off into sleep.

"Meyer and I just celebrated our third year of being paired. I still can't believe I found someone like him. I'm not sure how you felt about Father. But I hope you loved him. Because love is a gift. And, just like life," I say, softly, "it can be both broken and beautiful. I try every day to make life as beautiful as possible, like you asked me to."

Tears sting at the corners of my eyes and I draw in a breath to stay them. Maybe I do still cry out here sometimes.

"Bess moved out of Elore and is living a few miles from us now. I think you might be happy with her grandmothering skills already. She says that she'll do her best to spoil your grandchild for the both of you."

A hand grazes my arm, and I turn toward the most handsome face I know. Meyer grins at me. Then, he pulls up the cuff of his sleeve, revealing his antique watch, and examines the time. "Are you ready? We're meeting Ben soon, and we don't want to be late for Sanda and Aron's pairing contract signing."

"Did Corra say she was coming? I know she's busy," I ask.

"Yeah, she's bringing someone she wants us to meet. I was going to tell you about it on the way."

I nod. I'll be glad to see Corra. It's been a while. "Okay. Can you give me a minute more?"

Meyer smiles widely, and the sight of it makes me melt. I hope the feeling never stops—even in fifty years. He reaches out and runs his fingers gently over our child's head and then grazes my cheek. "Did you tell them the name, yet?"

I look down and then back up to him. "No, I was getting there."

"I'll wait back at the pod." Meyer kisses my cheek and then gives me the space I need for this. I turn, and a feeling of tremendous calm overtakes me.

"I have to go soon, but I wanted both of you to meet my daughter."

I tip my baby just forward and hold her out for them to "see."

Her pale complexion is set against a mop of dark hair and I'm not sure if she takes after Meyer or me most. I often wonder as she grows if she'll develop a spray of freckles that seems to run in my family. And, to be honest, I hope she does.

A gentle breeze skips by and I watch my daughter's dark hair flutter, and I smile.

The people in my life transformed me. I know who I am now and because of it, there was only one possible name.

A gift.

An invocation.

"Meet my daughter. Her name is Joy."

Dear Book Lover,

Thank you so much for your support. I am truly humbled. I would be incredibly grateful if you took the time to leave a review on Amazon. Short or long is JUST fine. Your review will make a big difference and help new readers discover The Configured Trilogy.

I would also love it if you joined my book club at JenettaPenner.com. When you do you will receive a FREE printable Configured YA coloring book, as well as news on my newest releases. You can also follow me on Facebook, Amazon and Twitter.

XXOO,
Jenetta Penner

FINAL THANKS

In January of 2015, I closed my bedroom door and, in secret, handwrote Avlyn's first words. Pretty much from that moment I knew her journey's last words. I knew they would take her full circle into becoming a whole person. A person who knew love fully and accepted herself for the individual she was, flaws and all.

To be honest, I can hardly believe that I've finished the *Configured* series. It's been a long road of learning, pain, joy, and tears. But I couldn't be more thrilled to share Avlyn's entire story with you.

And on to the thanks:

Thank you to every single one of my readers. You are amazing! And an extra big round of applause goes to my ARC readers. You are all the best!

To my husband Jon and my girls, Ohana and Lynn (who's probably read "Configured" five times), thank you for supporting me.

Thank you to my friends and family who have read the books

and encouraged me.

Thank you to my editors Chase Night and Jesikah Sundin, who made "Actualized" so much better and kicked my butt a few times.

Thank you to my author BFFs David R. Bernstein and S.L. Morgan #CatGifsForever.

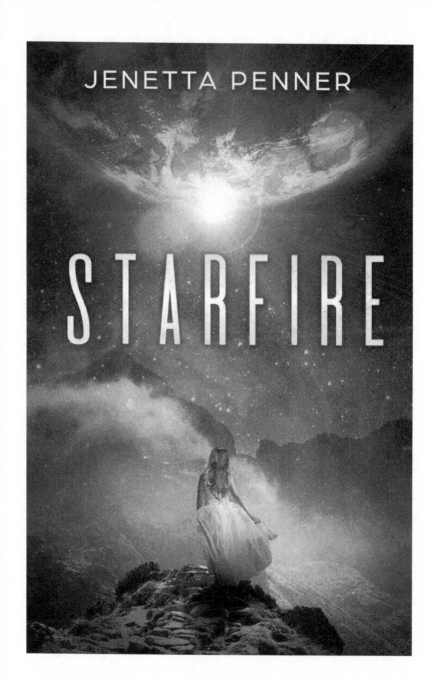

STARFIRE SNEAK PEEK

JENETTA PENNER

Chapter One

My father named me after the stars. But I've always preferred to keep my feet on the ground.

Ironically, I'm hurtling through space in a gigantic starship twenty-million light years from Earth. The only life I have ever known was there—school, my friends . . . Mom. This journey was Mom and Dad's dream, not mine, and she's the one we left behind.

I fumble for the simple gold band, encircling my right ring finger, and twist it. Now all I have left of her after she died is this simple piece of jewelry.

I'd rather have her.

The muscles in my stomach tighten and I exhale loudly. I glance at a glass computer panel, which displays a glowing image of Arcadia—the new Earth—our destination. It pretty much looks like old Earth but the continents are all mixed up, and it boasts two moons. For some reason the atmosphere of this planet also glows a strange shade of cyan. I'm told that, on the occasional night, the atmosphere creates amazing patterns like the aurora borealis.

Ten years ago it was Isabel Foster, my mom who discovered how the atmosphere was similar to Earth. My parents had worked tirelessly with the World Senate to streamline Arcadia's settlement. It'll be fifty years, at least, before the first permanent international colony will set foot onto this planet, my parents were told repeatedly. Yet, we'll temporarily disembark at the Sky Base orbiting above Arcadia in less than eight hours.

Without Mom here Dad's moods are mixed, but most days he's still excited. Though, once our starship voyaged out of the Turner Space Fold, I've barely seen him so I wouldn't know his mood today. To ensure safety, the captain programmed our exit point for a seven-day lightspeed journey to new Earth. Since we dropped from the fold, Dad has been too busy making all the preparations, or meeting with people I don't know or care about. I guess when you're the man who envisioned every aspect of how humans will live on Arcadia, people seem to think you're important or something.

His importance is evident by the cabin we were assigned, consisting of two good sized rooms plus a small office for Dad. There's even a little eat-in kitchen with a set of barstools at the counter and a living room. The refrigerator is stocked with food and, if the supplies start to dwindle, a cute delivery guy shows up to replace the missing items.

Most of the people down below are lucky to receive a bunk and a nutritional food pack for the day. Ninety percent of these individuals won a lottery ticket to the planet. But, the privilege also entitles them to a lifetime of indentured servitude on our new

"Eden." I doubt many will ever repay the incurred debt just from the journey's ticket price. Arcadia needs willing workers, however, and most had lived in slums and were starving while on Earth so they probably won't mind being indentured.

The remaining voyagers bought their way onboard. They're the types who typically have piles of money to spend, and no doubt bored with Earth too. Coming to a new world was hyped up as the chance of a lifetime and, if you have the cash to blow, why not blow it on building a new colony?

Princes and paupers. Not many passengers in-between.

I return my attention to my Earthscape lesson. Apparently, in my distraction, my entire simulated society suffocated from a lack of oxygen in their domed city, the result of poor planning on my part. I sigh and tap off the program. When both of your parents specialized in terraforming new planets, the expectation is that you'll do the same especially when you began to understand the concepts before you were five. When I want to focus I do have a knack, but not the passion. I'm only seventeen, why do I need to know what I'm going to do with the rest of my life? Maybe I want to be a painter. Don't need to travel across the galaxy to make that dream a reality and Mom never pushed me.

I stand, brushing my wavy, strawberry blonde hair out of my eyes, and go over to the nightstand beside my twin bed to search for a clip. Mom's jewelry-making tools—colorful beads and glistening gems and an array of metal fasteners—cover the surface. She was in the middle of teaching me her hobby when… we ran out of time. We did fashion a few pieces together though, and I even managed to partially cobble together a ruby tie tack on my own. After it's done, I plan to give it to Dad when we reach Arcadia. I might not be excited, but he is, and I love him.

I pick up a sapphire clip Mom made and affix it to the right side of my hair. Then I grab my green sweater hanging across the chair's back and then run my arms through the sleeves. This particular shade of green—a deep emerald—not only matches my eyes, it's also my favorite color. Fashion and matching eye color aside, there's an odd draft that always seems to be present in the corridors. I'm not sure the mystery breeze is a good thing, but the colonization site on Arcadia tends to lean toward tropical. I'll never be cold again.

Exiting my room, I amble through the silence of our unit. Once I enter the living area, I stop momentarily to stare at the blur of stars outside of our window. The blackness streaked with white light made by our forward motion takes me farther away from mom and everything I left behind. With a gulp, I resume my pace to the door and tap my hand on the release. The door whooshes back and reveals a brightly lit hall.

I step from the unit and glance back at the door. To the side is a bronze placard.

Richard Foster
Cassiopeia Foster

The names are listed as if we were some sort of movie stars or something. It's weird. No one else on our wing has names on their doors, only unit numbers. I shake my head and veer to my left, towards Dad's dedicated workspace. Maybe he has a few minutes for us to grab lunch and talk about tonight's gala planned for after our Skybase arrival. The party's a good distraction, and I'm sure he needs a break too.

Halfway there, I check the time on my Connect: 11:17 AM. I exhale in frustration. I know Dad, he'll be engrossed in some project until closer to noon. My best odds for pulling him away are to waste the next twenty-five minutes, so I take a right toward the atrium wing. The space is quiet, and the crowded plants spark memories of family trips we used to take to visit Grandma, who lived out in the country.

The five-minute stroll and elevator ride a few floors up is worth every second spent. My shoulders relax a notch as I stroll through the gigantic, nearly park-like setting. I scan the space for any other people, but there's no one. It seems like everyone else is working all the time. Looking up, I watch as simulated white, puffy clouds float across an equally simulated blue sky. Around me, buzzing worker drones—roughly the size of pigeons—tend to trees heavy laden with fruits of all kinds. The bots pollinate, prune, and dispose of dead leaves and any overripe produce. If I squint hard at their white, pearly bodies, I can pretend they're real birds, as if I'm outside, instead of inside an artificial atrium. Even the soothing sounds of a rolling breeze and the chirping insects are fake. Not that the pigeon drones would allow any insects into their perfect orchard.

I approach a tree and reach for a blushing apple. With a snap, I pluck it from the tree limb. I rotate the apple in my hands and study the impeccable skin before biting into the crispy flesh. Tart and sweet, the juice floods my taste buds. Pink Lady, my favorite. Then I grab a second and tuck it into the pocket of my sweater for Dad. They're his favorite too.

Slowly, I take my time perusing the trees and manicured gardens, hard pressed to spot one blemish. But, with the lack of foot traffic, I'm not even sure why the ship is equipped with an atrium. Our journey is only the week and everyone is working eighteen-hour shifts. Work, eat, sleep. Rinse and repeat. No time for nature.

With a sigh, I toss the core in my hand to the ground. The second it hits the grass, a drone buzzes in and gobbles the apple into its belly's trash compartment where the organic components will break down into usable compost. In real life, I'd never litter. But it's entertaining to watch the hungry pigeons. Even if they're not real birds.

I glance at my Connect again. This clear device accomplishes quite a bit for a small piece of tech. If I tap the face and interactive holograph will appear I can use to relay communication or as a computer. But, mostly, I use it for a watch. 11:38 AM. Close enough and it will take me a few minutes to get to Dad, anyway.

I exit the atrium and pass a few unfamiliar, busy looking faces along my way to meet Dad. Everyone holds such serious expressions. You'd think there would be more excitement. I hope that once we arrive at Arcadia, people will receive much-needed down time to enjoy their new lives. But, I have the feeling none of that will happen.

I chew the inside of my lip as the elevator rolls up, releasing my lip when the doors slide open at deck twenty five. From my vantage point, I spot Dad wearing a tan jacket and hustling down the corridor and away from me. He always complains about the mysterious draft on the ship too. Even though no one else seems to notice the breeze. I open my mouth to call out to him, then quickly snap it shut when realizing he's too far away and I would have to yell to get his attention. Shouting is something the snooty people in charge look down on around here. As I step out of the elevator, my father makes a left down a wing I haven't visited. Then a group of sharply dressed people I don't know come into view, following him.

I tap my Connect and bring up a hologram of his itinerary. No, he doesn't have a conference scheduled until 3:00 PM. And Dad is a stickler for schedules. Maybe those fancy-attired people aren't even with him.

My stomach grumbles, ready for a more significant meal than an apple. I glance around for any signs that the wing is off limits, but there are none, so I head in the direction he took. I turn the corner just as the last of the group behind him files into an unmarked conference room. As the door slides shut I hear Dad's angry voice rumbles through a nearby wall. Just my luck, he *is* in there.

Defeated, I decide to retreat and spend lunch in solitude. Typical. But the door makes a scraping sound on the track and then grunts when it sticks about a half inch open. Once more, Dad's voice, thick with negative energy, pipes from the narrow opening. Grumbles from voices I don't recognize step over whatever it is he's saying.

I shrug and look around again. No one is here and I've got nothing better to do, so I might as well be a little bit nosey. What can the Board do to me? I'll just confess that I was here for lunch and looking for my father. Which is true. A slap on the wrist is the worst they'll dole out.

I creep toward the door and position my ear as close as I can without being noticed. As an only child growing up, I had many opportunities to sneak around and listen to grown-up conversations I wasn't really supposed to hear. I always felt guilty, but I never could stand being out of the loop.

"You can't let *her* get away with it," Dad pleads.

Grumbles and several voices meld together through the crack in the door, and I lean my ear in closer to discover just who *her* might be and what exactly it is that she can't get away with.

The clop of heavy boots on cement echoes from around the corner and my breath hitches. I scan my surroundings and dash for the nearest escape. Luckily, ten-feet away, a short hallway connects a grouping of offices. On my toes, I dash for the safety of the hall. Just as I round the corner, a woman's frame comes into view.

I let out a breath, knowing she didn't see me, and then squat to peek from my hiding spot.

Oh—*her*. Elizabeth Hammond. Mid-sixties, with dyed white blonde hair and a scowl as a permanent accessory. The President of the Board . . . and my Dad's archenemy. I should have known from the disdain in his voice. The woman has spent her career mostly objecting to my father's ideas. He's always had innovative concepts, and the Board is conservative, especially Hammond. She's a rule follower to the core.

Oil and water.

She slams her hand to activate the door and it slides back with a scrape. I grit my teeth from the sound and the hairs on the back of my neck stand on end. Hammond doesn't flinch. And, instead of entering, she stands in the opening. The conversation inside goes silent.

"Dr. Foster, I am unclear why I was not invited to this meeting," Hammond says, her voice thick with venom.

"President Hammond," Dad finally speaks up.

His voice is strong, but I know him well enough to pick out a tinge of fear. He's using the same tone he had when he told me a year ago that Mom had been killed in a vehicle accident. I'll never forget every minute detail of the moment Dad telling me Mom will never be coming home again. It changed me and I stuffed it away as much as I could. Then something simple like the manner of someone's voice rushes it all back.

"You are not unaware of our . . . difference of opinion on this issue," Dad continues. "And by the look on your face, I get the impression that inviting you here would have been fruitless."

My pulse races in my ears. Everything in me wants to run to my dad and tell him everything is going to be okay. But doing that would get us both in trouble.

Hammond crosses her arms over her chest and throws her weight to her right side. "Then it's fruitless for you to have the meeting in the first place. No decisions are made without my consent—"

"But these people have information I hadn't even considered," he says. "I needed to hear them out and compile the data. Any repercussions will emerge on the Earthscape program. When you see it, you might change your mind."

"I don't need the data," Hammond growls. "I have all I

require to make the best choice for the people." With that, she spins toward the door and marches out with weighty boot steps.

Before the door scrapes shut I hear my father sigh. "Not *all* of the people."

CHAPTER TWO

I smooth out the skirt's pale pink silk on the full-length formal dress I chose for the Arrival Gala. In only a short while, we'll drop from light speed and Arcadia will come into view. I'm sure there will be plenty of "oohs" and "aahs" from the party goers, but I've pretty much stared at Acadia every day for the last ten years. I know this planet like the back of my hand.

I glimpse myself in the mirror fastened to the back of my bedroom's door. Tilting my head, I push away a fallen tendril of hair, loosened from a very amateur chignon over my left ear. Mom was always better at hair than me.

"This will have to do," I mumble, and I adjust the thin dress straps on my shoulders. Everyone will be looking at Dad anyway unless I do something stupid like slurp my soup too loudly or take a tumble down the stairs.

A tumble? Perfect reason to wear flats instead of pumps. Much safer. I spot the silver pair of ballerina flats in my closet, grab the shoes and shove my feet in.

Outside my room, I hear Dad groan a few curses. The sound makes my stomach clench. He only swears when he's under extreme stress. Whatever happened today with President Hammond plus Mom's absence has to be weighing heavy on his heart. And there's little I can do about it.

No. I can do *something*. I reach for a small box that I wrapped in a red bow. I didn't get to enjoy lunch with Dad today, so I spent the afternoon completing the tie tack for him.

Clutching the gift in my hand, I exit my room.

"Dad? Everything okay?" I call out.

"Uh . . . fine," he answers from the living room. I smile at the familiar sound of his deep voice, one I've always thought was kind. "I just can't get this tie knotted right."

As I walk into the living room, our eyes connect in the mirror hung over the sofa as he stares at his reflection. Unable to stop myself, I chuckle. One end of his tie hangs down about six inches too far and the other end six inches too short.

"Let me help you with that," I say as I lay my gift on the side table. I'm not good with hair, but I can knot a tie.

"Thanks, sweetie. Where would I be without you?" Dad wears a sheepish look on his face as he unwraps the tie from around his neck.

"Where would we be without each other?" I take the strip of blue fabric from his hand. "We're a team."

Dad smiles and his green eyes twinkle. His eye color is about the only physical feature I inherited from him, everything else was from Mom's DNA. He's 6'2", I'm barely 5'4" and, before his hair went nearly gray, it was chocolate brown unlike Mom's and my strawberry blonde tresses.

"Team Foster," he says.

"Forever. Now hold still so I can do this right."

He obeys, allowing me to run the tie around his neck. I make quick work at my specialty, a Windsor Knot.

When I'm done, he checks himself in the mirror and straightens his charcoal-gray suit coat.

"There, now," I say and look him over. "Almost ready."

He peers down at himself. "Almost? I don't think I can handle much more."

I smile and grab my red-bowed package. "I have a gift for you."

"A gift?"

"Yes, open it." I hold out the box and present it to him.

He takes it, slowly unties the red ribbon, and then removes the paper. Before he opens the lid, his lips pull into a smile. "You didn't have to do this."

"Dad," I scoff. "The last ten years of your life is being realized tonight. Arrival is an important occasion."

"But it's not as if *you* want to be here."

"Well, I am." I smile. "Now open it."

He pries open the top and reveals the bright, ruby tie tack inside. "Wow," he says grinning from ear to ear. But as quickly as it came, the smile drops from his face, and he turns and plops onto the sofa.

My heart plummets into my stomach. "You don't like it?"

Dad rubs his free hand over his face. "I love it. But tonight is not what I intended it to be."

"You mean Mom?" I carefully sit next to him and straighten

my skirt. My heart aches for her to be here with us too.

He nods. "Yes, but there's so much more than even that."

He's referring to that horrible conference this afternoon, but I can't breathe a word that I know about it.

Dad straightens and looks me straight in the eyes. "Cassi, if I teach you one thing in this life, let it be this . . . always follow your principles."

"You know I do."

"Yes, yes," he says. "But there are times when no one will understand your reasoning. You will need to find a way to hold your ground."

"What do you mea—"

Before I get the chance to finish, he taps his Connect. "Oh . . . look at the time. We need to go." He grabs the tie tack from the box and pins it on. "Look okay?"

"Yeah, Dad," I say, still full of concern and confusion.

He pops from the couch and gestures me to the door. "It won't look good if we miss the unveiling."

❀ ❀ ❀

As soon as we enter the glistening gala hall, the on-location management team immediately descends on us. The staff members are dressed in black to blend into the background when their services are not needed anymore. Two men and one woman, with comms in their ears and tablets in hand, escort my father out of sight and to his designated place for our Skybase arrival.

Of course, the workers don't care about me outside of duty. A glove-clad staff member supplies me with a sparkly drink called a Grape Galaxy.

"Take a sip," The lady with a tight bun says.

Like a good girl, I smile and sip the dark purple beverage. The thing is overly sweet and fizz shoots up my nose. But I nod at her and hold my hand in the air, indicating that I'm fine, so maybe she'll go away.

"Have a good time honey," she says and then leaves me to my own devices.

As I watch her buzz off like a worker bee I run my free hand over my arms. The prickly hairs stand on end. In our excitement to leave, Dad and I forgot our coats. The winter temperatures someone is fond of keeping this ship under are more extreme than ever tonight. Yet, if I try and slip out to return to my unit, someone dressed in black will only drag me back here, saying the unveiling will happen soon. I drop the mostly undrunk drink on a tray belonging to the first server who passes by.

Unfamiliar, fancily dressed adults sip drinks all around me. Drinks with sillier names that I'm sure, unlike mine, are full of more than juice. Everyone seems to have a lot less concerns than I do, laughing and speaking way to loudly, probably from the alcohol. Or maybe they really just don't have any worries. Human and bot servers attend to their every need and circulate the room with trays of strange looking finger foods. Gigantic floor-to-ceiling windows line the space, but the curtains are all closed in anticipation for the big reveal. The only stars we see are the twinkling lights from multiple crystal chandeliers.

I wind my way through the jungle of tables, towering floral centerpieces, and party-goers. Finally, I spot my place card on a table and walk toward my seat, relieved. At least if I sit, I can grab a roll from the basket without anyone noticing. On the way, I can nearly taste the crusty French bread with a smear of butter—

"Cassiopeia Foster," A deep voice says from behind, drowning out the room chatter and ruining my chances at a roll. "I was hoping to run into you."

Disappointed, I spin around to see who's calling me. It's not like I really know anyone on the ship except Dad and few of his associates. A tall boy, almost a man really—since I'm pretty sure he's older than me—stands about five feet away. His wavy brown hair falls over his forehead and casually across his left eye, though I can still see shades of blue peeking through the strands.

"Do I know you?" I ask, fully aware that I've never seen him in my life.

He struts toward me, hand extended. "No, we haven't met yet. I'm Luca Powell."

I smile sweetly and assume the role I'm here to play tonight: supportive daughter of Richard Foster. Without hesitating, I take his hand and give it a firm shake and look him in the eye.

He grins and releases my grip. "Confidence. I like that."

"My father taught me well."

'I'm sure he did." He says as he stares at me.

I cross my arms over my chest, not sure what to do with my hands from the lack of pockets in my formal gown. "So, Mr. Powell," I say and look around at the other patrons. "You're a bit younger than the rest of the crowd. What are you doing at the Gala?"

He chuckles. "I know what you're thinking. This must be some rich guy's son who bought his way into the party."

"The thought did cross my mind."

Luca puffs up slightly. "Well, you'd be wrong. I worked my way into this position. You're looking at the newly inducted assistant to President Hammond."

My throat tenses. Hammond? If he's Hammond's assistant, this guy must know about the rift between her and my dad. What if she sent him to be *friendly* just to get information on me? Especially after this morning.

"Oh?" Is all that comes out of my mouth.

"Yeah." He leans in close, smelling of spicy cologne. My nose tickles worse than from the fizzy Grape Galaxy. "I was thinking, since your father is high ranking and I'll be taking on more responsibility when we reach Arcadia, you and I should be friends."

Hammond definitely sent this guy to spy on me or maybe even to keep me in line.

"I . . . I'm sure you're going to be very busy. Too busy for someone like me." My mind spins with possible ways to make an exit, but none of my ideas end in success.

"Ms. Foster?" a new male voice comes from my left.

"Yes?" I say a little too quickly. Another boy my age, dressed in black attire like the crew, a color representing my salvation. He's shorter than Luca with straight, spiky blond hair and grey eyes. I know nothing about him, either. But, I'm pretty sure he's not another one of Hammond's assistants, so I already like him better.

"We're about to arrive and I've been requested to escort you to your position," the boy in black says.

"My position?"

The boy shifts his feet. "Yes, miss."

I glance at Luca, and he nods as if I should go. "Maybe we could meet up later and visit the observation deck to get a better look at the planet."

"Um . . . I'm not sure—"

The blond boy taps on his tablet. "I can see that Miss Foster's schedule is quite full tonight."

It is? What does he know that I don't? I strain to get a peek at his screen, but he drops it to his side before I get a chance. Anyway, at this point, I don't care what's on that screen since whatever's there is getting me away from Hammond's assistant.

"Maybe another time, Mr. Powell," I say as the boy guides me away. But I don't mean the invitation.

"I'm sure we'll be seeing more of each other," he says. "And it's Luca."

"Mmm-hmm," I mumble.

The boy leans into me once we're out of range. "You know . . . you should have just told him you didn't want to meet him on the observation deck."

I chew my lower lip. "It was that obvious?"

He chuckles lightly. "Oh, I'm certain Mr. Powell was oblivious to it. He's too busy trying to work his way up the food chain. But me? I have a talent for listening between the lines." My savior turns to me slightly, and his lips twist into a sweet smile. "I'm Max—Max Norton."

I grin. "It's nice to meet you. I'm Cassi—but I guess you already know that."

"Yes," he answers, his smile shifting from sweet to amused. "It was on the 'schedule'." He leads me to a row of ten empty chairs. Beside the seating gallery, is the podium where Dad will make his speech during the unveiling. "Here we are."

"But no one is here yet," I say.

"They will be in five minutes or so, and you needed an out. I gave you one." He gestures to the first seat.

But I don't sit. Instead, I grab Max's upper arm. "Think you could stay with me until then? In case Mr. Powell comes back?"

He taps his tablet screen to bring up the time. "Sure, I don't have anything else to do." He raises his eyebrow.

He probably has a million things to do, but right now I don't care. I'm short on friends around here, and Max seems like a safe bet.

"So . . . how do you like your job on the . . . event management team?" I ask.

Max shrugs. "It's a temp job. A buddy pulled me in for the night. Most days, I help escort members of the Board and other big wigs to meetings. Kind of like security, but not quite that important. I'm really more like a tour guide." He leans in. "You'd be surprised how loose people are with information around me, though. You'd think I was invisible."

Curiosity at his words creeps up on me, but I remain silent when a lady in a tall hat passes by where we stand. She takes her place in the row of chairs. It must be almost time. I lean toward him and keep my voice down. "Like what?"

"Oh, mostly news of how the installation is going well on Arcadia. But, as I said, I'm good at reading between their words. And then there's the tension." Max puts his finger to his ear as if he's listening to something in his comm.

"Tension?"

"Mmm-hmm," he mumbles, but I'm not sure if he's speaking to me or to the person in his comm. "Your father is coming out for the presentation in one minute. Would you mind taking your seat, Miss Foster?"

So there are more influential people than just Dad who disagree with Hammond. Or, at least, tension.

I nod, but wish we had more time to talk.

"Thanks for helping me," I say.

"No problem. Enjoy the show." Max smiles and I can only hope this is not the last time I run into him. He gives me hope that maybe Arcadia won't be so bad.

"Ladies and gentlemen," a man announces over the sound system and the room hushes. "Please take your seats. We are about to begin."

I turn and watch Max hurry away. The gathering of people mostly stop their conversations while locating their assigned chairs around the dining tables. I lower myself into my seat in the special row, next to the older woman in the tall hat who had breezed past me just a minute ago.

"This is so exciting, dear." She leans over to me as I sit.

Politely, I nod and fold my hands in my lap over the ripples in my puffy silk skirt. The rest of the "big wigs,"—as Max called them—file into the row, making me feel distinctly out of place. Hammond, dressed in a sequined blue gown, takes her seat at the opposite end of me. But, when Dad steps onto the stage, looking handsome in his suit and still wearing the ruby tie tack, I let out a breath and relax.

The patrons erupts into thunderous applause.

Dad smiles and holds his right hand up to quiet the crowd. "I'll make this short because I am fully aware it's not my face you're here to see this evening."

The gathering lets out a low chuckle at his joke.

"Thank you for joining me. I have been waiting for this moment for the last decade, and there were days I thought it might never come," he says. "But it has. While you were enjoying hor d'oeuvres and drinks, we very quietly dropped from light speed and arrived at our new home."

Dad raises his hand high in the air. As if by magic, the floor-to-ceiling curtains fall, revealing a spectacular view of the blue and green planet flanked by two moons. A haunting mist of glowing cyan fogs over the globe.

Chills rush through my body. The crowd, including myself, release a collective gasp.

"Welcome to Arcadia," Dad says. "The salvation of the human race.

CHAPTER THREE

"Why do I have to go down to the surface with you today? I can always go when the rest of the passengers do," I ask Dad as he leads me down the brightly lit, white corridor toward the Skybase connector bay. "There's nothing for me to do except follow you around, cutting ribbons and stuff."

He gives me a look peppered with frustration. "Cassi, everything is a ceremony around here, and the passengers can't begin disembarking until the Board and higher ups, such as myself *and you*, make the journey first."

I scoff. "It's not as if there aren't workers already down there. They've been building the city for two years already."

Dad tips his head and reaches into his jacket pocket, feeling for something but pulling nothing out. "You're just nervous."

A chill from the corridor settles over me and I pull my sweater in a little tighter.

Seeing the planet last night was incredible, I'll admit that. But I want to tell him I'm just not ready to go down there without

Mom. I brush her gold band on my finger. It's too final. At least on the ship, it still feels like I don't actually have to face a new life without her.

"But without Mom—"

Dad's face softens, and he immediately stops walking and pulls me into an embrace. "Mom is why I'm so excited today. There's something about Arcadia that brings me closer to her," his voice cracks with emotion. "When that curtain fell last night, I saw our dream right in front of me. It was as if your mother was standing right at my side, cheering me on, and supporting me." He releases me and pulls back. "This planet is everything. *Everything* Cassi. And I need you by my side to help everyone see that there's so much more to Arcadia than we're even aware of. I know you don't understand yet. But you will. So we need to get down there. You're going to love it." His eyes sparkle in a way I haven't seen for over a year.

Confusion stirs in me. How would he know this for sure? This will be his first trip to the surface, too.

I nod and reach for his hand. "I'm with you, Daddy."

He smiles and gestures us forward.

When we arrive at the docking bay, a sizable group of anxious patrons wait to transfer onto the Skybase. After that, we'll board a transport ship and descend to Primaro, the lone city on Arcadia. I've seen all the photos and videos and everything about it should be amazing. All the buildings are meant to mimic and blend into the existing nature to maintain the appearance that the planet is untainted by humans. Eventually, humans will expand over the surface; but, Dad believes that keeping everything contained was the smart thing to do until we learn more about how to successfully live on Arcadia. It was one of the few points of little contention between him and Hammond. But that was only likely because his plan kept costs down more than anything else. Hammond is a stickler for a budget. Not that anyone can fault her for that.

"Quite a crowd," Dad says.

From the number of multicolored jewels, gold, and expensive fabrics worn by the majority of the patrons, I know these people are the richest of the rich. They bought first dibs for the privilege of setting foot on the ground before any of the other passengers.

But then I see Hammond make her way to the front of the assembly and my excitement fizzles out. In contrast to the sequined dress she wore at the Gala, she's now dressed in a sharp black pantsuit and a pair of flat shoes. Her hair is pulled back into a low, short ponytail. The hairstyle highlights the sharp angles of her face and pinched mouth. I look to Dad, but he's admiring the buffet.

Lining the wall behind us is a massive spread of mostly untouched breakfast foods. Piles of bagels are loaded up on one end of the table, bowls of cut and uncut fruit wait to be eaten alongside a variety of breakfast meats. The energy of the crowd is nearly electric, and I can't help but let it affect me. My mind buzzes with activity.

I sneak another peak at Hammond and wind up staring straight into her ice blue gaze. I quickly look away, shivering, but from the corner of my eye, I can see her motioning someone closer. Luca Powell appears and she whispers something into his ear that takes at least thirty seconds to spit out. He pulls back with a quizzical look and taps on his tablet for a brief second before rushing away without comment. Hammond's eyes find the back of Dad's head and a sick feeling seeps through my stomach.

But, before I have time to think much further on it, she steps onto a platform ahead of the entrance to the SkyBase.

"Thank you all for coming today," Hammond says.

Applause fills the room, and Dad and I join in.

Hammond smiles coldly and continues. "We would not be here today without your generous support. As Dr. Foster stated last night . . ." She looks to my father and nods. "Arcadia is our salvation, a chance to begin again and do it right this time. This new Eden will give the human race room to expand. We will thrive once again. And very soon we will discover all the riches Arcadia has to give."

From what I know about Arcadia, it does have much to offer. It's a lush planet, untainted by humans. The surface is loaded with new minerals, precious metals, and probably a number of undiscovered energy sources.

But that bounty scares me, too. People are still fighting over how those things are best used on Earth, and the supply there is dwindling quickly. Money talks. Money makes the decisions. And how much people like Hammond are influenced by wealth, I don't know. As I look at the patron's dripping riches, I'm sure they want good returns on their sizable investments in developing Arcadia.

"Thank you again." Hammond's voice snaps me from my thoughts. "We will be disembarking to SkyBase in a few moments. Please be patient."

I link my arm into the crook of Dad's. At least there are still good men like him. He has a clear voice in this situation.

Hammond exits the platform.

"I need to take care of something, Cassi," he says and wipes a bead of sweat from his forehead. "Wait here, and I'll be back in a few minutes."

"Sure, Dad."

He pauses and removes his jacket. "Will you hold this for me? I think all the excitement is getting to me and I'm feeling a bit hot. You think you'll be okay?"

I take the jacket and nod for him to go. "No problem, I'll be just fine."

After he leaves, I spend a few moments scanning the bay, but the cavernous, white space is pretty boring without someone to talk to. And no one around here really wants to talk with a teenage girl, even if she is Richard Foster's daughter. Maybe Max is here. He did say he performed a form of security for the "big wigs" and these people are about as "big wig" as they get.

I look around the crowd of maybe two hundred patrons and staff. But disappointedly, I don't see Max's spiky blonde hair from here.

With a sigh, I check the space for Dad again. He walked off toward the stage but, other than that, I'm not sure where he went. I know he told me to stay put. But there's no harm in looking around a bit for Max. Plus I want to grab a bagel since I forgot to eat breakfast this morning. Tired of holding his jacket, I thread my arms through the too big coat and pull it in close. I have no idea why Dad was hot. It's cold in here.

I stroll over to the buffet and pluck a cinnamon raisin bagel from the pile of assorted pastries. I scan the table for a topping like cream cheese, but I don't see any. No butter, no jam, no nothing. You'd think with such a lavish display the staff wouldn't have forgotten the spreads.

At the other end of the display stands a buffet attendant, his back to me. At least, I think he's an attendant. Most of the people here are probably used to being served, so it makes sense someone would be helping. But his rumpled gray uniform is not exactly what I expect from the quality the patrons demand.

"Excuse me," I say to him as I grab a plate and a knife. As if he doesn't hear my question, he remains with his back to me. "Um, do you know if the buffet is out of cream cheese?" I try again and move closer to his position and speak over the room chatter.

This time, the boy with bronzed skin and jet-black hair twists my way. A look of surprise washes over his face and he furrows his brows in confusion. He raises his hand to his chest as if to say, *are you speaking to me?*

"Yes, I need some help," I say. "I was looking for the cream cheese and wondered if you had any in the back."

His brown eyes grow wide and, instead of answering my question, he turns from me again and dashes into the crowd of patrons.

I stand in confusion. What was that about? Maybe he's not supposed to be here. I drop the bagel, plate, and knife back onto the table and follow him. He's tall, over six feet, and I don't know if it's the particular, unkempt uniform, but something about him makes him stand out from the crowd, even as he weaves through the people. Strangely, the scene is almost as if he's swimming through water, his moves are so graceful. And yet, none of the patrons he avoids seem to notice him.

With ease, he picks up his pace, but I do too, keeping my eye on him. The strange boy nears the edge of the crowd, and the opening to a corridor waits ahead of him. I'm going to lose him if he makes it there. Too many easy exit points after that point and I'm not really familiar with this wing.

I speed up to catch him and, while moving full force, accidentally slam into the shoulder of an older woman. She looks down at me in shock, and I'm pretty sure she's the same person I sat next to at the Gala last night. When her surprise wears off, she lets out a loud yelp from our collision. The boy whips around toward the sound. He looks at the lady and then straight into my eyes. And, when we lock stares, a wave of freezing energy surges my body. I gasp, but quickly shake it off.

"Sorry ma'am," I pant.

The dark-haired boy tears from my gaze and spins away, rushing for the corridor. I push past the woman to get a visual of him again. I can't let him get away. Ignoring the complaining woman, I surge forward and push from the crowd. But, when I reach the edge of the hall, he's gone—vanished.

Behind me and from the opposite end of the bay, a scream pierces my ears. Momentarily I forget about the boy and pivot toward the distress. I hope it's not that woman. I really only tapped her.

But, before I have the chance to find out, a burst of orange and white light fills the room. A cry of help sticks in my throat as intense pressure, followed by heat, slams my body into the back wall of the corridor.

I hope you love Starfire so far! To read the rest of book one of The Starfire Saga you can buy it on Amazon.

XXOO,
Jenetta Penner

94355874R00207

Made in the USA
Lexington, KY
27 July 2018